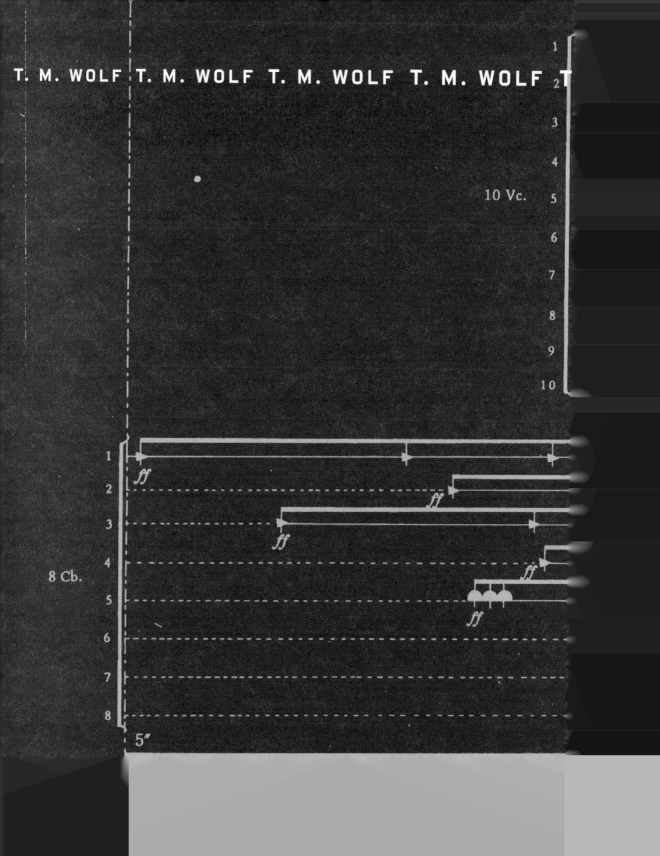

FABER AND FABER, INC. ///// AN AFFILIATE OF FARRAR STRAUS GIROUX ///// NEW YORK

FABER AND FABER, INC. ///// AN AFFILIATE OF FARRAR STRAUS GIROUX ///// NEW YORK

FABER AND FABER, INC.

AN AFFILIATE OF FARRAR, STRAUS AND GIROUX

18 WEST 18TH STREET, NEW YORK 10011

COPYRIGHT © 2012 BY T. M. WOLF

ALL RIGHTS RESERVED

DISTRIBUTED IN CANADA BY D&M PUBLISHERS, INC.

PRINTED IN THE UNITED STATES OF AMERICA

FIRST EDITION, 2012

ILLUSTRATIONS: PAGE VI © ISTOCKPHOTO; PAGES VIII–1

COURTESY THE LIBRARY OF CONGRESS

OWING TO LIMITATIONS OF SPACE, ALL ACKNOWLEDGMENTS

FOR PERMISSION TO REPRINT LYRICS CAN BE FOUND ON PAGE 367.

LIBRARY OF CONGRESS CATALOGING-IN-PUBLICATION DATA

SOUND / T. M. WOLF. — 1ST ED.

    P. CM.

    ISBN 978-0-86547-850-3 (ALK. PAPER)

    1. YOUNG MEN—NEW JERSEY—FICTION. 2. BOATYARDS—

NEW JERSEY—FICTION. I. TITLE.

PS3623.05526 S68 2012

813'.6—DC23

                          2011024953

ENGINEERED BY QUEMADURA

WWW.FSGBOOKS.COM

1 3 5 7 9 10 8 6 4 2

//// TO MY FAMILY—MY FATHER, MOTHER, AND SISTER—MY FOUNDATION ///// TO MY FAMI

I was once told records are made to be spun, not to be read. You can pick up a stray white label and run your fingers over its surface, but you can't decipher its sound in the feel of its chan-
nels and microscopic bumps. Instruments and vocals, rhythms and melodies, layer upon layer,
pressed into a wafer-thin disc. So full in the air, ear, mind. So flat at hand.

 So, put the record on the turntable and press the power switch. Feel the belt hum as it pulls
tight. Swing the arm over the vinyl's whorling dark stream, and plunge the needle in the gro
ov
e
.

WORDS BY *Cincy Stiles*

RECORDED, PRODUCED, AND

ARRANGED BY *Tom Lynman*

Side A

the truth

(GREETINGS FROM

THE JERSEY SHORE)

When the university cut off my grad funding, I did the only thing I knew to do: I went back to New Jersey. Back to a city I hadn't called my home for years, that my whole family had abandoned, like I'd never left in the first place, like the whole time between leaving and returning had been a waste. I'd entered the university's doctoral program three autumns prior, hepped up on four years' worth of undergraduate philosophy, and ready, finally, I thought, to devote myself to the academic life. For the first year and change, I spent my mornings and afternoons cloistered in the university reading rooms, studying metaphysics and teleologies, string theory and eschatology. I spent my evenings writing. I owned virtually nothing, lived in an apartment the size of a broom closet, ate cereal and noodles for most of my meals.

The first signs of trouble came in the months after I passed my general examinations. A whole summer that I should have spent developing my dissertation abstract slipped away. Then the September submission deadline passed and I was still empty-handed. The graduate committee gave me another semester, and yet another. Time I should have been in the library;

time I spent lounging in my apartment or wandering through the outer reaches of the city, picking my way through cemeteries and train yards, burned-over brownfields and scraggly parks. When I'd pick up a pen to lay down my thoughts, all sorts of things passed through my mind:

A first thought.

    A second, tangentially

    related to the first,

    at best, completely

    contradictory, at worst.

        Memories.

           Projections about

           the future, things

           I made up.

And on, and on. I needed to unify them, was told I had to unify them to say something valu-able. Thinking, writing didn't help: my thoughts were too different, too discordant to harmo-nize. Each fragment was seemingly right, but not entirely; each wrong, but not entirely. None worth abandoning; none worth building around. Each singing through its own space with its own trail of notes scrolling behind it, all seemingly traveling in parallel toward some same but unknown end, and, at some point, all running at the same time,

Thus

So

Not so

until one day—maybe it was in the library stacks, five stories below ground amid leaking pipes and decaying treatises, while I tried to recall a conversation that, on further fevered reflection, I realized hadn't happened; maybe it was in my living room, just as I took the first bite of a blackened slice of bread I'd left in the toaster a bit too long while I looked to the ceiling in pursuit of some missed connection; or maybe it was in a desolate depeopled subway car, staring at the ghostly half-reflection of myself in a key-scarred pane of safety glass until the conductor told me we had reached the last stop—I realized I'd reached a dead end.

And so did the committee.

No continuance meant no funding, no funding meant no food.

And, as it turned out, the market for my eighteen-year-old self in Jersey—the one who knew his way around a marina, who could operate a winch and weatherwrap a boat—was better than the market for my twenty-four-year-old self anywhere else, so I put up an ad for a subletter, packed my bags, and caught the first Greyhound to the Jersey Shore, with an offer for a new job from my old boss stored in my cell phone's saved messages, my mind lined with the burnt ends and ashes of thoughts.

Southward, oceanward. The bus roared through a late-night, deep-spring fog. Our progress was marked at uneven intervals by familiar green-and-white road signs that receded as quickly as they emerged from the milky white margins of the bus's headlights: Sandy Hook, Seaside Park, Monmouth Beach, Lavallette, Asbury Park, Point Pleasant Beach, Belmar, Spring Lake, Bay Head. As the bus banked a wide slow curve, its headlights sluiced through the rusted center guardrail, projecting fresh stands of shadows into the fog, row upon row, rising from sapling to adult before withering and falling in a mobile time-lapsed forest. I leaned my head against the window and closed my eyes.

Lunch time we traded dusty breaks on secondhand Maxell tapes / After school Cool DJ Red Alert

"   "

The Yankees' season starts tonight.   Tonight? No, tomorrow night.

The bus jolted and began to rise. The window grew cooler, the bus now eighty feet above the mirror-flat waters of Barnegat Bay and rocking in the breeze that kicked off the ocean. As we crested the bridge, the amusement area flashed into sight, the boardwalk, the piers, the water park, all a cloud of multicolored lights nestled in a chalky pink haze; the center-city motel district dotted with busted lettering: MPRES KRON SEA BR GHT; the blocks to the north and west shining golden edged with green; the whole area luminous, lapped by the black Atlantic tides along its eastern shore.

MC greats / Late night Mr. Magic, Pete Rock and Marley Marl / Writing

" "

OOOooO~~oooooooOOOo~O~o~oo~OOOoo~oXXXXXXXXXXXXXX00~ooOOO~oo~o~O~oOOOoooooooo~~Oo

The bus corkscrewed down the off-ramp and continued northward along the edge of the bay. Its wheels skipped rhythmically over the seams in the concrete-plated roadway like a needle on a cracked record, on past the illuminated expanse of Braxton Memorial Field, its outfield cross-hatched in a green parquet pattern, farther still the old vinyl-sided social clubs with their battered Italian and Irish flags, around the bend, past St. Vitus's School and its acres of blacktop playgrounds,

I dropped my backpack on the floor and sat down at the kitchen table, loosening the burlapy plaid tie all the lower school boys wore. I opened the backpack and filed past the phonics book with the matching plaid cover, the vocabulary builder, the Holy Communion prep book, grabbing for my math workbook, soft-covered and clear-contact-paper-wrapped, a year's worth of problems listed on the pulpy pages inside. I gripped my pencil with a full fist and got to work, milling through multiplication problem after multiplication problem, the numbers getting longer and longer, the procedure staying the same: start from the right, multiply, write down the digit, carry the ten, multiplication ultimately becoming addition, all the values totaling up to a single value at the end, the whole process neat, orderly.

along the edge of the city maintenance yard and its slumbering salt trucks and retired police cruisers, into the low rumble of the city bus terminal, a long, zigzagging canopy stranded in an oceanic parking lot. The bus's air brakes hissed and the engine shuddered to a halt as I clambered out onto the terminal deck. The driver placed my luggage—a suitcase, a duffel bag, a boombox—in a pile at my feet.

She caught my eye for the first time, waiting in a pool of light at the far end of the canopy.

Is it just that you're the finest little thing that I ever saw / Or is my imagination running too far

"

Snow gathered on the plaza outside
the university library. I caught her eye
as she pulled a book off the shelf,
perched up on her tiptoes, neck craned,
hair pulled back. Her eyes were brown,
almost golden. Something I could warm to.
She looked down with a smile.

> She let her fingers play through the tangles
> in her hair, let it ripple off in blond threads in
> the breeze while she rolled up her beach towel
> and zippered up her fleece.

> > The waxy green leaves of a magnolia bent
> > around her. The cicadas choired invisibly.

> > > I've never seen
> > > anyone like her.

"

She stepped onto an idling NJ Transit bus, disappeared as the doors closed behind her with a hiss of escaping air.

"   "

Coming or going?

She turned as I approached. "Hey, I'm"

A green digital display glowed above the bus door: OUT OF SERVICE.
Her bus rounded the corner at the parking lot's edge and headed bayward, away from me.

She stood in a pool of light.

Damn.

A horn sounded elsewhere in the terminal. All the other passengers had slipped away. I stood alone amid the shuddering and wheezing buses.

I shouldered my duffel, grabbed the rest of my stuff, and walked toward the exit, past a pack of drifters waiting for the late-night Atlantic City express. They were passed out on the benches like heaps of old clothing, some clutching half-empty wine bottles, others the complimentary bus tickets that the casino reps doled out on the weekdays to keep the bars and craps tables filled with bodies. The terminal's front doors opened with a whoosh.

It was well past midnight. The parking lot was silent and lily-padded with glowing car roofs. Out beyond the lot lay the Boulevard, which ran spinally along the city. Beyond that, the train line. I took a deep breath, feeling the cool night fill my lungs. Out here, away from the buses, the air was fresher, tinged with summer slowly approaching.

A train rocketed past, blurring up the bayshore. Across the Boulevard, beneath a wheeling flock of gulls upset from their roosts by the train's signal blast, a few figures picked their way along the side of the tracks, their hands grasping overstuffed trash bags or tugging children. A lone man stumbled along the far sidewalk, his form hidden and revealed in turn by the images of fast-food logos and neon store displays that slipstreamed along the rolled-up windows of passing cars.

“   ”

[   ]

Hey, tough guy!

Tom sat on the porch-wide hood of his cream-colored '84 Chevy. In the glow thrown off by the thirty-foot neon sign that leaned over from the lot adjacent, he looked pretty much like I remembered him, no different for all the years we'd bridged through e-mail: the same red-and-black plaid shirt, the same rugged, weatherbeaten face, the kind you might see on local sailors buffeted by decades of salt spray and cold easterlies.

He'd never sailed in his life. He always thought all the tacking and jibing were too indirect.

You too?   How you doin'?

Good to see you, man. You look like shit.   **Let's get going.**

He frowned and shook his head.

"   "

Meh.

I settled down in the Chevy's passenger seat and rested my feet on a mess of old magazines. Three brittle air fresheners hung off the rearview. A rip ran along the ceiling. I tugged on the seat belt. It didn't budge. I fiddled with the shoulder strap as Tom fired up the engine and rolled the car out onto the Boulevard. We headed northward along blocks of halogen-bathed parking lots and floodlit facades that hung flat and glossy like photographs clothespinned to the power lines running and dipping high above the road. People stirred in the blue-blackness around us, picked up in the headlights or in the glow of storefronts: two men shaking hands in a darkened doorway; a woman slumped atop a shopping cart, its cagework glinting then dimming in the passing beams; along the highway shoulder, day laborers and surfers pedaled home, hip-high in the dark on rotating arcs of reflected light that clustered and darted like swarms of fireflies.

The Yankees open tomorrow night against the Blue Jays in Toronto. Joining us on the phone is All Star second

So what've you been up to?

Bartending at the Diver's Bell, uhhh, gigging, you know, when I

baseman Robin ***

"   "

can keep a band together.

/ / / / / 11 / / / / / 11 / / / / / 11 / / / / / 11 / / / / / 11 / / / / / 11 / / / / / 11 / / / / / 11 / / / / / 11 / / / / / 11 / / / / / 11 / / / / / 11 / / /

For all the hours Tom put into his music over the years, he never seemed to take any joy in the playing, let alone the noisy musical accidents that came along with it. He just wanted to have the song down cold, to grind out his part with no mistakes and no detours from the line of notes in front of him. The feedback and flubbed chords that filled his parents' basement, my family's living room, our high school auditorium—that Tom pretended not to hear—sounded to me like the aural transcript of art labored over rather than loved.

He was even worse when he tried to rehearse with groups. He couldn't stand riffing, despised improv. The song was the song was the song. The writer for whatever loose ensemble he was in at the time had to show up at sessions with all the words and music fully notated, and damned if the band didn't play what was on the page. Which is probably why most of his bands ended up being cover bands, and cover bands to end all cover bands: Tom's groups didn't just play the old standards—the Drifters, early Springsteen, Southside Johnny—they played them over and over with such grim historical fidelity that they sounded less like real live musicians and more like oracles for the Classic Shore Rock Song.

Most other players didn't go in for that style, and so Tom usually played solo. Not that he wasn't always trying to scrape a group together. I think he realized that he couldn't have the songs he wanted without a full accompaniment. Sure, he could've moved through a piece part by part and line by line; played the guitar parts and sung the vocals, then slumped behind a drum kit and banged the percussion out. Each part on its own would have been enough for audiences to get a sense of the song, but no single part would be enough to get the song itself. So— through all the arguments, fistfights, and broken instruments—he soldiered on, bloodied and cranky, but still marching.

Do you think the bullpen will be *** *******

That's a shame.

I got into a fistfight with my bassist last week.　　　**He had it coming.**

*** *know, we have con***

"　　　　　　　　　　　"

Not as much as this mechanic, but

Tom pulled down an invoice from the driver's-side visor.

traffic and wr tog**   ****** *   ***

What's the damage?

I don't wanna talk about it.

He rammed the invoice into the glove box.

****   ***   **

C'mon

I don't wanna talk about it.

A green-and-red 7-Eleven sign reared up on our right.

Live and direct from Jerseeeeeeeeeeeyyyyyy   L-l-live and direct from Jersey JerJersey   Jersey Jer

Tom and I pawed through the circulars that came with the Sunday papers, looking for the best deal on a CD deck for the Chevy—P.C. Richard, Sixth Avenue Electronics, Circuit City, amps, woofers, sub-woofers, tweeters, and equalizers. We finally found what we wanted at the Wiz in Brick: a Pioneer system for a couple hundred dollars. We spent the rest of that day installing the head unit and speakers. My fingers shook in anticipation as we laced the wires through the doors. "Here goes nothing." Tom pressed the power switch and the system pulsed to life. The doors rattled louder as he leveled up the bass.

Tom jerked the Chevy into the parking area along the median and shut the engine off.

I could go for something.   Hey, wait

You hungry?

Tom was already outside the car, jangling his keys in hand.

You parked sideways across four spaces.

Something wrong?   **I have to park it like that. It doesn't**

"   "

go in reverse anymore.

" **"**
You comin' or what?

We mounted the sidewalk outside the 7-Eleven and strolled past a group of teens on trick bikes posted up near the front entrance.

" **"**
" **"**
Look at these d-bags.
            Nice car, lumberjack.

A soft electronic tone sounded as Tom opened the front door. The smells of burnt coffee grounds and shrink-wrap rose up to meet us as we loped past the Turtle Wax and car magazines and down the first junk food aisle. The store attendant peered at us over the edge of his tabloid, his eyes bloodshot and lids twitching.

                              I think so.
Did those kids say something to us?   **If you're gonna talk trash, you might as well**

" **"**
say it loud enough for someone to hear.

He grabbed a bag of Cheetos from an aisle-end display.

" **"**
Some things never change.

Maybe Tom's virtues weren't immediately apparent. But, growing up, I valued directness. In part because I couldn't figure out how to say half the things I wanted to say for myself. In part because my schoolmates had perfected their own Shore brand of passive-aggressiveness that made someone like Tom stand out as different, valuable, admirable. The kids outside were just like the kids I'd gone to school with; their whispered jabs and inside jokes the same kinds of things I heard in the halls, the locker rooms, the buses, the boardwalk, the beach. A constant chorus of halfhearted, half-throated snark. Was Tom harsh? Sure. But he stood up for his friends, he said what he thought, and because of that, you could trust him—an open book, never moving from that one page.

We wandered over to the Slurpee machine. I squinted at the tags over the spigots. The flavors weren't very descriptive; some were pretty menacing: Liquid Artillery. Fruity Chaos. Run with the Red Bull. Tom grabbed a big thirty-two-ounce cup and started filling it with some kind of silverish-gray slush.

"   "

C'mon, dude. For old time's sake.

I pulled a neon green cup out of the sleeve of twelve-ouncers and placed it under the Orange Lazarus nozzle. I opened up the spigot and Slurpee dripped out slow and goopy, like superviscous orange soda.

"   "

Those kids are looking in at us. Shouldn't they be learning to shave or something?

The clerk put down his tabloid as we neared the register. Next to the lotto machine, a dozen hot dogs spun on heated rollers, glistening with some odd moisture.

There isn't enough money in the world to get me to do that.

Ten bucks if you eat one of those.

The door toned behind us again. The kids were still out there, still watching us. As we drew even with the first kid, Tom lunged at him and barked. The kid fell off his bike in a rain of Mountain Dew and a chorus of laughter from his friends.

Little punk.

      We climbed back in the car and rumbled off again. As we drove, I nursed the Slurpee, try-
ing to skirt around a cold headache.

Jerseeeeeeeeeeeyyyyyyyy JerseyJersJerseyJerseeeeeyyyyyyyyy *** **

"   "

Man, this stuff is sweet. How'd I ever drink this?

"   "

Now there's trouble busin' in from outta state **and the D.A. can't get no relief**
Hey! You changed the station!
                              My car, my soundtrack.

      A line of cars scraped southward past us, packed with passengers and piles of clothes. Every
year, when summer started cropping up in radio ads, the city's houseless poor collected their
belongings from the cut-rate motel rooms and dilapidated bungalows they called home for the
off-season and headed out of town, traveling against the traffic on the Parkway and I-95 to make
room for the tens of thousands of vacationers that piled into the Shore for the high season. For
the time being, it was still early in the week and early in the season; we drove down blocks of
motels with nearly empty parking lots and NO darkened on their neon signs. The odd moment
of hollowing out before the summer's press.

"   "

I leaned over and reached into my duffel bag. Where'd I put that adapter? "Let us know when you get in." *My backpack slid
over my shoulders and slumped against the back of my head.* "Yeah, yeah, Dad, okay." *Where'd I put that thing?*

"   "

"   "

Oh, crap. I was supposed to call my parents. What time is it?   They turn their ringers off at night

"   "

Hey, Mom and Dad. I got in all right. I'll call

anyway. I'll just leave a message.

Who are you calling?

back later in the week.   I like to let them know where

Still got the lifeline out to the parents, huh?

I closed the phone and stashed it in my pocket.

I'm at.

Haven't spoken to my parents in years. After they paid that last tuition check, I was

"   "

Ugh. This Slurpee is making my heart skip.

X XX XxxX xXx

gone. Been living in shitholes since then, but whatever.

"   "

"Been living in shitholes." Speaking of?

So I was able to find this place on Springwood for a song. Moved in like two months ago.

Where were you living before?

Belmar, man. Tweekers ev-ry-where. Dudes we went to school

"   "

with, girls I used to hook up with. Shit was depressing.

Tom hung a right onto Springwood Avenue.

"   "

This new place isn't exactly, um, quiet, but the neighborhood's clean at least. And it'll be

My new neighborhood looked like a punch to the mouth: a line of three-story prewar constructions leaned and canted at odd angles, casting shadows like crooked teeth in the bright yellow glare of the streetlamps, the shadows broken only by gaps where buildings used to stand. Most of the buildings we passed were in various stages of renovation: windows missing, insides gutted, brick walls and crossbeam ceilings exposed. The street was lined with heavy-duty Dumpsters overflowing with gummy pink insulation and spindly metalwork.

We finally came to a stop in front of the lighted awning of a Laundromat. Tom motioned to the apartment on the sagging second floor above.

" "

This place probably won't be here a year from now.
Home, sweet home.

As I waited for Tom to pop open the front door, a police cruiser zoomed by, sirens blaring, lights flashing. Tom glanced over his shoulder.

" "

Do-oo-oo *not* mess with the cops here. They've been on some other, other shit recently.

Wood creaked and moaned underfoot as we climbed up the stairwell. A half moon peered through a dirty-paned window at the top of the steps, bathing the landing in a pool of silvery-blue. Pausing in front of the door, Tom finessed the locks in an almost ritualistic way. A click, a sound of the lock's tumblers falling, and Tom stepped inside. I followed close behind, letting my bags fall to the floor as he threw a switch that flooded the place in flickering yellow light from a bare overhead bulb.

The apartment was luxurious in a raw, abstract sense: big windows, an elaborate fireplace, lots of space; depressing in a lived sense: flaking paint and warped floorboards, wall cracks and rippled ceilings. The living room was littered with magazines and newspapers, Chinese food cartons and pizza boxes, reams of old notebook paper that massed around the feet of chairs and tables like drifted snow. Dark gray foam egg crates hung staple-gunned to the apartment's walls.

Yeah.

Great.

It's kinda like a time capsule.   **Kinda cool. Don't worry, man.**

He slapped me on the back.

"   "

We can fix it up, make it nice.

I sat down on the sofa. I was too heavy, I guess, for its fragile springs: I sank almost to the floor. A pile of newspapers fanned across the floor at my feet. February 7, 2006. December 29, 1916. August 1, 1995. December 30, 1898. August 24, 1999.

The people in here before us must have been some real pack rats.

The papers were perfectly clean, ivory white, edges sharp like they'd just come off the press. I panned back over the room, my eyes fastening on the egg crates again.

What's up with those?

"   "

I pointed to the wall.

Echoes?   When who plays what?

Those? They help cut down on echoes.   **Yeah, when we play.**

No.

I didn't tell you about that?   **Yeah, the band comes in like once or twice a week to re-**

Once or twice

hearse and record.   **Don't *worry*. We're usually done by two in the morning.**

Tom crumpled his way across the apartment to open the windows. Sounds of cicadas chirp-ing in the treetops outside eddied in as he slumped into a rusty desk chair opposite the couch and began to fiddle with a laptop that sat glowing on an old drafting table. A tiny computer microphone rested near the mouse pad; two boxy speakers bookended the desk.

"
                                                 "

Check it out, man, I'm running a whole production suite off this thing.

A set of teal-colored sine waves ran in parallel across the screen.

"
                                               "

We've been cutting covers and getting 'em pressed up to play in the jukebox at the Bell. All

"   "

on the sly.

He leaned back in his chair.

On the sly?

We're tryna replace every album in the box with our own cover. Hopefully, no

Why don't you want anyone to notice?

one will notice the difference.   **Because if no one notices,**

"   "

then we know we nailed it.

Tom turned back to his computer.

"   "

Things started going a lot faster when I got this place. I just download the tabs from the Web,

"   "

revise 'em a little, then we record and mix basically all of our songs right here. You ever

Uh-unh.

mess around with this stuff?   **Tell you what, grab that mic over there. It should still**

"   "

be hot.

Tom nodded toward an old mic that stood in the corner of the room. Its head looked like
an old satellite, dull silver and ringed with steel filaments.

Where'd you find this thing?   Is it any good?

          A garage sale, can you believe it?   **That thing's so sen-**

                                                  Isn't all the trash

sitive, it can probably pick up what you're going to say before you even say it.

in here bad for the sound?

          Nah, man, it's exactly what we need. It makes everything all dusty-

"   "

sounding.   You got the mic? Take that thing to the far side of the room and we'll put

"   "

something together real quick.

I dragged the mic toward the kitchen. Its cord trailed across the piles of trash that covered the living room floor.

Yeah.

You good?   **All right.**

Tom clicked his mouse twice.

Like what?   Nah, man, that's not my bag.

Say something.   **Anything. Rock the mic, dude.**

Tom clicked the stop icon. I crossed back over to get a better look at the screen. Two short sine waves glowed at the top of the display. He dragged his mouse over the PLAY icon.

Say something.   *Anything. Rock the mic, dude.*

Like what?

Cool.

Yeah. We record all

"   "

these things onto different tracks, layer 'em on top of each other, and boom, you've got a

"   "

record.   **Well, it's a little more complicated than that, but not much.**

Tom copied the sine waves into clean tracks beneath, shifted them slightly forward in time, then pressed PLAY again.

Say something.   *Anything. Rock the mic, dude.*

Like what?

Say something.   *Anything. Rock the mic, dude.*

Like what?

Tom leaned back in his seat.

I just listen while I

So you've really never dropped a rhyme? With all the stuff you listen to?

write other stuff.   No, not really.   You know, philosophy stuff,

Not music.   **So, like what, exactly?**

academic papers,   You're not the only one.

You've lost me already.

My head lurched down the steep back end of a sugar rush. The edges of my vision pulsed with some rippling rainbowy border.

I'm shot, Tom. I think I'm gonna call it a night.

Yeah, cool. I'm gonna warn you, though, your

All

room is full of crap. Some old books, boxes and shit I didn't get a chance to clean out.

right.

"   "

I pressed my fingers to my temples.

I guess I'll deal with it later.

"   "

I opened the door to the second bedroom and peered in.

One thing Tom doesn't do is lie.

The room was a mess—piles of yellowed newspaper on the floor, water-stained boxes of water-stained books on the desk and under the bed, bureau drawers hanging open, filled with ancient moth cedars and Te Amo cigar boxes holding corroded pennies and broken crayons. Yard-long cracks ran down the walls.

I turned on a lamp near the dresser beside the door. Hunched against the window was something that looked like a liquor cabinet or a heat register. I inched across the room, trying not to trip on anything. A black power cord extending from the bottom of the thing lay unplugged. Its sides were lined with dusty brown mesh, like stereo speakers. I traced my hands along its top, its grayish-brown lacquer cracked and peeling, two hinges on the window-side edge greened and flaking. A depression in the side opposite the hinges was just big enough to fit two fingers. A hatch. Beneath the hatch, a turntable.

A record cabinet.

I plugged the power cord in and flipped the red power switch that lay beside the needle arm. The turntable spun; the needle arm swung across and dipped down to touch the record that wasn't there. A dull hiss leaked from the speakers.

I always wanted one of these.

I rooted through the boxes, looking for records to play. Nothing. Just books. Books everywhere, in fact: on the window ledges, on the shelf in the closet, even laying on the unmade mattress. Many of the volumes older than me, older than my grandparents. Some of them crumbling, some beautifully bound.

My eyes were burning, sore in their sockets. I retraced my steps and clicked off the lamp. In the dark now, I felt my way back to the bed and lay down with my hands clasped behind my head. The box spring squealed underneath me.

Standing in a pool of light. "Excuse me, miss"

The streetlight projected the shadow of a spider onto the far wall. His arms knitted back and forth as he inched out the threads of his web, cycling slowly out from its center. By his fourth go-round, I was out, sleeping a dreamless sleep.

dock on the bay

I woke the next day to the muffled heat of a closed-windowed room on an early April after-noon. I rubbed the corners of my eyes. The tree outside my room pitched crazily, its crown of leaves hanging in midair to the right of the trunk.

Huh?

I jerked the window open. The tree stood tall, whole.

It's just my window.

The view up and down the street was obscured by the tops of trees that fizzed in the ocean-borne breeze. A jackhammer rattled somewhere in the distance.

I rustled across the room, pulled my boombox out from the pile of luggage by the bedroom door, and plugged it in.

It it it's the new the the new it it's the ne ne newwwwwwww It's th th the new

I don't know quite when I started listening to music the way I did—incessantly and immer-sively. But I have a pretty good idea why. The music was space-filling. The voices were warming accompaniments for the wide cold stretches of winter. It dulled harsh edges and amplified warm tones like the late evening sun.

I saw something even more in the hip-hop I first picked up years back on staticky radio broadcasts from New York. It added rough depths to glossy surfaces, bass to life's treble. It seemed to fit a pattern: The songs I caught never let things extend indefinitely; they looped and repeated finite bars. Every few seconds brought you back to the same beginning before rocket-ing you out in a new, unexpected direction . . . only to return again. They made circles and ovals out of straight-line time, swirling over and over with slight changes. They were futuris-tic and historical simultaneously, the true present, flipping the old into something new, or some-thing old-new. Crate-digging and loop-building: a chop, a slice, a scratch, a quote. Laying layer upon layer into jagged mountains of sound.

I pulled on a fresh T-shirt, buckled the belt on my jeans, and wandered out into the living room. The clock on the wall read 1:17.

I hated sleeping late, hated the weird sense of disjointedness when my early became every-one else's late and my late meetings became early ones. I was due at the Trenton Boatyard and Marina at four to meet with its owner, J. D. Trenton, about a shift-manager position he had lined up for me. J.D. had been a high school friend of my father's and a father figure to my friends and me growing up—a quasi-caretaker back when we didn't have anything better to do than wander around the docks and wharfs, a summer employer when we hit high school. Even though I hadn't spoken to or seen him in almost a decade when I called his office in March, I knew I could count on him to help me out.

Getting the job was easy; getting there was going to be a little more difficult: it was hard to move around down here without a car. I peeked into the other bedroom, the living room, the kitchen. No sign of Tom. Trash everywhere. If he had left a note, I wouldn't have been able to find it. I scanned the refrigerator for a bus schedule. The routes were easy enough to remem-ber—if nothing had changed: one line of buses traveled around the city clockwise, the other counterclockwise. I just needed to get in the right loop.

I dug through the drawers in the kitchen, pulling out wads of old unused napkins, broken pencils, pieces of string, screwdrivers and matching masonry screws, unspooled Scotch tape and thread, keys on chains with water-streaked tags, cans of crusty shoe polish and chamois with blueberry-like polish stains, nothing valuable, everything except what I was looking for.

The living room windows shook. Outside, an NJ Transit bus was lumbering up Spring-wood.

And there we go.

I threw water on my face from the kitchen sink and raced out the door, down the stairs, and out onto the sidewalk. The ground felt rough underfoot.

I'm not wearing any shoes.

I stopped and watched the bus chug up the block and around the corner, trailing black clouds of exhaust in its wake.

I guess I'm walking.

I went back upstairs, slid my shoes on, grabbed a stale bagel from above the fridge, and hit the street again.

The boatyard sat on the extreme north side of the city, amid the wharves on the bayshore. As the oldest yard in the city, it had the most coveted position on the bay, right at the inlet's mouth, its docks and bulkheads washed daily by the freshwater that flowed seaward from the Manasquan and Metedeconk Rivers and the salt water that surged in from the Atlantic through the inlet's narrow neck. It also marked the head of the Intracoastal Waterway, or its tail, depending on which way you were headed or which way you held your map, or neither, if you were one of the rugged Loopers—sunscreened-up, recreational-yachted-out—who saw the Waterway as just one stretch of the waters that circled the eastern half of the continent, from the Mississippi River to the Great Lakes to the Gulf of Mexico, who saw our tiny city as a backwater stopover on the way to New York City, Chicago, or New Orleans.

My walk through the wharfside played like an old album with the needle on the ridges rather than in the grooves, everything spinning along a familiar path, but slightly displaced. I passed marinas with their fleets of 120-foot trawlers for deep-sea fishing and double-decker paddle-wheels for downbay cruising, rows of ramshackle crab huts and fish markets, convoys of re-frigerator trucks that ferried food in and out, strip malls with tackle shops and greasy generic delicatessens sitting back from bleached and cracked parking lots, the air heavy with diesel fumes and seafood scents, soot and brack and breeze. Turning slightly northward now, draw-ing closer to the inlet and its rocky jetties, the gateway to Trenton's peninsula was guarded by a nautical graveyard—a field of gravel and scrub littered with yachts with holes punched in their sterns, sailboats with sun-blistered decks, steel skeletons and fossilized wood, all scattered among the remains of bigger tankers and steamers, nothing more now than lopped-off smoke-stacks and sheets of tempered iron, multistory hulls pitched sideways, edges rusted and ragged, coated with striations from collisions and barnacles from stagnation like beached whales pre-historic in size. Farther still to Trenton's, jutting out into the bay on its narrow sandy spit, joined by the Inlet Surf Shop and Digger's Clam Shack.

I walked along the length of the yard, shaded by the blocky blue silhouettes of warehouses and outbuildings that the westward-arcing sun draped across the roadway. On through the yard's front entrance, pushing through an unlocked gate topped with a cyclone of rust-streaked razor wire. The main building looked more like a diorama of an office than a real office, its street-facing wall just a bank of windows looking crosswise into a boating supply shop and a warren of work spaces overflowing with paperwork and diagrams and nautical memorabilia. A single window stood open on the second floor.

J.D. was perched on the edge of a desk in one of the first-story offices, rubbing his neck while poring over a pile of curled-up cash register receipts. He looked up at the sound of my fist rap-ping against the glass; a smile emerged from the complex wrinkles on his face. He held out his hand in an open-palmed pause sign. Turning down to his desk, he picked up a folder and strolled out to meet me.

"   "

Cincy. Great to see you.

J.D. shook my hand with an eagerness that betrayed his affectless voice. If he hadn't inher-ited the family business, he probably could have made a career as a voiceover actor for children's movies or a narrator for audio versions of kids' books. He had a preternaturally calm tone, a kind of put-the-kids-to-bed timbre that was soothing even when the words themselves were threatening or angry. My friends and I used to call him "The Captain," less for his role in his business or the downbay E-Scow races than for the role his voice seemed to foist upon us and him equally—the steady, unflappable presence, a sort of salt-breeze- and diesel-smoke-wreathed Stoic of the Bay.

"   "

Let me show you around. The yard's changed a bit since you were last here.

J.D. led me by the shoulder across the lot.

"   "

The lockers and showers are still over there in the outhouse.

J.D. pointed to a long, gray concrete building with a white-shingled roof that extended bay-ward from the main building.

"   "

We added a break room on the back. I think you were here when we built the first big warehouse,

"   "

The struts arched
over a freshly laid
concrete pad.

right?

A four-story-tall warehouse loomed in the middle of the lot. Its corrugated metal sides were interrupted at even intervals by semitranslucent bay doors.

"   "

Let's cut through here.

We ducked through one of the partially open bays into the warehouse's interior. Normally, the warehouse held several yachts being prepped for sailing or storage, each sitting in midair on elevated platforms that moved up and down like giant forklifts. For now, the elevators were empty; it was still too early in the season for any major jobs. Our footsteps echoed as we crossed the space. J.D. pressed the UP button on a dirtied red toggle switch that hung at the side of one of the far bay doors.

"

"

We had to build a second warehouse just to handle the bigger boats customers started to bring by.

We circled around a smaller, stark white warehouse with one massive door on each end. It was the perfect size to pass a single large yacht from the back lot to the bay and back again.

No more sails?

I had to sell off the sailmaking business to make room.   No more salvage either. Too

"

"

much paperwork, not enough money. These monsters

He slapped the side of a sixty-five-footer wrapped in weather-resistant blue plastic.

"

"

are where the money's at now.

We continued on into the undeveloped acres in the rear lot, weaving through a maze of large motorboats and yachts, some wrapped up, some already undone for the season—house-size Egg Harbors and Sea Rays, pocket-rockety Wellcrafts and Chris-Crafts, big-masted Catalinas and O'Days—occasionally passing the unmistakable two-pronged shapes of catamarans and the long slender hulls of M-Scows and E-Scows. Most of the boats seemed new, or like new, but scattered throughout were others that didn't even seem seaworthy, their sides breached and unrepaired, their fittings stripped, masts snapped in two.

"These have just been building up over the years. Owners keep writing checks, but I don't think they're ever coming back."

He pointed to an off-white catboat with weather-faded benches lodged against the back fence. Green creeper vines crept across its hull.

Is that my mom's catboat?
               My mother slathered zinc across our
               faces as we rocked along with the bay.
                              Yeah. We've been trying to sell it for years. No takers. "Shame, too. It's a beautiful boat."

We headed toward the bay again, rounding the edge of the new warehouse, and strolled along the yard's branching dock. Our feet clopped on the dock's sun-split gray boards. A line of trawlers returning from their early morning fishing expeditions loped downbay, sending rhythmic surges crashing against the yard's wooden bulkhead. We sat down on a bench looking out over the water. Our feet searched out clean spaces amid the impasto of gull droppings and cracked shells that covered the dock.

Out across the water, a sprawling condo development was taking shape. A new yacht club had already overtaken the far shore, replacing the sandy wooded coves with a three-story clubhouse and two broad flanking docks where masts bobbed and dipped tidally, the whole complex roosted like a giant osprey testing its wings for flight. Out beyond the clubhouse, a golf course stretched, flat, lush, savannah-like, dotted with sand traps and imported cypresses. Beyond the links, the peaks of condos peeked over the treetops, joined by a new water tower, green below the tree line, blue above, UPPER BAY stenciled on its side.

I just hit a dead end, you know.

So you need to take some time off from your work?   You're in good

Yeah, yeah, I'll think my way through it eventually.

shape, though? You feel all right?   You think so?

I think I'll think through it.

"   "

I tossed a jagged shell out into the bay, watched it flash in the sun and then slip out of sight under the surface.

Never mind.   So what's the plan? What do you need me to do?

Shift-manage. You know the

How many

boats, the yard. We'll get some people to work under you, and you'll be good to go.

people are we talking?

"   "

J.D. looked down at his splayed fingers, ticking through something in his head.

"   "

Seven or eight. A couple of heavy-machinery guys then a couple of attendants. I'm staffing up

"   "

more this year because of that.

J.D. motioned toward a massive white ferry moored at a landing just east of us.

A lot of people using

The new New York ferry. Gets folks here from Midtown in under an hour.

it?   Have you hired anyone else yet?
  Does the pope go to church?   I grabbed some union guys to han-

"   "

dle the lifts, but we're still looking for the attendants.

J.D. picked up his folder and began meandering back toward the office.

So, basically

I've had ads out for a couple of weeks. I got five applications for five spots.   We'll in-

"   "

terview these guys, but they're pretty much hired unless they're crazy, so

The sound of tires on gravel greeted us as we set foot back on dry land. A customized Caprice—body blue and mirrored, chrome work reflecting its surroundings at oddly pitched angles—rounded the edge of the main office and pulled to a stop in the customer parking lot. J.D. altered his course toward the car; he motioned for me to follow.

The driver, when he finally, slowly unfolded out of the car, was easily six and a half feet tall: he hid J.D. completely in his shadow.

"   "

J. D. Trenton. Nice to meet you. You must be Mr. Hawkins.

Yeah. But my boys call me Tone.

"   "

Glad you could make it today. This is Cincy, he's one of the shift managers for the yard. He and

"   "

I am?   Um, what's up?

I'll be interviewing you.   Don't worry about it.

What it is?

Tone's hands were as big as baseball mitts and about as rough. He had to be two hundred and fifty pounds, although the tablecloth-size black T-shirt and baggy black knee-length shorts he wore might have had a slimming effect.

"   "

Why don't we head into the break room? And sit down?

"   "

The main building was perfumed with a faint must mixed with the scent of spray-on fitting lubricants.

Your car's pretty cool.   You just get it

"   "

You like that? That's my chrome-plated woman right there.

washed?

"   "

I polish her every day. I like to keep her looking clean.

J.D. led us through the lobby and into the first of the front offices. The silver plates and tarnished medals in the memorabilia cases outside the room trembled as Tone passed. J.D. and I took seats behind the desk, our backs to the window. Tone's head brushed the chain dangling off the ceiling fan as he stooped to sit. He scanned the room and then leaned forward, resting his folded hands on the tabletop between us. The massive gold crucifix hanging around his neck swung back and forth. A thin skein of sweat glistened on his bald head.

"Can I get you something to drink?"

Nah, I'm straight.

He pulled a black bandana out of his pocket and mopped off his head sweat. I looked in the folder J.D. had handed me.

"   "

Résumés. Nice.

So you're an old pro, huh? Three yards in the last three years?

Yeah. One in Wilmington, North

"   "

What does this Post-It say? "References check out. Marine tech? Forty an hour."

"   "

Carolina, one in, ahhhh, Norfolk, Virginia, and then one down there in Baltimore.

He scratched at the carpety beard that covered the lower half of his face. His skin was coated in a fine flowing black script that swirled out under his sleeves and along his forearms, past his wrists, and onto the backs of his hands.

"   "

What'd you do there, exactly?

A little bit of everything. Power cleaning, towing, repairs, sales in the

When'd you move to

"   "

supply shop. I trained up and got my marine technician license in Baltimore.

Jersey?   Where're you from originally?

"   "

A few months ago.   **East Savannah, Georgia, is where I call**

Everywhere?

"

home. But I've spent time nearly everywhere. **Yeah.**

He started counting off cities on his fingers.

" "

" "

So, I was born in East Savannah, but my family, they were from the Bronx. Then we moved out to

But you didn't stay out there.

" "

L.A. when I was a kid. **Nah, I didn't really belong out there. I left home**

" "

" "

after high school and started working my way back east. Houston, Nawlins, Memphis, a couple

" "

" "

months in each of those places. But I've been moving up the coast for a while now. Figured I'd check

You by yourself?

" "

things out up here, see if I couldn't get something jumped off. **I've got some, ahhh,**

He rubbed his index finger along the side of his nose and sniffed.

Interesting. I couldn't really place your accent.

" "

cousins off there in Long Branch. **I picked up a little**

"

      You have a Jersey boating license?

bit from everywhere.   **As a matter a fact, I just got it last week.**

He reached into his pocket and pulled out a laminated card. He held it up to the light like he was inspecting a diamond, and, then, with a nod of approval, slid it across the table to us.

Cool. So you can handle a motorboat all right?

      Okay. I

Inboards, outboards, even sailboats, yeah.

"   "

      What

have to ask this. No offense meant   Okay.

Charged. Never convicted.   **I beat that case. Pro se.**

"   "

kind of case?

"   "

You two are looking a little shook. I promise to the Lord Himself I'm not caught up in that knuckle-

" "

" "

head bullshit.

      J.D. shot me a quick look. It wouldn't have been the first time he'd ever given someone the benefit of the doubt.

"   "

Forget I even asked. You said you've got your cert? We've got a ton of outboards around the yard

"   "

"   "

that we were going to sell for scrap. Unless we can fix them. You think you could help us out?

"   "

"   "

"   "

Let me take a look at 'em and we'll see.

We led Tone out toward the garage.

Used to be bigger. They used to do custom fittings for sailboats, salvage, you

"   "

This joint is huge.

name it.

This is it here.

"   "

J.D. stooped down and grabbed the garage door handle. The motors were inside, packed in like a terra-cotta army in a Chinese emperor's tomb.

"   "

They seem to break really easily.

Shit. There's gotta be fifty of those things in there!   **Let's see. What**

"   "

"   "

are these   some fifteen-horsepower joints   A few bigger ones   Evinrude

"   "

What do you think?

Mercury   Yeah, I've seen plenty of these.   I'd have to take a couple of them

"   "

"   "

apart, but

He picked up one of the fifteen-horsepower outboards, popped the gas tank, sniffed, and then mounted it on a bracket extending from the wall; he gave the cord a few tugs. Nothing. He removed the hood with a screwdriver and peered inside.

"   "

Sure, go ahead. We'll be back in the main building.

Mind if I fool around with this for a little bit?

"   "

"   "

Cool.

It was one after the other like that for the rest of the evening: J.D. didn't waste any time, scheduling all the interviews back-to-back. Next up was Mike Hathaway, a high schooler. He stumbled into the office, skateboard in one hand, the other pushing his hair out of his eyes.

"   "

Mike! How're your parents?

F-fine.

I flipped through the folder. No résumé. Just a sheet of paper with his name and number on it. And a note: "Give him ten family favor."

"   "

Let me introduce you to Cincy. He'll be your shift manager.

"   "

I held out my hand for a shake. Mike took one step forward, a second, then tripped over his untied shoelaces. His skateboard clattered on the floor as he pitched forward. He averted a straight-out fall by shooting out his hands to brace himself against the glass display case beneath the register. With a sheepish grin, he half-straightened into his normal posture—something like a comma—and stuck out his right hand. His palm was clammy.

"   "

           Why don't you sit down?

Nice to meet you.

He slumped in the chair, his feet splayed out to the sides in a lazy V.

"   "

So, you're still at Shore High? Must be getting ready to graduate soon.

           Almost done with my jun-

"   "

      Do you have a boating license yet?

ior year.   I can wakeboard pretty well.

He had a beatific grin on his face. I sniffed the air.

           Yeah.

Know anything about sailboats?

      They still have those?   Aren't they from the country times?

He fingered the rimey, water-shrunk hemp necklace that hung loosely around his throat.

"   "

Country times?

      You know, back when everyone used to live in the country.

J.D. blinked and frowned.

"   "

Ever been in any trouble with the police?
                              Well, there was this one time when my brother and I

"   "
"   "

were smoking a blunt down under the boardwalk in Avon and a cop caught us, but it turned out

"   "
"   "

he was friends with my brother from high school or something and they used to do that all the time

                              So he didn't arrest you?
"   "

when they were younger, so he smoked the rest of it with us.

Mike's brow furrowed.

"   "

They leaned against the wall or laid out in the tall
grass that crowded up against the rear of the theater.
Moffo split the Dutch Master open with his thumb
and gutted the tobacco. O'Toole drizzled some crum-
bly green weed into the Dutch; Moffo licked it, rolled
it back up, and passed it over O'Toole's lighter. The
scent hung heavy in the air. "You want a hit?" "Nah,
I'm cool." Some things never change.
"   "

Nooooo. Not that I can remember.

I sniffed again.

Are you high right now?   Weed?

                                           Could you   could you not show up
          Um   yeah.   Uh-huh.

"   "

like that in the future?   All right, so
              Yeah, um   I think so.   I could try.

    Mike stood up.

"   "

Where are you going?   Don't you want to hear our terms?
              I thought the interview was over.

"   "

                          Yeah.   We'll pay you ten dollars an
Terms? Like   I   I'm hired   terms?   Uh   yeah   totally.

"   "

hour for six shifts a week. Sound good?   Awesome. We'll start next Monday.
                          Sounds great!

    I shuffled the sheet of paper with his contact information to the back of the pile.

Huh?   My week? It's been, um, all right.

"   "

How's your week been, Cincy?   Your week, how's it been?

Yeah.   Definitely.   See ya Monday.

"   "

That's good.   Awesome.   See ya!

Mike sauntered toward the door, his smile wider by a few inches.

So, what was it like in the country times, J.D.?

You learn something new every day.

Next up was Corey. He sat with his hands in his front pockets, a toothpick dangling from his mouth. The toes of his pristine Top-Siders leaned up against each other.

"   "
"   "

Before we get started, I've got photocopies of my boating license, my social security card, and

"   "
"   "

my driver's license here.

He pulled some folded papers out of his pocket and tossed them across the desk. They were rumpled along the edges and damp with hand sweat.

"   "

Oh, great, thanks.   So, you live down here year-round?

I've been here for about four years.

"   "

Where were you before?

"   "

His head was cocked to the side, as if he were paying close attention to J.D.'s questions. It was hard to tell, though—he was still wearing his sunglasses.

"   "

What's up with that?

"   "

Back in Connecticut, where I grew up. Moved down here to take a job as a sailing instructor at

Is it bright in here, or is that just me?

That's a nice club.

Inner Harbor.   Very nice.   Must be you. I'm

"   "

"   "

fine.

Two convex versions of my own face reflected back at me from the lenses of his glasses.

"   "

You're not working Inner Harbor anymore?

I'm getting a little tired of the club scene. I want to

"   "

A mix of everything. Pumping out bilges, try something different. What's the basic day like?

"   "

gassing up yachts, maybe patching some hulls. We've got an ice service for fishermen, you know,
"   "

"   "

carting out coolers of ice for them to carry on board. Winterizing and dewinterizing boats. De-
"   "

"   "

pends on the time of the week and the time of the summer.   As far as pay
                                                    All right. I can do that.   So, we'll

"   "

                                                                        Yes.
have a lot of contact with the boats going up and down the bay, right?   Okay.

I flipped through his packet of photocopies. A Xerox of a speeding ticket from 2010 was tucked in with his IDs.

What's up with this?
"   "
"   "

I slid the Xerox across the desk.

"   "
"   "

Just a ticket I got a while back. I wasn't sure if you were going to do background checks or some-

                                                          A ticket for sixty in a fifty-five is
"   "

thing, so I figured I'd just get all my paperwork in order up front.

all you've got? That's not even criminal.

Any questions?

I believe in full disclosure.

"   "

How about now? You're hired.

When do you think you'll make decisions about hiring?

Corey pushed his chair back and began to stand up. He didn't even crack a smile; instead, he looked down at his watch and frowned.

"   "

Next Monday, 8 a.m.

Great. When do we start?   Okay, see you then.

He turned and began to stroll out.

"   "

Wait. About the pay   Twenty an hour

Oh, yeah. What are you paying?   Okay, whatever.

That was the last we heard from Corey until the first day of work.

The final interviews—with Oz and Deuce—got off to kind of a weird start.

A man was hunched forward on one of the benches in the lobby, fiddling with a fitting he'd probably found sitting by the register. His skin was a sort of translucent white with a pink undertone, his hair yellowish, cut close around his temples and ears, but thicker on top, like a crown of popcorn. A pair of wraparound shades teetered on the edge of his nose.

Jeremiah Knight?

"   "

The man sitting on the bench looked up at me with near-purple eyes peeking over his shades, then looked back down at the fitting.

Arthur Knight?   Cincy. I'm a shift manager here.

      That's me. I go by Oz.   What's going on?

He held out his hand to dap me, but, as I moved closer, his brow knitted for a second and his fist unballed for a shake.

Why don't we head down the hall?   Where does "Oz" come from?

      Cool.   Not really sure, just always

"   "

been called Oz.

He stopped at the threshold to the office. J.D. looked up from the desk and his folder of résumés.

      Yeah, it's at the end of the hall there. I'll be in here

Hey, I gotta piss. You got a bathroom here?

when you're done.

      Got it.

I settled back into my chair and waited, tapping a half-chewed pencil that I found sitting in an empty tin can on the desk. After a minute or so, Oz passed by the office, heading left to right across the doorway.

Hey, Oz, the bathroom's right down there. Just keep going.

What?

Isn't that?

      I'm not Oz.

He looked just like Oz. The same eerily pale skin, the same broad and flat nose, the same shades, the same loosely fitting pants and T-shirt.

Wait   What? Who are you?   A.k.a. Jeremiah Knight?   And "Deuce" because?

"   "

Deuce.   Yeah.

You applied for a job, too, right?

"   "

I don't really know. I've just always been called Deuce.   Uh-huh.

Are you related to Oz?

Identical twins?   Do you guys nor-

That's my brother. We're twins.   Yeah.

"   "

mally work together?

We're kinda a package deal. At our last job, our boss just had us work all

That's kind of a jerk move.

"   "

the same shifts and called us by the same name.   Yeah, it wasn't really

"   "

Why don't you take a seat?

a good situation. Some European dude.   Cool.

Deuce sat down and looked around the room.

"   "

Tell me about it.

This place needs some work.

Oz came back in and sat down next to Deuce.

"   "

"   "

"   "

Sorry about that.

I looked at one, then the other. They were identical, down to the last detail.

                              No, it's that. I just

"   "

                                        Nah, he's just never seen twin

You look like you've never seen twins before.

                    Nooo, I

"   "

albinos before.

                    Look, man, you don't have to front like we aren't a little, um, unusual.

"   "

                                        Albinism is really rare, isn't it?

It's not like this is the first time people looked at us kinda funny.

"   "

                                        How do people tell you

"   "

"   "

Yeah. You'll probably never see something like us again in your life.

apart?

"   "

If you look real close at our eyes, you can see that they're different colors.

Mine are kinda

"   "

"   "

And mine are green.

purple.

They took their sunglasses off to show us. It was hard to see their irises, though, with them squinting against the light.

You want me to shut the light off?

"   "

That's what sunglasses

It's all good. We're just a little sensitive.

"   "

"   "

are for.   We still got a little melanin, just not much. Some SPF sixty will get you

And sunblock.

"   "

Um-

right.

It's kinda like being white, just with all the negatives and none of the pluses.

"   "

hmmmmm. Alright, so you guys were working until a month ago?

"   "

"   "

It didn't take a whole lot of lobbying to get them to take the jobs. The only thing they seemed to be concerned about was whether they'd be able to wear long-sleeved T-shirts.

After Oz and Deuce left, we walked back to the garage to check on Tone.

"   "

"   "

This one's ready to go.

He tugged the cord and the motor roared to life.

That was quick.

Let me tell you a bit more about the

I've done a few a these before. Very easy.

"   "

job. Your team's going to work six eight-hour shifts a week and

I'm not really trying to work a

"   "

Don't worry. You'll be on eight a.m.

graveyard shift. These night jobs are gonna be the end of me.

"   "

to four p.m. most days. A few evenings here and there.   Given your magic touch with the

Pay?

"   "

engines, we can pay you forty an hour. Sound good?   Welcome aboard.

Yeah. Sounds real good.   **So**

"   "

You got the job.

I got the job?   **Thank you, thank you.**

Tone clasped J.D.'s right hand with both of his.

"   "

I beat that case.

So this is our guy?

Your first shift is going to be the eight to four, next Monday.

See you then.

The sound of cracking gravel accompanied Tone all the way to his car. He revved his engine once, twice, and disappeared in a cloud of gravel dust and bass pounds.

UHHHH The rawer the 'caine, the flya the product / The harder the slang, the thicka the wallet

The sun had dropped to the edge of the horizon, plunging the yard into deep shadow.

I don't know   I guess

So   Don't overthink it, Cincy. You'll figure it out.   It's a boatyard, not a space

"   "

shuttle launch. You'll be fine.

my new
favorite
song

Within a few days, I had fallen into a routine, waking up early, bustling around the yard, re-turning home exhausted, collapsing into my bed, then doing the same thing again the next day: the early season in the yard had a ceaseless, manic pace, way different from school, but refresh-ing after years of drifting.

And just a few weeks of the daily grind were enough to get the team clicking: Corey took to the job immediately, unwrapping boats at a rate that almost had me worried for their uphol-stery, speeding boaters through the refueling lines, moving what seemed like a metric ton of ice to fishermen, the only real downside to all of this being what seemed to my eye like too many of his friends—some from the ferry, some from around town—stopping by to chat. Tone had also become a bit of a local celebrity on the strength of his motor repair skills, fixing major me-chanical problems faster than anyone else on the bay and reviving dead outboards left and right.

Oz and Deuce seemed to be getting the hang of the job, although any of the problems I had with them were probably my own fault. Not knowing the difference between the two, I'd send both of them to do the same task, thinking that I was just repeating instructions to one of the two who was having a particularly slow day. Mike showed up at the start of every shift, apparently with a buzz that he rode like a pilot flying a powered-down plane on a daylong descent. Weed high and all, it was good to have a younger kid on the team—he didn't look at me like I was crazy when I asked him to rake rocks, hose down boats, or pull weeds, and he kept the rest of the guys loose. Plus, he had a good manner with customers in the supply shop when he wasn't faded.

On my days off, I worked on the apartment, slowly cleaning the place out, running back and forth from the recycling center with loads of discards in the trunk of Tom's car. And in the evenings? I took the city for a few spins.

■ ■ ■

Reflections from the TV coated the inside of the pizza parlor's grease-painted window.

After a sluggish start, the Bombers have really turned it on. Six and oh since they beat the

I saw Finnerty a few hours ago. Said you had a run-in with him today at the auto body.

"   "

Tom lowered the nub of his near-finished sub and glowered at me.

Sox at Fenway. They're riding the hot bat of number ten, Phil Rizzuto, who's hitting nearly

Nothing specific, just that you were giving him a hard time.

What did he tell you?   **Listen**

He shoved the rest of the sub into his mouth.

three-

What?

I

He swallowed hard and chased down the rest of his soda.

ninety in eighteen plate appearances

"   "

Forget it. We're late for drinks anyway.

We tossed a few dollars on the parlor's crumb-covered table and headed out the front entrance onto Decatur, sidestepping the overflowing trash bags and empty silver Coke syrup canisters that were scattered along the curb. The night air slipped and mingled around us as we
sauntered beachward, our steps interrupted by sycamore roots that pried through the sidewalks
or by ridges in the cross-streets where it seemed whole sections of different cities had been run
together. Decatur had once been the hub of the city's western half. Now it was tired, dusty,
packed-away: its parking meters headless, most of its shopfronts storm-shuttered. Old lettering
cobwebbed along the walls of weatherbeaten brick—WOOLWORTH'S MEN'S CLOTHING
HAIRDRESSERS. Here and there, newer plastic signs smoldered—BAIL BONDS, ARMY
SURPLUS—their yellows and whites sputtering behind the hands of green leaves that fanned
them with salt breezes.

From as far back as I could remember, the place we called home had been a salt-air corroded,
neon-laced no-man's-land, its welter of candy-colored Victorian houses and towering apartment blocks hanging on the grim end between decay and revival. Growing up, we had heard
all the stories about the city thirty, forty, fifty years ago. The boards. The Carousel. The crowds
of vacationers, from pineys to New York bankers to American presidents. Everything had been
bigger, brighter, cleaner back then. Our fathers came up on roaring strips and packed pavil-
ions; we made do with litter-strewn promenades along abandoned boulevards and low-slung
clubs bomb-sheltered in the shadows of aborted beach condos.

It didn't take long for me to see how the city was changing. With each passing day, the city
was becoming less and less like I remembered it. Newly minted millionaires were building
minimansions upshore and down. Closer to home, demolition crews were imploding the burnt
remains of the motels and apartment buildings that had once crowded the beachfront; in the
place of whole blocks, craters; around the craters, chain-link fences; on the fences, a paper-thin
city in watercolor and pasteboard, equally 1890s, 1920s, and 2020s; above the watercolors, new

buildings in brick and steel and shiny green glass. Watching the tourists piling off the south-bound trains into the cavernous arrivals hall, the roofers scrambling to patch up the Carousel's caved-in ceiling, the new cars lining the sidewalks along Ocean Avenue, it was hard to deny the boosters who tooled around town whistling "Glory Days." The city seemed to be getting younger as it aged, at least as long as you didn't notice the fractured blocks that the developers hadn't touched, the way history kept piling up in the alleyways and abandoned lots. The way it seemed to me, the city's development wasn't erasing or retracting time; it was bending it into a spiral.

We passed beneath the Boulevard overpass. A flock of pigeons, purple-headed, green-winged, milled about like an oil-slicked puddle. The overpass's columns were clean, covered with a patchwork of beige paint blocks.

A semi rumbled across the overpass above us, sending flakes of green paint snowing off the road's underbelly. Tom stood on top of an overturned shopping cart. We hissed curling lines of black paint across the overpass's concrete stanchions, paint fumes mingling with exhaust creeping through the bandana that covered my mouth and nose. One more turn of the wrist and I closed the loop. "Done." I tripped over my gym bag and algebra-stuffed backpack backpedaling to get a better look at our tags. "This stuff can't be good to inhale." Tom looked up. "I hear it causes memory loss." "Where'd you hear that?" "I forget."

"   "

So, every time I bring my car into the shop, it's a different thing. Flat tire, a blown belt, a

"   "

jammed window motor   and that's just the past two months. I'm sick of   Hold up,

" "

let's cross the street here.

Tom was a habitual jaywalker, always looking for the most direct route from wherever he was to wherever he was going. With the first lull in traffic, we broke up the street toward the far corner.

Palace Amusements hulked to our right like an old steamer anchored in new seas, its sides barnacled with bleached posters, brittle and peeled from the ocean breeze. Looming over us from the roofline was the Palace's famous portrait of Tillie—its weird boy-man mascot, part clown, part huckster, hair parted and pomaded, blank eyes staring out over the beachfront. He'd seen and heard everything from the rooftop: from the hotel fires of the forties, to the new boardwalks in the fifties, to the shuttering of the Convention Hall in the eighties, smiling the whole time as if to keep from crying, the smeared and pocked freckles on his cheeks looking more like tears with each passing year.

" "

Whoa, hey, look at that.

One of the Palace's metal-leaved fire exits hung open.

" "

Let's go in.

We snuck inside, drawing the door shut behind us. Sickly silver moonlight illuminated shallow rainwater puddles that had accumulated in the carpeted arcades, the linoleum-tiled snack bar, the gouge-ridden roller rink that together filled the Palace's block-wide space. Fresh clouds of dust puffed up with each step as we wended through the rows and clusters of darkened rides, here a carousel frozen in time, each of its horses rearing and straining but getting nowhere, farther along a minitrain overgrown with vines that had forced their way through the floor.

Rows of video games and slot machines were covered with tarps. Piles of old bedding, cig-arette-burned and water-stained,

I pulled the arm. Seven. Seven. Seven. Twenty silver plastic
coins poured out of the blackjack machine into my gray
paper cup, piling up on top of coils of red two-point
tickets. Five thousand more and that Nolan Ryan rookie
card was mine.

rested against the concession stand, surrounded by empty Sterno cans and charcoal ash, wet newspapers and rat droppings. Light slipped through the splits in the plywood that covered the main entrance. I crept close and peered out.

A crowd buzzed under the Palace's bulbless marquee, their heads and shoulders limned by the streetlamps winking on in the gathering dark. They were knotted around an overturned garbage can where a dealer, fitted cap low, head bobbing, swirled three tent-bent cards in rhythm with a boombox thumping at his feet:

Rollin' deep with the Jersey fam / Pullin' sticks, doin' vicks / Whippin' the fly Land / But that was just a
Ay ay, scare money don't make money.   **Whatchu got, money?**

dream that got shattered / In the
Which one, which one? Where you at?

The whoop of a police siren sent me jumping and the crowd scrambling for cover. In the mad dash, the trash can tipped and scattered the dealer's china-patterned cards across the pave-ment like porcelain shards. The police horse-collared two members of the crowd and slammed them against the hood of the cruiser. Quick pat-downs, rooting through pockets. The boom-box, upended in the rush, fired bass lines and drum kicks into the sidewalk. The sidewalk an-swered back with a muffled roar. The sounds of the siren echoed off the walls of the abandoned blocks behind us. Blue and red flashes pulsed on the plate glass windows on the far side of the street. Thin glassine Baggies shone white in the street light. The cops pocketed the Baggies and hustled their captives into the backseats of the squad cars. A siren burst and they were gone.

Yeah.

Let's get outta here.

I inched the exit open and surveyed the street.

It's safe.

"   "

We continued on past the boarded-up entrance to the Asbury Lanes.

"   "

Where was I?   Right   I'm sick of sinking all my money into that damn car. And

"   "

I'm sick of Finnerty getting rich off it. How many years did we go to school together? And

"   "

he can't give me a break here and there on a spark plug?

A right off Decatur and onto the Circuit, the long avenue that circled the city's oceanfront blocks. Oceanside, all the obstructions that crowded in on the Boulevard—the towering bill-boards and fast-food signs, the rows of utility poles lined up like an armada's worth of masts—fell away. Along the northern horizon, Lower Manhattan shone like a fluorescent bar graph, dwarfed, at least here, by our city's own skyline: the Free Fall, the Sling Shot, the Ultimate Rush. Along the water's edge, the boards' booths lay heaped like paling embers. Faint sounds of washing waves mixed with the dull bumping of stereos from the line of cars loping up the Boulevard toward us. A blocky Escalade truck on chrome rims, a bone white '80s Thunder-bird, and a low-riding '64 Chevy.

"   "

Right. If it were, there wouldn't

I ask Finnerty to check the alignment on the thing. Easy, right? Just twenty minutes or so.

"   "

be a story.

I'm sitting in that waiting room for two hours before he finally comes back. *Two hours.* He

"   "

[   ]

comes back saying the alignment is fine, but that I need new brake pads. I just *got* new ones

"   "

True.

from him six months ago. He says I'm driving the car too hard, too much start and stop.

"   "

Not likely.

I tell him that I think he sold me a bum set. He's like, if I weren't such a cheapskate, my

"   "

Probably right.

pads wouldn't be worn out. I'm like, maybe I could put a better set on my car if my buddy

"   "

[   ]

would give me a break on the price. He says he can't. His dad's tired of him giving out fa-

[   ]

vors to his friends. I'm thinking, all right, so he's been helping other people out, but not me?

"   "

Oh no. Here it comes.

Who the fuck does this guy think he is? Or better yet, who the fuck does he think *I* am.

So what did you say?

[   ]

I said, "Who the fuck do you think I am?"

The Tides Bar glowed at the northern edge of the boards. A cluster of silhouettes lounged on the ramp that wrapped around the outside of the bar. Near the door, other shadows sipped drinks against the still chilly ocean drafts in the drowsy early evening. Inside busier by a little, a light warm-up for the high season.

The count's three to one on Cano.   *That's strike two.*

No way! Really?

[   ]

Yeah, I said it.   When have I never *not* said what I mean? He deserved it.

Full count, runners on first

"   "

He has a point.

There he is. **Yo, Frisco!**

Tom headed for a table overlooking the ocean. The shiny scrape-scratched hardwood floor creaked and groaned underfoot. The inside of the bar was all flat screens and picture windows, vistas of the ocean tiled along the walls with scenes from ball games and surfing videos, shots of tropical oceans blending with the water outside in some unstable mosaic. At the right time of day, at the right angle, it was hard to tell where the images on-screen ended and the real ocean began, the televised depths in their plasma flatness sometimes seeming deeper and more lively than the ocean itself.

and second.   ***Hernandez throws to first. Berra slides back safely.***

"   "

Frisco who?

Frisco, Frisco, long time, no see, man.   **Hey, this is my roommate,**

What's up, Tom?   Ditto.

Hernandez checks first.

What's up?

Cincy.   **How long you been here?**

Jeff Frisco. Good to meet you.   Thirty minutes or so.

He ran a hand through what was left of his hair as he reached his other hand across the table to stump out a Camel in the ashtray, laying it next to three other identical butts. He was wearing a polo shirt with a wavy worn-out collar and a pair of stylishly ripped jeans.

and he slides in for the Yanks' second run of the inning. Cano gets an RBI on the play and Berra's advanced to third.

"   "

There's money in advertising like that?

Drinks? They're on me.   Humor me. Seems like you could

The Giants' pitching coach is going to try to calm Hernandez down. Let's take a look at Cano's hit again. He laced a

For a month or so, yeah. The starving have to stick to-

"   "

use a handout anyway. You live with this bum?

nice long single off the center-field wall.

gether.

He's a professional philosopher.

Starving? That's a little extreme. You a musician like this guy?

Strike one to Winfield

But now?

"   "

Say no more. I was into all that at one point.   Not really. So what are you doing down here?

The second pitch to Winfield. Just misses the inside

I'm on leave. I've been working at a boatyard to make ends meet.

"   "

Boatyard, huh? Now *that's* unneces-

corner. Ball two.   **Winfield is entering the game batting two-fifty lifetime against Hernandez in twenty**

I don't think

"   "

sary hardship. You should go into the ad industry.   I had the same doubts before I started.

previous plate appearances.

"   "

What doubts? I didn't even get a word in edgewise.

"   "

I wanted to write screenplays, but my undergrad loans were heaaa-vy. Some friends said copywriting

Hernandez goes right down the center of the plate for strike two.

How's the writing going?

"   "

would be an easy nine to five that would give me time to write.   Haven't writ-

Two and two to Winfield.

And you're happy about that?

Me neither.

Frisco's been pretty successful.

ten anything in three years.

Hey, I

Cano's taking another long lead.

Hernandez releases and

What's the secret?

What's the score in the game?

"

"

figured out the game early and haven't looked back.

Listen closely, something this

CANO'S OFF FOR SECOND! And the throw from Giancanni is just

"

"

If he doesn't say so himself.

"

"

good doesn't come along twice.

Frisco rolled up his sleeves and lit another Camel.

for his tenth stolen base of the season!

"

"

"

"

Pretend I've got my PowerPoint here.

He wiped his hand down an invisible computer screen beside him, then took a drag and smoothed out his shirt.

Mantle swings and

"

"

"

"

There are two, and only two, types of people in the world. Hold on   HEY, COULD YOU MUTE

“   ”

“   ”

THIS TV? I hate baseball anyway.   So, yeah, there are two types of people in the world: naïve

“   ”

“   ”

consumers and cynical consumers. The naïve ones believe anything you tell them and want anything you

“   ”

“   ”

show them.

He drummed his fingertips on the table.

“   ”

“   ”

Cynical consumers are trickier. They won't believe anything you tell them, but if you tell them what they

“   ”

“   ”

won't believe like you don't believe it yourself, they'll probably end up wanting what you show them.

“   ”

“   ”

It's like they let themselves indulge in the product as a reward for figuring out how the ad works. I design my

How?

“   ”

ads to hit both of these groups simultaneously.   Okay, this is the ad that landed me my first gig. It

“   ”

“   ”

was a spot with testimonials from people about what they'd rather do than eat a Whopper.

Frisco held his hands up to focus our attention on his face.

"   "

"   "

"I'd rather go hungry than eat a Whopper." Then a shot of a Whopper. Then, "I'd rather go to school

"   "

"   "

naked than eat a Whopper." Whopper. Then, "I'd rather electrocute myself than eat a Whopper."

"   "

We crashed into the hard plastic booth after five hours on the
road. The moon hung high over the Pine Barrens. Out across
the parking lot, cars zipped in and out of the filling station.
I bit into the Whopper and followed it with a swig of extra
sweet Coke. Man, I could go for a Whopper right now.

Stop, no. That's how they get you.

"   "

Whopper. Then, "I'd rather be buried alive than eat a Whopper." Then, a final long shot of a Whopper,

hmmmm

"   "

with an overlay that said, "Fine, Have it *Your* Way." Annnnnd cut. So?   Well?

So it's like two different routes to the same end.   I can't think of any-

"   "

Yeah. Pretty liberating, right?

thing more depressing.

"   "

And if you like that, I've got more for you: I don't even write ads anymore.

"　　　　　　　　　　　　　　"

"　　　　　　　　　　　　　　"

I've got a stable of copywriters working for me back in the city. All I do is fob the ideas off on corporate

How

"　　　　　　　　　　　　　　"

types and cash the checks.　　　　How do I look myself in the mirror every morning? Easy. When I'm in

"　　　　　　　　　　　　　　"

"　　　　　　　　　　　　　　"

my suit, I'm "Jeff, Ad Professional," and I say what I have to say to touch target demographics and create

"　　　　　　　　　　　　　　"

Does he answer these questions a lot?　　　　Is he even paying attention to what I'm saying?

"　　　　　　　　　　　　　　"

brand identity blah blah blah blah blah. When I'm not, I'm "Frisco, Twenty-something," and I go plot the

"　　　　　　　　　　　　　　"

"　　　　　　　　　　　　　　"

proletarian revolution and grow my own organic flax and whatever else we're supposed to do at our age.

"　　　　　　　　　　　　　　"

"　　　　　　　　　　　　　　"

Maybe if I was pushing anthrax or coke, I'd have a problem with it, but it's just burgers and soda. So,

"　　　　　　　　　　　　　　"

"　　　　　　　　　　　　　　"

back to the eternal question: drinks or no drinks? There's only one answer, my friends.

Frisco snapped a fresh twenty out of his pocket, chuckling, and strode to the bar.

Like what?

He wasn't always like this, you know.

Tom puffed an invisible cigarette and thrummed his fingers while jerking his head around, wide-eyed.

Really?

Totally. Back in college, he had this kind of chill, Zen thing going on. He went totally

"   "

off the rails after graduation, though. Between you and me, I don't think he even believes

What do you think he actually believes?

himself. He's too edgy to be sold on what he's selling.   I

"   "

have about as much of a clue as he seems to. Just don't get too down on him, though. There's

Number 27 Jack Baldschun

"   "

a good guy in there somewhere.

Frisco reappeared with three Coronas.

his last three appearances. He'll face the Rays' Evan Longoria, with Fred McGriff to follow.

Yeah, it's beautiful down here, right?

"   "

Awww, mannnn, it feels good to be down the Shore again.   You're

Not at all.

"   "

kidding me. Please tell me you're kidding me.   *Beautiful* is the last word I'd use to describe this

Strike one to Longoria.

So why do you come down?

"   "

place.   Let's put it like this: The upside of being in a place where you feel

Baldschun sends that next pitch wide, evening the count. The bullpens for both sides are

"   "

"   "

like you're always about to get jumped is that no one gives a damn what you do. There's no pretense here.

wearing a bit thin. We've seen five pitchers from each team today.

"   "

"   "

If I want to sit in a lawn chair out by the curb and drink my ass off, so be it. My neighbors will probably

The third pitch is a ball, tight inside. That brings the

I

"   "

come out and join me. Satisfied?   Look, it's not going to get this place into *Travel and Leisure*, but it's

count to two and one.

I've never found another place like it. It's   Yeah, it's home.

home.

the truth, for what that's worth. You?

Longoria checks his swing. Ball three.

"   "

It's got its own rhythms, you know what I'm saying?

Seriously, this is Jersey we're talking about.

Swing and a miss. Full count now.

"   "

Well, now that you mention

There's got to be something you don't like about this place. Anything?

The Rays could really use a hit.

"   "

it. I could do without some of the dudes I went to high school with.

"   "

Tom took a swig of his Corona. He paused as he went to place it back down on the table.

Longoria fouls the Baldschun

"   "

Wait, wait. Who's that?

Where?

Tom pointed to a girl at the bar.

Baldschun better match his

"   "

How do you know her?

Oh, her? Her name's Aimi.   Friend of a friend. I'll get her over here. Aimi!

She turned around with a smile.

pitch total.

"   "

"   "

Come meet some friends of mine.

She strolled over.

And Baldschun sends a sizzling fastball down the middle of the

"   "

"   "

Aimi   Tom, Cincy. Tom, Cincy   Aimi.   Join us?

Okay, but just for a bit.

Tom turned his back to us and boxed Aimi off from the rest of the table. She was pretty, in the way that all the girls Tom ever linked up with were pretty: average height, blond hair, eyes wide with an excitement that usually revealed itself to be some kind of low-level neurosis after a few weeks. The trend started in high school with Jen Monaghan. Every girlfriend he'd had since looked like a new version of her, like he was hell-bent either on overcoming the time she dumped him the day before junior prom, or hell-bent on reliving it. If he hadn't told me otherwise, I would have assumed that the pictures he sent through e-mail during college were shots of him and her, maybe with a different hairstyle, maybe a little older, but still, fundamentally, the same girl—the same looks, the same personality, the same story.

JUST WIDE

He doesn't play, does he?

"   "

Frisco pulled another cigarette from his shirt pocket; a few loose ones peeked out from the foil packet.

Swing

Sure.

Let me ask you a question.   Are you really cool with your life down here? Don't you think you'd be

and a miss. Longoria's out on strikes.

Oh,

Where have I seen *her*?

She stepped onto the dock.

She jogged by on the promenade.

That's the girl

from the bus stop.

happier in New York? Making real money?   You there, man?

Vera!

Vera wandered in our direction, pulsing in the light split and sifted by the ceiling fans circling overhead. She was about five-nine, slender and curved, like the curls of smoke rising from the flaring end of a cigarette. Perfect.

She settled onto the stool next to me.

Hi, I'm Cincy.

beautiful. Really beautiful.

Nice to meet you, I'm Vera.

"   "

Her eyes were dark and deep and glossed with twin smudges of white light. I couldn't read them.

Huh?   There's

He still has half a pack left.

"   "

Is there a place to buy cigs here?   Cigs. Where can I get them?

a 7-Eleven on the Boulevard, like a block from here.

"   "

I'm just going to step out for a second. You need

I'm good.

No, thanks.

anything?   Vera?

Vera glanced over at Aimi and Tom.

Don't worry about him. He's harmless.

"   "

Our eyes met. The corners of her mouth rose, then she turned back to the drink she was swirling in her hand. She began to stroke her calf with her free hand, biting her lip and look⁄ing down.

"   "

"   "

Hey.

Her head turned. A waiter sidled up to the table.

"   "

Who is *this* guy?   Maybe that's a good thing.

          Heeeeeeeey.   Out and about. Things have been

Hey, Vera.   Long time no see. Where you been?

"   "

kinda hectic recently.   Nice shirt.

          I've missed you around here.

She touched his elbow.

Who *is* this guy?   Wish I could say the same.

Sure you did.   I know you.

I wore it just for you.   What? You doubt me?

Why's she even talking to him?

Nothing, Aimi. He's just trying to flatter me.

Appetizers,

What're you two up to?   Is it working?

I think we're good.   If we want anything, we'll let you know.

anyone?   Nothing?   Ooooookay.

Vera turned back to Aimi and me.

Flirting with the wait staff, are we?

Stop it! I just don't want him to spit

Vera's a bit touchy-touchy.

in my food, thank you.   I don't want a pack of rabid admirers.

She has a pack of rabid admirers.

I don't want the attention. I Ohh, I LOVE this song!

The pack seems to get bigger every day.

She grabbed my wrist.

I was a fool from the start / Fooling around with my mind instead of my heart / I was young and fine and

"   "

"   "

you plucked me clean / But you didn't know that I didn't know that you didn't know what I mean

"   "

His voice was perfect. Just listen.

I watched her rocking back and forth to the jukebox, a smile playing across her lips. As she leaned forward to say something to me, her hand pressing down on my knee, her face drawing closer, the Tides's time signature slipped for a second, the pulse of the fans, the rolling of the waves, the ebb and flow of the conversations around us contracted and expanded. Listening to her was like hearing my new favorite song for the first time,

a blurred melody   She's a friend of mine from school

a half-heard lyric

Yeah, you?

everything rising up for a beat

Definitely.   the blush of the familiar

Once or twice

a heart skip, a thrill

All ready to rewind and press PLAY before it was over, to get another listen, to start putting it all together.

The rest of that night—an hour, a minute?—passed in the blink of an eye. Before she left, she punched her number into my phone and pressed SEND.

I've got it. See you soon.

Call me? Or should I call you?

She and Aimi walked out through the front doors. The crowd washed in behind them.

Split and sifted. Here then gone.

I cupped my hands over the candle as it burned out,
letting the smoke curl inside the hollow between my
palms, one more moment of warmth. "Hey, hold up!"

Tom punched me on the shoulder.

Wha   what?

Wake up, man.

byrd lives!

(ANIMAL HOUSE)

A few days later, I was strolling along the beachfront promenade on the way back from my lunch break with a bag of sandwiches in arm for the guys back at the yard. The air was slowly warming up, the shadows of buildings and lampposts lengthening on their west–east crawl away from the sun, street noise bubbling with the convecting waves of heat that rose from the blacktop. A crowd of children, necks darkened by the sun, coasted by on flat-pedaled bikes, chanting the hook from some song or another off the radio. My phone rang.

My dad.

Yeah, I think I'm in a nice groove. The team's good, business has been steady.

Settling in?   J.D. hasn't

Mostly day shifts, usually a day completely off each week. Not bad.

been working you too hard?

Ssssure.

Uh-oh.

Could I ask a favor?   We're getting ready to show the house and the front porch

Okay.

Crap.

really needs to get repainted.   I would've done it myself the last time we were up,

Yeah, well, that's kinda rough work.

Why didn't you get a painter?

but my back couldn't handle all the crouching.   I bought all

"   "

[   ]

the supplies, though. There's a belt sander and paint in the shed in the backyard. Do you

Yeah, I can do it.

I leaned back against   I really want to say no.
the porch railing, tired
after three straight
evenings of work.

think you can handle it?   Great.

"   "

[   ]

Combination on the lock is the same. We'll treat you to a big dinner the next time we're up.

When will that be?   No problem.

That's the last
time I let an
insurance
salesman
cold call me.

Soon. We'll keep you up-to-date. Thanks again.

A swim in the ocean would have been refreshing; instead, I wiped the sweat off my forehead and looked out over the breakers. A hundred yards off Casino Pier, a cluster of cranes ducked and swooped. The tangled form of a ship was rising in the water at their feet: the recreated wreck of the *Morro Castle*, an ocean liner that ran aground in the shallows off the boards in the early forties. Back when the *Morro* first foundered, Shore entrepreneurs ran motorboat tours out to the wreck, a tidy racket that kept a steady stream of tourists flowing to the beach until the ship's rusted remnants slipped beneath the waves. Anchoring a new *Morro* off the shore had become a way of anchoring our changing vistas . . . or that's at least how the developers explained it. Good enough for the crowds that were gathered on the beachfront to gawk at the process of building something destroyed.

Gawkers, walkers, sunbathers: the whole shorefront—from the sand to the bars and restaurants lining the promenade—was bustling, couples strolling, sand-covered toddlers scampering around the foot washes, skateboarders weaving in and out of the crowds. The city's giant central jetty parted the water to my right, slick with seaweed and dusted with shattered shells.

The nor'easter lurched into our latitudes that afternoon, real, pounding, menacing, the multicolored swirl of rain densities and cloud formations that we had tracked during a week's worth of study halls and lunch breaks now rain, wind, waves, waves too good to waste on a high school history class. So we snuck out between periods and headed for the beach, stopping home for just a few minutes to grab boards and wetsuits, then out on the water. An hour into it, breakers fifteen feet high, surf taller, faster than we'd had all summer. The storm surge flowed around, over, nearly through me. I crested a wave and crashed down into its trough. My surfboard slapped an aborted breath out of my lungs as I hit bottom. Fifty yards upshore, Tom strained against the break. I had drifted far from where we started, from the broad open beach by the promenade to the shadows of the old casino and the whitewater cut up by the city's craggy jetty. The ocean dipped as a new breaker rose in front of me. This was what I'd been waiting all day for, all year for. I didn't even think about it: I just went for it, swung my board beachward and dug into the water with a double overhand stroke. My hands ripped through the froth. I shot forward just as the wave broke. I slid down the wave's face, braced my hands against the top of the board and swung into a standing position, zipped southward again as the top of the wave foamed above me. I pushed hard with my right leg and started to climb. Tiptoed along the crest, down again. Leaned left, leaned right, left again, right and then . . . I hit a phantom chop and my left foot slipped. I caught myself staring at my foot hovering out in space. Then the wave buckled. I hung airborne as the board shot forward, leaving me behind. The barrel of the wave tackled me, tightening, ripping, snarling now. My leash pulled taut, yanking my right leg first, then my whole body. I rag-dolled in the jaws of the wave, until I slammed into the jetty and

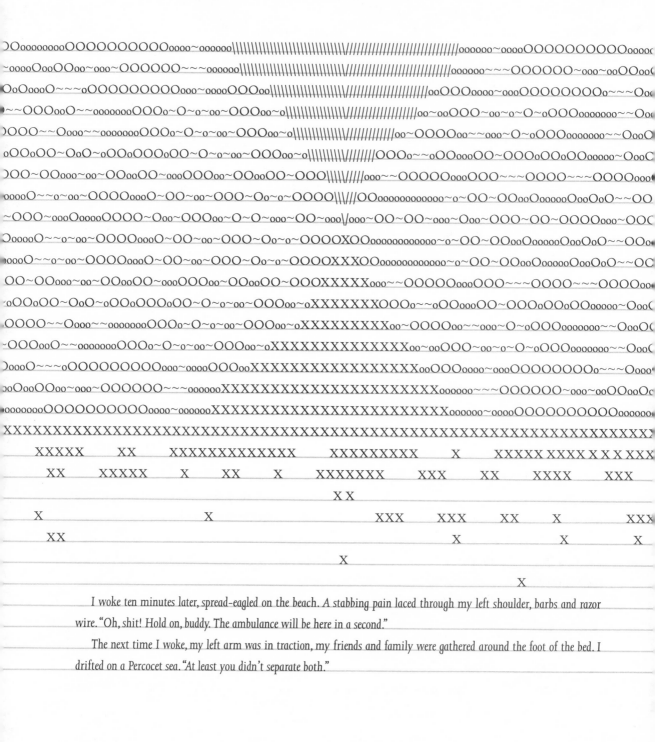

I woke ten minutes later, spread-eagled on the beach. A stabbing pain laced through my left shoulder, barbs and razor wire. "Oh, shit! Hold on, buddy. The ambulance will be here in a second."

The next time I woke, my left arm was in traction, my friends and family were gathered around the foot of the bed. I drifted on a Percocet sea. "At least you didn't separate both."

I reached up under my left shirtsleeve and ran my fingers over the scar that crept down the crown of my shoulder like a tree root.

A disturbance rippled my way along the promenade. The crowd parted. A stranger half-brushed, half-bumped me, then continued stumbling southward.

He was overdressed for the weather, nearly bursting through a rough flannel suit, sweating through a wrinkled white shirt. A tie hung loosely from his collar, its knot oddly thick and twisted out of shape. His face was full, puffed and shiny, his skin dark under a film of sweat. His fingers—thick, ashy, and calloused—folded and unfolded in stringless cat's cradles.

Li'l Phil and I, we'd go to the Hi-Hat, the Reno with some mezzirolls. KC was hopping back then,

we'd watch those cats cut, light up a mezziroll and watch those cats cut because   you know

Because   because   He wanted it and he got it. It was the only way it could be, since

I mean, when you really look at it   because, you know

A yo, the FUCK are you doin'?

The stranger crashed into another man lugging a cooler, sending a dozen bottles of beer spilling across the promenade. Despite the commotion, the stranger remained fixed on his hands.

But, but, you see, and, and   But but but because I know, I know it because be-

Are you retarded?

cause because

Are you going to

A woman stepped in between the two men. Vera.

Sir. Sir, calm down.   Give him a break. He doesn't know what he's doing.

"   "

But this son of a   **If you**

The stranger continued to stare down at his feet.

                              Do you want me to help you pick these up?

"   "

think I'm gonna let this   **I want you to get outta**

        He doesn't even know what's going on.   No, *you* look.

"   "

my way so I can   **Look**

She gave the tourist a hard stare and shoved the two bottles into his hands.

Take. Your. Beer.

"   "

"   "

It was hard to tell who was more confused at this point: the mumbling stranger or the tourist taking orders from a woman half his size. The tourist was silent.

It won't happen again, trust me.

"   "

"   "

She grabbed the stranger by the elbow and led him away from the gathering crowd.

Byrd.   Byrd!   Byrd, go home.

See back in K.C., at that time, woooooooooo we   Li'l Phil

She snapped her fingers inches from his nose and shot him the same hard stare she'd given the tourist. Byrd stopped speaking, then turned, slowly, fingers still working, and shambled away. A stumble, a misstep, a lean, and he disappeared behind a bank of parked cars.

That was great. You normally tough-talk Bennies and bums?

The Bennie or the bum?

I know him.

Liberty Byrd, the mumbler from Liberty. I mean, from around. He lives down the street from me.

Square?

"   "

Liberty Square was one of the city's unreconstructed back blocks, marooned out on the west side of the tracks, home to acres of ruined motels covered with creeping vines and white paint flaking off in the salty air. *No one* lived out there.

You live on Liberty Square?

"   "

She exhaled.

So what's

I messed this up royally. I do social work at a shelter on the Square. Byrd's a regular.

the big deal?

We're not really supposed to interact with guests outside the house. And we're defi-

"   "

nitely *not* supposed to point them out to other people on the street. So, can you keep a secret?

Tell me more. Maybe I'll forget.

"   "

She smiled.

What's Byrd's problem?

I don't try to label people. He just talks in these endless circles. Kind of the

That must be pretty weird.

same five or six topics. If you don't stop him, he can go on forever.   It's

"   "

the same thing with everyone that comes in. They just need a blank screen for their own thoughts.

So you're a

The less of me I put in there, the better for them.   I'm whatever they want me to be. It's

"   "

all in their heads.

Her phone rang. She paused, then looked back at me.

"   "

Just a sec.

She turned to the side and hunched over her open phone.

"   "

What's up?   Sure.   Okay.

She turned back to me.

What's up?   Well, before you go   What are you doing

I have to go.   Umm Something came up.   Yes?

Saturday night? I would've called, but you're standing right here.   You accepting?

                                                     You offering?   No fair!

          All right. You and I, Saturday night. Let's walk the boards. Meet at D Street and Ocean

I asked first.

Ave.?

"   "

          She paused.

     Okay, see you then.

Sure.   Yeah.   See you then.

     I was tempted to call it a day after that, but I still had the guys' sandwiches.
     The rest of the walk was easy. Even the wharfside seemed like a bright and happy place. I
might've even had a little strut going as I walked into the break room.

                              Me?   I'm Cincy.

                                             Mike, you high?

All right, Corey got the subs, Co-rey-got-the-subs.   Um, no.

"   "

     You're gonna wish you had all this time you're wasting back.

Yeah.   I'm not even really that blown.

"   "

     Hey, Cince. You notice that dude across the street?

Just a little.

I followed Tone's finger. A man was leaning against the pay phone outside the Inlet Surf Shop and fiddling with his nails. His face was hidden beneath a mop of curly hair and blocky black wraparound shades. He didn't look any different from the hundreds of surfers who wandered around the wharf this time of year.

Nah. Should I have?   What do you think he's

I've seen him hanging around here the last few days.

"   "

up to?   No clue.   I'm

I think he's a narc. You know about anything going down around here?   Nothing?

"   "

clean.

What about you, Mike?   Just keep an eye out, cool? Shit's going down all over the place.

Nah.

Tone tossed me a newspaper.

A police raid?

Police raided a raucous party at 1126 Fifteenth Street Sunday morning.   Mayor's new Animal

Yeah, man. I was there that night;

"   "

Is that even legal?

House initiative   drug arrests marijuana, ecstasy, cocaine   State and federal

The police horse-collared two members of

the crowd and slammed them against the

hood of the cruiser. Thin glassine Baggies

shone white in the street light.

they arrested damn near everybody they could get their hands on.   **It is if they "find"**

"   "

prosecutors seeking illegal drug suppliers

something on you while you're waiting to get processed. And if I'm reading this paper, right? With a

mayor like the one we've got here, and the feds, all hunting for drugs? You *know* they're "finding" a

lot. Just giving y'all a heads-up.

Over the course of the afternoon, I tried to keep an eye on the suspicious surfer through the front office windows. He'd leave his spot for brief periods, sometimes going into the surf shop, sometimes the clam shack, but he'd always return soon thereafter. He didn't do much of anything while he was out there—no phone calls, no note-taking—just scanned the yard.

A camera panned the office. I appeared in the center of the viewfinder, head down. Click,

shutter, capture, click shutter capture.

Why would the cops be monitoring our yard? *"I think he's*

[   ]

a narc." That seems kinda off-base.

How would Tone even know?

[   ]
[   ]

"I beat that case." What case? *"They arrested damn near everybody."* For what? Dealing drugs? Using them?

Before I left for the evening, I climbed the stairs to J.D.'s office. I found him leaning back in his chair, eyes to the ceiling.

Something wrong, J.D.?

Should I bring it up with J.D.? Like every other surfer, "I think he's a narc." Forget it. I don't want to open that

Nooo, I just got fed up with that book I was reading. It was a complete

"   "

can of worms.

waste of time.

He pointed to a fat volume splayed on the floor. The office was a mess: the walls papered with maps covered with handwritten notes in black ink, random pieces of navigational equipment and fittings scattered across the floor, the only clear space seeming to be the window looking crossbay toward the yacht club and golf course. J.D. was seated in the corner by the window, behind an old claw-footed oak desk covered in hardbound books.

You've been putting in a lot of time up here.   I thought

I'm planning a dive with a friend in England.

you gave up salvage?

I did too, but then David called me up about this Spanish galleon. It's been

He found it?

lost for four hundred years.   No, but we think we have a pretty good idea where it is.

Aren't people using GPS and robot subs and stuff to find these wrecks now?

That takes all the fun out

So   wait   You're reading books

of it.

I stooped down and picked up the fallen book.

old travelogues to find it?

If only. There are so many conflicting accounts. If the wreck even exists,

"   "

it could be anywhere in here.

He pointed to the map behind his desk. A cluster of thumbtacks stuck out of the waters off the southern coast of Portugal. J.D. had drawn a rough circle around the tacks.

So what're you going to do?

I'll keep reading and try to shrink the field down. But, at this juncture,

But you don't know exactly

it looks like we're just going to go out in September and start diving.

where it is.   So you'll hire a crew and take a ship out to some spot in the ocean, just because some

And?

Dutch sailor thought there might have been a wreck there centuries ago?   And not even be sure that

Yes.

there's something there?   Because?

Yes.   There's nothing like that split second before you break the

Or nothing.

surface on a new stretch of ocean. There could be anything down there.   Or nothing.

I

You're right. But it's the uncertainty that makes the search worth it.   At some point, you just have

How

to take a deep breath and dive.   Why don't you come see? I'll be flying out after Labor Day.

I don't think I'd be a great crew member. I've never   Yeah.
                                        You've crewed boats before, right?   This

"   "

won't be any different. You have to be certified to dive the wreck itself, but I'm not asking you to

"   "

do that.

J.D. pulled another map from a desk drawer and tossed it to me.

"   "

Think about it.   For now, though, let's get out of here. It's late.

The map was soft and creased, tissuey with age and refoldings. I stuck it in my back pocket and followed J.D. downstairs. As we passed through the lobby on our way out for the night, J.D. disappeared into a closet near the front offices. He emerged two minutes later, empty-handed.

What was that about?   Cameras?
            Just changing the tape in the cameras.   The whole yard is wired

"   "

up. See?

J.D. pointed out one camera in the corner of the lobby, aimed inward toward the cash register and another in the storage space behind the register that faced out toward the front entrance.

Why go through all the trouble? Have you been robbed before?

No, but you never know when they'll

"   "

come in handy.

ice cream

Who cares what else happened that week? I didn't. Saturday couldn't come fast enough; the boardwalk—and Vera—couldn't be close enough.

Ever since I could remember, I loved the boardwalk's minor chaos. Its visual overload: broad, searing white sands; the glittering surf; spinning, neon-skeletoned Ferris wheels; Day-Glo and deep pastel signs splashed with art-nouveau / art-deco / art—Home Depot swirls and stylized types; the garish, flashing arcade lights. Tactile frenzy: the sun beating down on your shoulders; skin tightening with drying sunblock; the rough sand; full-body immersion in the ocean and the muggy air; the boards burning underfoot; sea breeze flowing around your body; slow salt encrustation; the heat. And the smells: pine tar; fried everything; sticky sweet candies and shakes; the sand's earthy musk; the salted air; hot, wafting blacktop; chlorine from the massive waterslides; garlic; grease; cheap cologne.

But it's the sounds that really got me. Sounds like a crowd of bathers escaping from a shark sighting, a surf line stampede of noises, grabbing each other by the head, shoving each other down, surging forward and falling, breaching the wash for another breath: thumping bass; car horns; idling engines; crunching driveway gravel; propeller planes overhead, dragging yards of flapping banners; rolling breakers; children's laughter; blaring tinny radios; lifeguards' whistles; zooming ATVs; swooping kites; ice cream trucks with their "Pop Goes the

Weasel" calliopes and cowbells; frying steaks, chickens, and shrimp; arcades—the thwacking of pucks and paddles on air hockey tables; buzzing, whirring, exploding video games; rides—slamming bumper cars; swoosh-rumbling roller coasters; whooshing multiarmed scramblers; games—roulette wheels clacking; water whizzing; balloons popping and bells ringing at the clown's mouth shooting galleries; flinging ringing coins and hoops; softballs banging against steel-lined bottles. And the voices—criers, hecklers, riders screaming, the overflowing bars, beaches, gulls.

throbthrobthrobwhooooooshsqueaaaaaaaaaaakrrnnnnhnnnnripripripripropᵖʳᵒᵖrattlerattlerattlerattlerumbferumbferRUMBLERUMBLERUMBLERUMBLERUMBLEWHOOOOO
OOOOOOSSSSSSSSSSSSSSSH thwap YOOOOOOOOOOOOOOOOOOUUUUU thwapHEEEEEEEEELP! °ping °ping °ping PINGAHHHHHHH!
PingpingAHHHHHHHHHHHHHHHHHHHHHHHHHHHPing °PingPing °ping °pingSHUFFLEpifffffft ppifffffft °pifffffftpifffpifffffftpifffffftslapPOP° pifffffft
pifffffftpifffffft POP POP POPslapPOP pifffffft pifffffft pifffffft ppifffffffftpoppoppoppifffpifftpopPUNKTPUNKTRING SHUFFLEYOOOOO
OOUUOUOUHOOOOOO °OOOO hssthssthssthssthssthssthssthssthssthssthssthssthssthssthssthssthssthssthssthssthssthssthssthssthsst pifftPOP
pifftpifft ʺAHHHHHHHHHHHHHH wooooooooooooAHHHHHHHHHHHooooooooooooooooooopifffffftpfffftpifffffft° pifff
ffftslapPOP° pifffffft pifffffftpifffffftPOPPOPPOPPOPP° pifffffft pifffffftpifffffftPOPPOPPOPPOPpifff
throbthrobthrobwhooooooshsqueaaaaaaaaaaaaaaakrrrnnrrnnnnripripriprip
ripropclickclickclickclickclickclickclickclickWHOOOOOOOOOOOOOO
OOOOOSHrattlerattlerattlerattlerumblerumbleRUMBLERUMBLERU
MBLERUMBLEWHOOOOOOOOOOOOOOSSSSSSSSSSSSH

By the time I reached the southern pier at D Street, the sun was already dipping under the rooflines to the west. I sat on the edge of a bench on the side of the boards and stared off across the dunes, watching the ocean speeding from blue to purple to black in the dying light.

"AHHHHHHHHHHHHHHHHHHHHHHHHHHHHHH! Fuck, Doc!" The muscles in my left shoulder clicked and strained as I windmilled my arm, eyes fastened on the knot of yellow-colored muscle on the generic musculature chart that hung over the therapist's desk. "Good, good. Again now." I gripped the one-pound plate, letting my middle and ring finger hook through the center hole and pressing the edge of the weight against the heel of my hand.

O~oOooooO~~o~oo~OOOOoooO~OO~oo~OOO~Oo~o~OOOOXOOoooooooooooo~o~OO~OO
ooOoooooOoooOoO~~OOooOoOOoOooooO~~o~oo~OOOOoooO~OO~oo~OOO~Oo~o~OOOOX
XXOOooooooooooooo~o~OO~OOoooOooooooOooOoO~~OOoooOo~OOO~OOooo~oo~OOooOO~ooo
OOOoo~OOooOO~OOOXXXXXooo~~OOOOOooooOOO~~~OOOO~~~OOOOoooOOooooo

I tried again. *"AHHHHHHHHHHHHHHHHHHHHHHHHHHHHHHHHH"* I was sweating just two rotations into my first physio session. *"How many more of these today?"* *"Rotations?   Five."* *"How many more until I'm back to normal?"* *"Maybe a thousand. Maybe ten thousand. Maybe never. You got banged up pretty badly."*

And here I thought you were standing me up.
Hey.

Vera smiled.

Shall we go?
"   "

It was the height of summer. We were awash in crowds, people everywhere, buzzing inside the arcades, milling around the edge of the grandstand, loitering outside the bars and restau⁄rants, stumbling down the boards with giant gangly stuffed animals.

All my life.   From birth through high school.
How long have you lived here?   All?

Her eyes met mine.

I left for a while. You?   Where'd you move
I moved here last year after I got my master's in social work.

from?   Where are you originally from, though? Where's home?
I'd been out West for school.   I've moved

"   "

around a lot.

I raised my eyebrow.

My dad worked overseas for a while. There's nowhere I *haven't* lived for at least a month.

did he do?

He was a consultant to foreign companies. My brothers and I used to joke that he was

Wouldn't you be able to tell?

a spy.   It's not like all spies walk around wearing tuxedos and drink-

And he never explained what he did?

ing martinis.   I wouldn't have wanted to know even if I could.

Why not?   You keep a lot of secrets?

Some things are better left unsaid.   I don't think I

I'm very much into "Say what

have to let everyone know everything that's on my mind.   You?

you mean, mean what you say."   Then I don't say any-

But what if you don't know what you mean?

thing.   How could I?   What if anything short of the whole truth is a lie?

Nothing?   Tell part of the truth.

Yeah.   Every day.

So you just keep quiet?   That cause problems?

The horizon opened up as we cleared Casino Pier. It was bright as day under the board-walk lamps. Out where the ocean curved, the lamps of idling tankers winked. The surf pil-ing up on the beach reflected the tallest rides in zigzagging bands of light. Circles of red and orange from the Ferris wheel pulsed across the water as it beat a quiet, steady measure on the shore.

Vera wasn't the first woman I'd taken for a stroll down the boardwalk; like most Shore guys, I considered the boards my default first summer date. Not that it would have made much of a difference where I had gone with women in the past: on the boardwalk or off, they all seemed to be too much a part of the place—glowing blond and tanned with bottled sunshine; great for a night, great to make me feel like summer, but never enough to ease the feeling that they'd fade away in the fall when the Tilt-a-Whirl folded in its arms and the Ferris wheel stopped spinning.

Maybe it had something to do with the light—or the lights kaleidoscoping redpurple-yellowgreenblue across Vera's skin as we walked side-by-side down the boards, flashing, exploding out of the arcades and the booths; but every glance I got of her was like a snatch of a fragment of a facet, shifting, different with each degree, all beautiful, no two quite the same, something in the arrangement of the shadows, her beauty in the darkness beneath her brow or nestled behind her ear, in the smile lines that resolved then disappeared, intriguing as much for what the shadows were hiding as the light was showing.

You like your job?   Why's that?

                    Too much.   The work takes a lot out of me. The people take a lot out

        But you're doing what you want to do, right? Doesn't that make you feel good?

of me.   I mean, yeah,

"   "

some days it feels great. Other days? I don't feel like I'm getting anything done, or even really

"   "

connecting with the people I'm working with. I give them a lot, you know, attention, advice, a

"   "

smile when they need it, and they take it all in. But when I look them in the eye, it's like they've

And you start to won-

wandered off into some space inside their heads that I can't really access.

der whether it's worth it.

Yeah. And then I get moody, or I don't want to go out, or   It's up and

So what keeps you going?

down, I don't always know what to expect.   Probably a bunch of things

"   "

that are asking too much.

Hey hey, what a cute couple!

I turned in the direction of the catcall. The hawker at the Skee-Ball Race. I looked at Vera. She blushed. I looked back toward the booth.

Yeah, you, man! I know you're ugly, but that girl there's good enough for two! You should go a round.

Should we?

Sure!

Vera and I strolled over to the booth. I slapped a five in the hawker's hand. Two rows of balls knocked into the sleeves at the base of the ramps.

Bell goes, you start rolling. Ready?

The game was easy enough. I'd played it hundreds of times before. Normally, I'd win, but . . .

And that's a win for the lovely lady.

"   "

You threw that game!

She punched my shoulder.

No I didn't! My track was warped!   How?!
                    Uh-huh. I know you're lying!   I can see it on your face!

She was right. I was grinning like a fool.

Can you blame me?
   "   "

She pushed me. I took her by the wrist and pulled her closer to me. She laughed and tucked herself under my arm.

We set off again into the Midway. It was getting on in the evening, the night heavier. The next day could be millions of years away. A pack of bar-goers bore down on us on their way to the Aztec or the Tiki Bar or Avenue A, jostling one another, slapboxing and clowning as they passed through and around the crowds headed in the opposite direction. They stared us down as they passed, some stone-faced, others tilting their chins up toward us. Vera nestled against me.

                    Are you worried about something?   I don't think it's danger-
How safe is it down here?   I hear stories.

ous. Or, I mean, some parts of the city aren't the best places to hang, but I wouldn't take you anywhere
   "   "

I thought was bad.
   "   "

There'd always been fistfights and stabbings at the dive bars, car windows smashed and stereos stolen. The newer clubs had their own problems, too. But you could live here for years and never see a shade of it.

Huh?   Oh, they flash-fry Oreos in funnel-cake batter.

What's a fried Oreo?   Over there.   Ever have

        I'm more of an ice cream guy.

one?   So let's get some.

    The parlor's refrigerators hummed as we settled into a back booth with our Styrofoam ice cream cups. At some point, everything in the parlor must have been blindingly white, from the floor tiles to the fridges to the workers' smocks; now everything was a dingy gray, old with use. Vera sat looking out toward the boards, her back to the parlor's mirrored wall. Behind her, people's reflections floated like neon vapor escaped from storefront signs, illuminated along their edges by light from the pizza joints and lemonade stands, clouded in my view by the flecks of corrosion and veins of gold on the mirror's face.

    Vera leaned across the table.

                        I'm in grad school. I mean, I was in grad school.

So, what about you? What do you do?   What were

        Philosophy, but I   uh   Forget it. I'm not trying to be mysterious or anything, it's just

you studying?

that people have been asking me about school a lot recently. And I've kinda realized that I had no idea

    "   "

what I was doing. Like, it sounded good at the time, but it was all too abstract.

                                                            Are you going to go

        Who knows.   I'm a manager over at Trenton's. That's

back?   What are you doing in the meantime?

good until Columbus Day.   I think I'll be good to go by then.

                    And when the summer ends?   But if not?

My boss was talking to me about going on a wreck dive in Europe.

                                        Wreck diving? Have you ever

                    No.   It is, I guess.

done anything like that before?   It seems really different from philosophy.   I'd prob-

                                        Maybe.

ably go, even if I thought I was ready to go back to school.

    She shifted in her seat, keeping her focus on me.

"   "

I'm really glad you asked me out tonight. I

    She broke eye contact with me and shifted again to my right. Her smile faded. I looked in
the mirror again, but I couldn't make anything out of the reflection.

Is something   Everything all right?

        No, no, never mind.   Yeah, everything's fine.

    She twirled her spoon in the cup, pulling out a twist of softened ice cream.

            Walk you home?

Look, maybe I should go   Maybe you could walk me to a bus stop?   I mean,

"   "

I live more than a walk from here.

We made our way out of the ice cream parlor and back onto the boards. It was getting late: the crowds were thinning, the lights slowly winking out in the booths and arcades. It seemed noisier than earlier, though, busier. As we passed along the mirrors lining the funhouse wall, Vera . . . Vera's image . . . her doubles, triples expanded, contracted, and twisted at my side, more strands in the flashing lights.

"   "

Damn. I know how this is going to go.

We turned down the ramp to Avenue A. The bus stop sat in the shadows of Lucky Leo's Arcade, bathed in lamplight that sputtered along with some invisible rhythm. Vera walked an arm's length from me. I reached for her hand. She kept walking, her eyes fixed forward, maybe teetering a little bit farther away from me. We stood apart at the stop as the bus rolled in. "See you soon?" She looked down at her feet. The bus doors opened; she stepped inside and looked back at me. "Maybe." The doors closed, and then she was gone. I walked home alone, a single set of footsteps echoing down the sidewalk. Over the Boulevard and up Springwood, my hands in my pockets, head down.

We turned down the ramp to Avenue A. Police officers pulling the late-night shift leaned up against the sides of the cars; loose flocks of people wandered along the sidewalks, stumbling home for the night. The bus stop sat on the Boulevard, in the shadows of Lucky Leo's arcade, bathed in lamplight that sputtered along with some invisible rhythm. The bus was already rumbling up the block. Vera shuffled and looked down at her feet. The bus sighed into the stop.

I had already begun to pull away from her as the bus doors opened.

Well

"   "

Vera must have had other ideas. She pulled me to her and kissed me, long and slow, her body pressed up against mine.

"   "

"   "

She fell back onto her heels, smiling. It took my mind a second to catch up.

"   "

Where did that come from?   For real. That really just happened.

The doors closed behind her.

She didn't look back, didn't

    Vera grabbed me and kissed me,

    long and slow, her body pressed up

    against mine. Warm, there, real.

"   "

She turned to step onto the bus. I reached out across the space between us and pulled her close to me, close for a second kiss. She didn't resist. When I finally looked up, half the bus was looking on.

"   "

I'll see you around, Cincy.

She squeezed my hand and stepped off, looking once over her shoulder.

"   "

Call me.

loop diggin'

That night, I lay awake, replaying and remixing my time with her.

She smiled like She smiled like she meant it. She smiled like I could mean something to her. She smiled like I did mean something to her. "I'll see you around, Cincy." She squeezed my hand and stepped off, looking once over her shoulder. She smiled like she meant it. She smiled like I could mean something to her. "See you around" She smiled She smiled like she meant it. "Call me." "Call me."

Dreaming, feeling like I was walking a tightrope. Waiting for it to be pulled out from beneath my feet, thrilling from the heights. Play it again. Play it again.

endless summer (day)

She smiled   *She smiled like she meant it. "Call me."*   Huh?

    When I got to the yard the next morning, the outside door to the locker room hung ajar, its padlock lying broken on the ground. A few thin gouges, deep enough to expose unfinished wood, ran down the door jamb. The locker room itself was in worse shape: each of the lockers had been broken into, their combination locks clipped and their doors thrown open, the guys' stuff scattered all over the floor, the whole place a mess of work clothes, deodorant sticks and shampoo bottles, glossy surf magazines and old newspapers.

What did I have in here? *Razors, towels.*

    J.D., hair tousled, sleeves rolled up, entered from the inside door.

          Man. Have the rest of the guys seen this mess already?

It's always an adventure, right?   Yes. I told them

How'd someone even get in the front gate? Did you get anything on

not to touch anything. Not sure.

tape?

Quite a bit. Why don't you come take a look?

Over the course of an hour or so, J.D. took me through a stack of tapes, rewinding and pausing at the few places where the cameras got a clean shot of the intruder, or at least as clean as they were going to get in the dark: a white guy, skinny and ghostly, his right arm covered in some sort of sleeve tattoo, a ski mask over his face, his movements shaky. He first entered the camera's sight as he crept from the large warehouse to the main building, moving slowly but purposefully with a crowbar in one hand and a pair of bolt cutters in the other. He used the crowbar to claw the padlock off the door and then tried the doorknob with his hand. When the knob didn't budge, he jammed the crowbar into the space between the door and jamb and leaned on it until the inside lock gave way. Once inside, he made quick work of each of the combination locks with the bolt cutters, then reached into the lockers with both hands and spilled their contents out onto the floor, rummaging quickly before turning to the next locker. He didn't seem to find what he was looking for: he straightened up from the last pile and slammed the crowbar into the bank of lockers. Then he left the room the same way he came, tools in hand, and jogged back across the yard, disappearing from sight around the edge of the warehouse.

Cash?

What do you think he was looking for? So why wouldn't he break into the store and go for

I don't know.

the register? Can you do a once-over on the yard and make sure we haven't missed

Sure.

anything? I'm going to call the police and have them take a report. I'm counting on you to be my eyes and ears here, Cincy. Let me know if you find anything out, okay?

I spent the rest of the morning combing the yard from bay to back lot, reporting in to J.D. from time to time on one of the yard's beat-up walkie-talkies. A faint sense of unease washed in my stomach with my morning coffee as I checked doors and windows,

Was that locked? Let me test it again.

dipped through the rows of boats,

Something stirred behind one of the Blue Jays. "Hey! Stop!"

surveyed the warehouses,

A form sprang out
of the dark. A fist
crashed into the
bridge of my nose.

It's fine, it's fine. The winds gusted over
the bay, thunderheads formed in the west.
We nosed our boats back to land, passing
into the marina just as the first drops of rain
pattered over the water. We were safe.

From some things. The padlock lay
broken on the ground. The door frame
splintered.

hoping that enough looking would turn up something, anything that could tie the images on the film to a real person.

The only sign of an intruder I could find, though, was a small hole cut into the fence in the deepest reaches of the back lot, where the yard verged on the nautical graveyard. The hole was just big enough for someone to crawl through, or almost big enough: a swatch of white T-shirt fabric clung to a jag of fencing.

A million shirts would match that.

I ducked through the hole into the graveyard and inched through a gap between the Dumpsters that crowded up against the fence. A strangled bark sputtered out from the far side of a rusted steam engine. A guard dog lay on the gravel, his eyes cloudy, a mealy puddle of vomit pooled on the ground by his mouth. He whimpered as I crouched and ran my hands over him; his breathing was shallow, his heartbeat faint.

I struggled to my feet with the dog in my arms. The dog's head and body lolled and swayed as I carried him through the graveyard toward the attendant's shack, through a labyrinth of corroded steam turbines and busted boilers, multiton anchors and fractured propellers, the ground littered with gaskets and dials, links of chain, scraps of wooden decking. Nothing stirred, the silence complete.

As I neared the shack, the attendant rushed out. I laid the dog out on the concrete patio outside his door. He felt the dog's pulse, ruffled his neck, mumbled something about drugs. Without as much as a second word, he raced off across the graveyard, calling out the names of his other dogs.

Bella!   Warner!

I settled into an old deck chair in the shadow of the shack as the walkie-talkie roared to life.

I'm in the graveyard. It looks like whoever cut through
You've been gone for a while. Where are you?

the fence came in through here.   He drugged them.   J.D.?
Wouldn't the guard dogs catch him?

Don't worry about me, J.D. I'll be fine.

I've never seen anything like this before. You're safe?   Keep

"   "

me posted, okay?

The dog struggled upright, then lurched against the side of the shack, before falling again with a whimper. I cast around the shack for a bowl of water, a pillow, something to make things easier for him. Nothing, just corroded metal detritus. His whole life was probably spent wandering around the sharp corners and hard edges of the graveyard: a ragged scar ran along his flank, his skin pink and puckered, furless; a dirty bandage bound his left foreleg; a tiny triangle of flesh was missing from the tip of his ear.

We lowered ourselves through the cage of roots, down to where the engine lay, half-sunk in the marshy lowlands of the hollow.

It was a good ten minutes before the attendant returned, huffing back with a dog slung over each shoulder. He stooped and lay them beside the first.

Are they gonna be okay?

All of 'em. What did they do?   I'll call a vet. Don't worry about us, buddy.

He ducked into the shack, leaving me alone to pick my way back through the graveyard, through steam funnels wide enough to stand up inside, alleys formed by piled-up driveshafts and shipless rudders. The gutted carcass of an old tanker sat close on to the yard, a barnacled drogue lay in its wake; the chain that joined the two had long since broken, its rusty links now adrift on the gravel. I weighed one of the links in my hand; it was heavy, hand-staining, pungent with age, something solid to hold on to as I climbed back between the Dumpsters, back through the hole in the fence, back to the yard.

The sun was hovering directly overhead by the time I reached the basin. The sun glinted off the razor wire that ringed the yard.

My dad gagged on his mashed potatoes.
"You went where?" My neck reddened
above the collar of my acrylic school
sweater.

The wharfside wasn't the safest place in the city. We all knew that, I guess, growing up, when our parents shot us nervous looks as we gushed about our latest third-grade adventure traipsing through the marinas and running along the bulkheads, or when—early on in college, fake ID'd up—we caught cold stares from the longshoremen and fishermen those first chilly, furtive nights sneaking drinks at the dive bars that sat beneath the bay bridges, the kinds of places you thought you might see a fight, or, if you were lucky, get into one yourself—but I'd never seen, never heard of anything like what I'd seen this morning, never really understood what all the barbed fences and glass-topped walls were for.

The dog lay on the ground. Cloudy eyed. The fence bent inward.

Useless.

My hands had begun to sweat. Red rust from the link flowed out in rivulets between the fingers of my clenched fist. I pitched the link out over the basin, watched it crest over the bulkhead and disappear into the Barnegat with a splash, the spot where it pierced holding wound-like for a second before the tide washed it smooth again.

Out beyond the channel markers, a bihulled catamaran flying the Upper Bay Yacht Club burgee was gliding toward the yard, sails down, motor churning, trailing a greasy cloud of diesel smog. As the boat approached an open service slip, the boat's skipper leaped into action, cutting the motor then racing toward the front of the boat to sling the bowlines around the dock's pylons. Corey pulled them tight as the skipper darted back to fasten the stern line. Once everything had been knotted into place, he vaulted up onto the dock. He was decked out in full gear: a pair of gray-and-navy-blue rubber boots, padded hiking shorts, and a slim red life vest. A long-billed canvas hat sat far back on his head, exposing a sunburned forehead and a mop of lank blond hair.

We've got an expert on staff, don't worry.

I need someone to check out this motor, ASAP.

I pushed the call button on my walkie-talkie.

** Hey, Tone. We got a guy who needs some motor work. You got time?**

** I was gonna do

"

"

Actually,

lunch, but I can do it. I'll be up in a sec.**

You're not from around here, are you?

yeah, I grew up here. What makes you ask?   You?

Nothing in particular.   We summer here. We're

"   "

from up north. The City.

Tone appeared with his tool belt and a brown paper shopping bag.

He's right here.   Yeah, him. He's the best

So when's this expert of yours getting here?   Him?

"   "

tech guy on the bay. Tone, this is   Buddy, this is Tone Hawkins.

Buddy Woodbury.

"   "

Tone stuck out his hand.

"   "

I've got somewhere to be in two hours. Let's make this fast.

"   "

Buddy pulled a cell phone out of his pocket and strolled down the dock toward the office, leaving Tone with his hand hanging.

Forget it, man. Just another jerk. I'll keep him out of your hair.

The fuck?

I didn't have much to worry about. Buddy spent the next two hours pacing around the soda machine, yelling into his phone and gesturing wildly. Occasionally, he'd stoop down and pick up a piece of gravel and fling it sidearm into the marina, tracking it with his eyes as it arched through the air and plashed into the water. I watched him out of the corner of my eye while I surfed the net for fence repairmen and alarm installers, click after click through layers and layers of security:

electronic access systems   hand geometry   benching   biometrics
    user authentication   TCP/IP capability   live capture   lock-down
crossover error rate   read range   automated fingerprint identification systems
      binning   credentials   motion sensors   perimeters and pass codes
26/34 standard signal output   monitoring duress   anti-passback
dynamic signature   counter-direction intrusion   cost-effective security solutions
lock-open   verification speeds   voltage supply
      English language   prox cards   intrusion protection
          optical turnstiles Wiegand wire   challenge response   DET curves
    open-set identification   false alarm rate   hamming distances
identity governance

Algorithms and laser beams, heavy metal and razor edges, oddly soothing for all their men-
ace, dense enough to get lost in.

A scar ran along his flank.

Buddy still hadn't wrapped up by the time Tone was done. I waved to get his attention. He
frowned and turned his back to me. I tapped him on the shoulder.

We're good to go.

What is it? I'm on the phone.   About time. Look, I'll call you later. I said

"   "

I-WILL-CALL-YOU-LATER. Just put the repairs on the tab. I can't hang

"   "

around here anymore.

He shoved a twenty in my hand.

"   "

For your *trouble*.

He set off across the yard, stalking down the boardwalk and leaping back into the catamaran.

Whoa, where'd you come from?

Punk.   **I cleared outta there before he came back. I would've knocked**

At least he left a tip.

him smooth the fuck out if he even looked at me again.

I held out the twenty.

Go

Forget it. I wouldn't touch that dude's money with a ten-foot pole. Mind if I grab lunch now?

for it.

It's unreal the kind of appetite you can work up dealing with these folks.

He tapped his paper bag and strolled off toward the break room.

Hey, Tone!   Can you give

Crap. I've gotta work on the house tonight. How am I gonna get there?

Yeah?

me a ride home tonight?   Yeah.

You in town?   I'll stop by your office when I'm done working.

■　■　■

It was nearly three o'clock before the police arrived, evidence kits, metal clipboards, and carbon forms in hand. They photographed the hole in the fence, the doorway, and the locker room, snapping enough pictures from enough angles that they probably could have reconstructed the whole yard in three dimensions back at headquarters. When they were done with their cameras, they measured out the room then dusted the door frame and lockers for fingerprints, applying white powder with fine-haired brushes that they then lifted with thin strips of clear tape. The tape went into labeled plastic Baggies, the brushes and powder containers back into their evidence kit. An officer with a Dictaphone narrated all of this to tape while checking off items on his clipboard.

It seems like you col-

Tell Mr. Trenton we'll mail him a final copy of the report as soon as it's finished.

lected a lot of stuff.

That's just standard operating procedure. It might be important, or it might be junk.

You think we have anything to worry about?

Hard to tell beforehand.   This kinda stuff happens all the

You mean, the people don't come back, or you don't catch them?

time. Nothing usually comes of it.   Both

"   "

would be fair to say.

KNOCK *KNOCK*

Cince, you good to oh I'm just gonna wait out here.

The officer refocused on me.

No, I think we're fine.

Any other questions?   Well, you know where to find us if anything else comes

"   "

up. Have a nice day.

As the cruisers pulled away, I found Tone waiting out by the soda machine, head down, hands in his pockets.

What was up with that?   He was just here about the break-in.

I don't trust cops.   Yeah, well

"   "

Forget it, let's roll.

We drove across the city to my old house, first downshore along the promenade, then cutting in zigzags inland, the sun's white glow on white gravel and the ocean's surface gradually giving way to the softer green suffusion and deep shadows of the city's interior blocks. We glided past the elementary school and ironworkers' garage, the Masonic temple and the plumbing supply stores, the deep scents of baking blacktop and freshly cut grass wafting through our open windows. Loose groups of day laborers—toting handheld radios and oversized thermoses—wandered across the parking lot of the Acme Supermarket or huddled in the scraggly shade of the trees that lined the sidewalk near the bus stop, all of them waiting for the contractors who might or might not drop by to muster up for nighttime jobs at the construction sites that littered the beachfront. A few laborers clambered in the side door of a painter's wagon; a few others sat in the flatbeds of a fleet of pickups from a local construction firm. The familiar neighborhood sites continued to roll by: K&H Bathrooms & Kitchens The Clipper Shop Exxon First Methodist Church of Jersey Shore Chiropractor, all in steady rhythm, all where they'd always been.

I got that cheddar, mayne / That leather, mayne / You can call me weathermayne / Toss a couple ones / Turn

You have any clue what that break-in was about?

I beat that   I don't trust cops.

I'm telling you, you gotta keep your head on a

that rain into a hurricane / Then I let my trunk hang / And I let my speakers bang / Stayin icy sippin Tang / Silver

"   "

swivel. Shit reminds me of some old trap house shit, running up in people's cribs, snatching shit. I

lady on my hood lookin like a weathervane / And that's what's up, mayne / Say what say what say what, mayne? /

"   "

didn't realize y'all northerners were on it like that. And I didn't realize *you* were on it like *this*. This

*Please excuse my **RUN THAT BACK!***

"   "

is where you live? This big old house?

The house where I had grown up was a whitewashed three-story Victorian with a wide-floored, long-roofed porch, hedged around its base by privets with elastic branches that waved in the breeze like crowds bidding goodbye to a cruise ship on its maiden voyage across suburbia's green lawns.

say what, mayne? / Please excuse my attitude but I don't give a WHAT, mayne / 'Cuz I'm in that green

Nah, this is my parents' old place.

I know how it is. I still call Georgia home even though I haven't

thang / Candy paint, turnin lane HOLD UP! HOLD UP! turnin' lane

"   "

lived there for years. It's like you never really move out, you know?

I stepped out of the Caprice and onto the sidewalk. I reached back to slam the door.

Thumpin sumpin bumpin

"   "

Gently, ya heard? Gently.

The door closed behind me with a soft click.

And I'm 'bout to turn it up, mayne

"   "

Keep it real.

Tone crawled off, leaving me alone on my old block. Lawn mowers hummed and sprinklers machine-gunned up and down the street. I never thought my parents would even think of letting this go, would ever get over what captured them about this place years ago. Maybe it was just enough bedrooms for the kids they were expecting to have, maybe something to do with the ocean breezes that reached from the beach all the way down the street's length. They loved to tell the story of this house's transformation, from a crumbling fixer-upper with rotting floorboards and moldy kitchen to a home, gutted at the depths of the recession, renovated, re-decorated—buy cheap, reuse, live like a king on an insurance salesman's salary and an artist's commissions.

I circled to the rear of the house, past the fallow flowerbeds, around the utility room extension where the back stairs climbed up to the kitchen. I brushed aside a dewy cobweb and reached into the narrow space between the stairs and the ground, my right hand fishing around for the rusty Folgers can where we kept the spare keys.

I tipped the can over. Two keys, tarnished and dirt flecked, fell into my open hand.

I tilted the can over. Nothing fell out. I shook the can. Nothing.

Mom and Dad must have taken them when they left.

I walked over to the shed and popped the combination lock. The smell of earth and diesel greeted me as I stepped inside. Dad's snowblower sat in one corner, nearly buried under tarp-hooded lawn chairs, stacks of cracked and flaking pottery, bikes with missing tires, deflated basketballs and beach balls, spindle-armed umbrellas and bald tires. The belt sander, still in the box, sat on an old glass-topped table along with a couple cans of gray paint, a tray, and a few rollers. A thin layer of grit coated everything. I gathered up the materials and crossed the yard again, each step stirring up a sweet puff from the grass underfoot. As I crested the stairs, a black van crawled by on the street beyond.

The porch wrapped around two sides of the house, long and wide enough for a whole family to move outside for an un-air-conditioned summer. Its wood floor stretched out beneath my feet in a half-acre of cracks and pits.

I plugged the sander in and got to work, starting from the near corner and slowly fanning my way outward.

The sander hummed its way slowly through several layers of paint, throwing up flecks of gray, green, and white as it bore down toward the underlying wood.

I was on my hands and knees, sanding down the porch for the first time, shortly after my thirteenth birthday. My father's hand closed over mine. "Glide. You're not trying to drill through the wood."

As I inched streetward, the sander passed over a cluster of rust-colored spots near the living room window.

"Tag!" My brother gave me a full body shove and ran. My face cracked against the sharp edge of a steamer trunk that crouched under the window as I fell to the floor. I clutched my cheek to keep the warm blood in. My mother found me lying there a few minutes later. "Oh, honey!" I looked down at the porch through parted fingers, where blood had already spilled. "Dad's gonna kill me!"

Dad didn't kill me.

I continued sweeping streetward, setting aside the sander and taking up a scraper to hack away at patches of paint that had clotted in the knots of the wood.

By seven, I had finished the shorter arm of the porch and began carving away at the eastern corner.

We sat on the hammock, drinking raspberry Snapples and watching our feet glide back and forth over the worn gray deck with the pale wood grain peeking through like shale in a shallow stream. The pillars were cracked and scaled.

I swirled the sander in gentle circles, watching the wood slowly emerge.

I woke at two a.m., bedded down in a pile of beach towels in the deep pocket of the hammock. Turns out bugs bit at night, too. Worse. I raked my hands over my calves and stumbled to my bedroom.

As the sander reached the railing, it skipped over a set of deep notches carved into the porch. My initials stood out in gray relief against the smooth wood of the deck.

"Your dad won't care! Just look at the
sidewalk!" Tom handed me his Swiss Army
knife with its long blade already jutting out.

Dad minded.

By the time I scraped all the paint out of the cuts, it was well past eight. Sweat had long since leached through my shirt, which clung to my back closer than the humid evening air.

Man, I should've brought some water.

I checked under the rear steps again. Still no key. I tried the kitchen door. Nothing. I climbed back onto the porch and gave the front door a push.

I leaned into the door and threw my book bag
down on the floor. Home.

No dice.

■ ■ ■

I came back every night for each of the next four or five nights. The worries of earlier in the week sanded down along with the rough spots in the wood, disappeared as I primed the deck and rolled on fresh coats of gray paint. The only thing I could think of by the time I was done was sleeping.

A muffled drumbeat greeted me as I turned onto Springwood, the kicks and snares grow-ing louder and clearer as I mounted the stairs to the apartment. I stepped into the living room, straight into the middle of one of Tom's recording sessions. The drummer's sticks were wrapped with tube socks; strips of newspaper stuck out of the cymbals on his hi-hat. The bassist was playing with his pinky and ring finger taped to his palm; the rhythm guitarist was playing an old battered Stratocaster; Tom leaned toward the mic, both hands on his Les Paul, a lump of something crammed into the right side of his mouth. They were all wearing dirty, faded jeans, dingy white T-shirts with musty pit stains, and dusty-looking Pro-Keds. As the door creaked shut, the drummer missed a beat, pausing with his sticks above his head and his mouth hanging open.

"   "

Oh, jeez

I don't Wrico, wrhat the fwuck? Oh, hey, Cincy. Take five, guys.

I crossed the living room.

What are you guys doing?

Wrecording. Hold on.

Tom pulled a wad of tissue out of the side of his mouth.

Can't you just use the software to do that?

Sleep.

Just trying to get the right sound.   **We could, but that**

But it's not like the original singer sung with tissue in his mouth.

Sleeeeeeeeeep.

wouldn't be authentic.   **Sounded**

So what's up with the three-fingered bassist?

like it.   **The original bassist lost his fingers in an ac-**

"   "

cident. We didn't want Russ to be able to play any notes that guy couldn't. You ever meet

No.

"Murph" "Vinnie" "Scanlon"

the guys?   **All right, well, you got Three-Fingered Russ there on the bass**

Russ looked up from his water bottle, his eyes barely visible beneath the brim of the hat he wore low over his eyes and the hair plastered across his forehead.

"   "

"Fred"   "Taylor"   "Fred" "Fred's back?" "Yeah, well, there are only so many drummers."

There's Rico, the drummer.

Yo.

Rico was busy rewrapping the tube socks on his sticks. He stopped to push his Coke-bottle glasses back up his nose.

"   "

A second guitarist?

He's not very talkative. And that's Ben Christiansen on the other guitar. You remember him

"   "

That's a new one.

from high school?

Ben was sprawled on the couch. His eyes were crossed and focused on the smoldering tip of his cigarette. He didn't seem to notice, let alone care, we were there.

What's up with your clothes? You guys have some sort of uniform or something?

I'm sensing a bit of

No, no, it's just

sarcasm.   **You wanna be authentic, you gotta go all the way. It's like I used to**

or go home.

say in high school: "Go big or go home." Exactly. And I don't know what your little adven-

"   "

tures sanding your parents' porch taught you, but for me?

Tom grabbed his guitar.

"   "

Ain't no going home.

shelter

The next few weeks passed in a blur: waking up warm, spending days at the yard, evenings with Vera.

We swam through the electric tides on the boards,

      rocked gently back and forth while music leaked into the deep humid nights

I waited for her along the promenade, not sure where she was coming from, not sure where we were going, caring even less when she got there. The setting sun haloed around her head. She was hyperreal, barely there.

      We slipped away for a while, windows down while bass lines shivered and vocals stut-

      tered, harmonies melted, the two of us leaning off the warming air and syrupy codeine-

      slow jams.

Woozy, packed parties. All eyes on her. She strolled almost drifted through the crowd, six feet off the floor. Her hand laced through mine. *We floated above it all.* She drew me outside, we ebbed off with the smoke in the air. I ran my hands along the sides of her face, tilted her chin up to me, kissed her. Her cheeks flushed, her eyes

I could feel myself falling slowly into her, until one June evening . . .

Vera had invited me to the shelter where she worked, on the edge of Liberty Square Park, out amid the west side's acres of abandoned churches and ruined motels. As the sun slid beneath the western horizon, I steered Tom's Chevy up Heck Street, its macadam potholed and decayed, my way lit by filigreed brass streetlamps that sputtered and sparked to life in the thickening darkness. At the park's far edge, the husk of the old Metropolitan Hotel loomed. Green-leaved and purple-tendriled vines crept across the hotel's cracked walls and crooked porte cochere, reached inside through doorways and skylights and dragged the whole structure rightward, groundward off its foundation. A single bare lightbulb, visible through a dirt-flecked awning window, burned in the basement. The western wall had been frescoed into a memorial, covered in streaks and clouds of Krylon, tagged and retagged by the neighborhood crews.

A clump of newspapers tumbleweeded down the block, borne by the ocean breeze. The stoplight flashed red. A Dodge Neon with a cloudy paint job—hazards flashing, dome light on—idled on the shoulder. A woman sat in the driver's seat; her male passenger held his arm across her and gripped the wheel. Two small children were fastened into car seats in the back, a baby boy with a thumb in his mouth, an older girl twirling a pigtail in her tiny fingers, her eyes wide.

LET GO OF THE WHEEL!

AND HAVE YOU GET IN ANOTHER ACCIDENT?! YOU GOTTA CALM DOWN!

MAYBE I COULD *CALM DOWN* IF YOU WEREN'T OUT HERE FUCKIN' AROUND ON THE BLOCK!

AWWW,

MATTER OF FACT, WHY DON'T I LEAVE YOU OUT HERE ON THE BLOCK, SINCE THAT'S WHERE

C'MON!

YOUR HEART'S AT!

YOUR HEART'S EVERYWHERE BUT WITH ME!

The light turned green; the Neon stood where it sat, receding in my rearview as I crawled forward, around the north edge of the park now, along First Avenue. The Methodist church hunched along the northern side of the park, its steeple circled by a flock of gulls that lit in cottony groups on the splintered wooden beams that jutted like fractured femurs through the church's dome. The shelter, an old stucco building annexed to the back of a fieldstone Epis-copal church, hunched catty-corner on First and Grand.

Lights blazing on both floors of the shelter sent sloping yellow rectangles across its lawn, spotlighting a crowd of people who milled around outside the building's entrance. Cigarette tips burned and flared; old cell-phone screens glowed green. I pulled the Chevy along the curb. The sounds of hushed conversations followed me as I approached the front door, where a stocky guy in a skullcap lounged. I looked once to my left, once to my right, feeling the eyes that had zeroed in on me from all sides, then reached for the door handle.

I'm here to see Vera.   No, I   I think she works here.

You got business here?   She a guest here?   You

Yeah, I know so.

think so?   You a volunteer?

He pressed the button on a tiny box mounted next to the door. Something buzzed inside the shelter.

No, just visiting.
"   "

The door opened. Vera stood propping it open, yellow rubber gloves in one hand, a mop in the other.

Hey   hey, Vera.

The setting sun haloed

around her head.   Man, she is perfect.

How'd I luck into this?

Cincy!
"   "

She looped a loose strand of hair behind her ear.

"   "

All eyes on her at the party.
Like a curl of smoke rising
from the flaring end of a cigarette.
We floated above it all.
Could you take this?

She shoved the mop into my hands.

"   "

She was hyperreal, barely there.

"   "

Looks like you're volunteering now.

The guard hiked his jeans up and moved away from the door, leaving just enough room for me to creep past. I followed Vera as she turned back down the shelter's main hallway. Walls of white-painted cement blocks and moss green tile ran the length of the building. Vera strode purposefully down the hall, her footsteps echoing off the gray linoleum.

Where are you going?   I thought you were a social worker?
She strolled almost drifted
through the crowd, six feet
off the floor. Her hand laced
through mine.
　　　　To finish cleaning up.   We're understaffed.

What am I supposed to do?

The two of us leaning off

the warming air and syrupy

codeine-slow jams.

> *rocked gently back and forth while music leaked into*
>
> *the deep humid nights. No need for words. It was perfect.*

I do whatever I've got to do to keep the shelter running.

I looked down at the mop in my hand. A bead of water ran down the handle and onto my knuckle. She stopped halfway down the hall and turned to me.

"   "

Help. C'mon.

She waved me down the hall and disappeared through a doorway on the right. I heard her footsteps echo-shuffling down a flight of stairs. The corridors smelled of bleach; the floor tiles were still slick with a thin film of water. When I caught up with her on the basement level, she was standing in front of the door to the men's room.

"   "

Here.

She tossed the yellow gloves to me.

"   "

Could you mop the floor in there? It'd be a big help.

She walked into the women's room opposite.

The men's room reeked of urinal cakes and disinfectant, corrosion and mildew. A battered wringer bucket filled with ammonia-laced water sat on the floor near the sink. I rolled up my shirtsleeves and got to work, wiping the mop head across the bathroom's tile floor. As I passed the bank of sinks, I glanced at myself in the mirror. A line of sweat edged my hair.

After ten minutes or so, I'd mopped and remopped the whole room. I tipped the bucket over the bathroom's floor drain and watched as the smoky gray water rippled through the teeth of the grate and disappeared with a gurgle. Vera leaned into the bathroom.

Yeah.

Are we good to go?   Let's go up and let everyone in.

We climbed the stairs again and returned to the front door.

"   "

Okay, Johnnie. We're good.

"   "

Johnnie cupped his hands around his mouth and barked out.

"   "

"   "

Everyone line up! Let's go!

The folks waiting outside formed a rough queue outside the door that trailed out into the dark. Johnnie gave each person a cursory pat-down before standing aside. One by one they passed along the hall and down the stairs: some looked like they hadn't showered for days, maybe months—one carried her hair in a single thick lock wrapped in a green scarf; another stumbled past, the soles of his shoes separating from the toes with each step, revealing his dirt-caked feet. Others, though, could have just come from work, their ties pulled low and upper buttons undone, some loose hems on their pants or yellowed stains on their shirt cuffs the only hint that they were living in a shelter.

What should I do?

Be patient with everyone tonight, Cincy. It's rough out there for folks.   Can you

Not really.

cook? The kitchen staff might need an extra hand.   Man, you are *useless*. Clean some

Okay.

dishes?

The kitchen was on the ground floor, tucked into the back of a long, low multipurpose room that seemed to do a little bit of everything for the shelter: a dining area filled with round tables and metal folding chairs, a computer workspace with a row of boxy-screened PCs, and a TV lounge, all bathed in the yellow-green light of the fluorescent panels checkered across the water-stained drop ceiling. The air was heavy with cooking smells and sweat. Shelter workers in white aprons and matching latex gloves were handing out plates loaded down with pasta and salad to a line of guests, nesting the plates on top of one-ply napkins and mismatched silverware. The sink was already full with piles of plates stuck together with a cement of mozzarella and marinara. A motley collection of cups, mugs, and glasses lined up along the counter.

It didn't take long to fall into a rhythm, rinsing, scrubbing, and drying just fast enough to stay ahead of the dishes that mounded up on the edge of the sink over the course of the night. By ten, I'd probably passed over each plate in the place at least twice, as guests came back for seconds and thirds, eating until the foil catering trays were empty.

When I racked the last plate, Vera was sitting at one of the round tables in the center of the room, talking with a guest.

He looks familiar. Where have I seen him before?   *passed out on the benches like heaps of old clothing*   No

The stranger crashed into another man lugging a cooler.   *She grabbed the stranger by the*
elbow and led him away from
the gathering crowd. "Byrd."

His hands lay on the table, his fingers tapping on the cover of a folder overflowing with rumpled and soiled staff paper full of jagged notes and letters that spilled out beyond the staves into the margins of the sheets. As I approached the table, I tried to catch Vera's attention. She didn't look up, though; she just leaned toward Byrd, her eyes following his as they darted around the room.

"   "
"   "

KC was hopping back then. Crazy. All those cats were out there, cuttin'. We'd watch those cats

"   "

Byrd.
cut 'til one, two in the mornin'.

She placed her hand on top of his free one and gently lowered it to the table. His eyes shifted toward her.

"   "

I'm just going to get in the way here.
Don't you think it's time for bed?   Yeah.
You know how it is, right?   For bed?   Because, because, be-

I'm going to go over there.
[   ]
Sure.
cause

I wandered over to the bank of computers. Their monitors were the size of hotel minifridges, their towers and keyboards yellowed everywhere they weren't dusted with dirty fingerprints. I sat down in front of the closest computer and shuffled the mouse. An hourglass stood frozen,

half-tipped where the pointer should be. I joggled the mouse again. Nothing. Farther down the bank, a man sat in front of an open Netscape browser, his shoulders bunched up, his chin resting in his balled-up fists. Another man stood behind him; one of his hands rested on the first man's shoulder, the other traced an arc across the screen.

"   "

I've been here before.   I've *been* here. I filled in my form and waited for them to call.
                        This is brand new.

"   "

They never called.   I'm not gonna get anything off this.
                        They're hiring now.   Every time I try to hook

"   "

                                                            I'm just an old man looking for younger days.
you up, you say it isn't gonna work. What do you want?

I tapped the space bar a few times. Still nothing, not even a mechanical click or grind. Across the room, a circle of six men were watching a movie, their chairs scattered in a rough semicircle around a TV on a rickety nightstand. On-screen, a conversion van bounced along a sandy road in what seemed to be the Pine Barrens—scraggly jack pines reached skyward from beds of browned needles, their knobby and arthritic limbs blotched with poultices of white moss and crackling audibly in the breeze. An eerie zithery noise shrilled from the TV's speakers.

I walked over to the far side of the room, my footsteps unexpectedly loud as they bounced off the floor and walls. The guests clustered around the TV were all slouched in their chairs, hands behind their heads or buried in their pockets. They barely budged as I sat down.

Hey
                Forget it. They'll be pissed if I distract them.

The characters on-screen were building a fire, or what looked like a fire captured in night vision. The music intensified, the guests leaned farther forward in their seats. Back across the room, whatever negotiation Vera and Byrd had been involved in must have come to a close: he pushed his chair back from the table and began to shuffle across the dining area to the exit. His hands hung relaxed at his sides, his fingers completely still. Vera pushed her chair back and began making the rounds of the room, passing from table to table, talking with the guests, or, more often, just listening to them, her head tilted to the side, nodding faintly in assent to some point or another, a smile playing across her lips every once in a while, her hand reaching out to touch a guest on the arm, her eyes warming, someone's nervously tapping foot or hand coming to rest, uptight bodies untensing, heads raising, smiles emerging, staying long after she had moved to the next table. No one quite seemed to let go of her, even when her attentions had shifted elsewhere; all the guests' eyes followed her as she played about the room, their eyes softening as they soaked her up . . . or she them. The room was audibly calming as she went, the din of conversations rattling around the hollow space softening from a dull roar to a hushed whisper to silence.

The movie had spooled out, leaving nothing but a black screen in its place. More than one guest was startled when a wristwatch went off or a friend tapped him on the shoulder, bedtime, time to lie down and dream while Vera continued to round the room. By eleven, all the guests had gone off to the dorms or fallen asleep in their chairs.

"   "

Looks like you're the last man standing.

The guest sitting next to me was sprawled in his chair, his eyes closed, his head tossed back, mouth agape. A snore rattled from his nose.

So what do we do now?
                    Why don't we go back to my office and I'll grab my stuff. Then we can

"   "

go. The night's still young, right?

Vera led me down a hallway lined with rooms stacked with bunk beds. Most of the beds were filled by guests staring up at the ceiling with their hands behind their heads, or face down in their pillows like they'd been shot from cannons, others curled up in bundles of sheets and huddled against the cinder-block walls. Clothes hung everywhere, off the radiators, the ends of beds, towel racks by the in-room sinks, sweat-dampened shirts and old basketball shorts, some suits, collars undone, ties drawn down but not untied, jackets and pants limp and trailing.

We climbed up the center stairwell and continued down the far end of the hallway; her office sat in the rear of the second floor, its entry at a right angle to twin-leaved doors that opened onto the church. She flicked the overhead light as we entered.

So this is your space, huh?

That it is.

I landed on an overstuffed sofa that rested against the interior wall of the office. While Vera poked through the drawers of her desk, I scanned the books on the shelf behind her. Every-thing ordered, but no real order—all the spines lined up flush regardless of the seeming size of the book, but beyond that, nothing: a textbook on abnormal psychology next to a phonebook next to a museum catalog for a Chinese art exhibition; a French-to-English dictionary next to a copy of the Koran next to a bird-watcher's manual. The walls—the same white cinder block as the walls downstairs—were bare except for a few diplomas and, on the wall behind me, a large unframed print that she must have stared at for hours a day while she met with guests or searched for an escaped thought. It was something I probably should have remembered from a college art history survey or a museum somewhere: a woman, or what seemed like a woman, her face a patchwork of colored planes that intersected at odd, canted angles, some planes lighter than the others, the darkest lost in some indeterminate middle ground between flesh and emptiness, the extreme outlines of her face disappearing into shadow, eyes hooded, her gaze— or the suggestion of a gaze—directed somewhere in the distance.

Where's that painting from?

"   "

She looked up from her desk.

Is that supposed to be you?

A guest made it for me.   I don't know. Maybe.

She rose from behind the desk with a journal clutched to her chest.

Taking your work home with you?

This is mine. For personal things.

The edges of her journal were battered, the bottom cover pitted; more than half the paper showed frays and crinkling from being touched and written on.

Looks well used.   And it all goes in there?

There's a lot to write about. A lot to say.   Some of it.

She flicked the lights off as we left her office.

"   "

I try to keep these off when I'm not here. Drives the security guard nuts, but whatever.

We turned down the hallway, our shoes squeaking in the antiseptic air.

Well, I had some dinner ideas, but

So what are we doing tonight?

I watched the short hand crawl past the 12 on my watch.

I think it's a little late for that.

"   "

The Chevy sat along the curb. Nothing else stirred on the street. She climbed into the passenger side.

There's still time for a ride.   Does it matter?

                    Where are we gonna go?

I eased the Chevy onto East Main and headed northward, out of the city, over the bridges and across the lakes glittering with stars and the windows of condo towers, through the warrens of Interlaken and Allenhurst, all porches and widow walks, sycamores and elms giving way to Deal's stark flat geometries, synagogues and convents on beachfront plats neighbored with Rococo palaces and croquet grounds, modernist estates with toothpicky twin palm trees and perfect pools awaiting a bigger splash, onto Monmouth Beach's rambling surf clubs and chalk white wedding cake Victorians, sliding into Sea Bright, the beachside disappearing behind a story-high sea wall separated by the roadway and a narrow shoulder from the shore homes nestled on the sound side of the narrowest part of the island, barely a block and a half from the Atlantic, an inch high at best above sea level. Every two blocks or so, a wooden staircase arched over the seawall to the beach on the far side; in the near distance, a group of men in coveralls peered from the top of the wall, looking down at something on the beach. A line of panel trucks sat silently along the shoulder, hazards flashing. Army Corps of Engineers—Beach Reclamation Project.

    Vera grabbed my arm.

"   "

Could we pull over for a second?

I pulled off the road at the next staircase. Vera climbed out of the car, pulling me across the bench seat and out behind her. As we rounded the top of the wall, we looked southward where the engineers stood clustered. A bank of halogen floodlights leaned over their shoulders toward the beach below, where a team of earth movers and cranes ducked and shuddered, carting giant cement disks from the seawall to the tideline.

Let's get closer.

The sand on the beach was hard-caked and gravelly beneath our shoes, barely registering our footsteps as we walked. The beach up here was only a few yards wide, storm-shortened and eroded from nor'easters that must have pounded the shore over the course of the winter and spring. The whole tideline along this stretch of beach had been torn up, the cement disks inserted at alternating angles like a set of crooked teeth. In the area underneath the disks that were tilted inland, fresh piles of sand lay. These revetments would probably be good enough to add another few yards to the beach for the summer, enough to hold through the tourist season before new winter storms swept in and swept the beach away again.

Vera dropped my hand and reached toward the water that rolled gently onto the shore. As her fingers made first contact, she pulled back, clutching her hand to her chest.

What's the matter?   It's still early. It'll get warmer.
                    I didn't expect it to be so cold.

She looked up and down the beach. Out beyond the break, gulls bobbed on the surf, their feathers almost fluorescent in the spotlights.

ooooOooOOoo~ooo~OOOOOO~~~oooooXXXXXXXXXXXXXXXXXXXXXXooooo~~~OOOOOO~ooo
~ooOOooOoooo~~OOoooooooooOOOOOOOOOoooo~oooooXXXXXXXXXXXXXXXXXXXXXXooooooo~
ooooOOOOOOOOOooooooooOO   XXXXXXXXXXXXXXXXXXXXXXXXXXXXXXXXXXXXXXXXXXXXXX
XXXXXXXX   XXXXXXXXXX XXXXXXXX XXXXXXXX   XXXX X XXX XXXXXXXXXXXX
XXXXXXX XXXX X X X XXXXXX XXXXXXX XXXX   XXXX   XXXXX   XXXXXXXXXX
XXXXXXXXX   XXX   XXX   XX   X   XXXXXXXX   XXXXX

Vera touched my arm.

Ready to go?

I took Vera by the hand and led her back up the beach. By the time we crossed over to the roadway, everything was silent.

As I turned the key in the ignition, a bass line shivered through the Chevy.

Turn it up

Vera reached forward and dialed the stereo off.

I glanced at her as we eased off the shoulder. She smiled.

"   "

Let's try to keep it quiet tonight.

We rolled the windows all the way down. The breeze enwrapped us as we streamed farther up the coast. Near Sandy Hook, the road swung hard left and rose, soaring over the neck of the sound and climbing toward the Highlands on the far shore. A trawler slid into view from beneath the bridge, heading inland under full lights, its hold open and overflowing with bluefish shining slick and silvery.

We crossed onto the mainland, on solid ground now and winding past the Cape Cods and cedar-shake bungalows that clung to the sides of the hill that rose from the banks of the sound. The road continued corkscrewing upward, the houses disappearing into dense thickets of birches whose limbs interlocked above the road like praying hands. As we banked the final turn, the night sky opened above us, the carpet of stars broken only by the shadowy spire of the lighthouse, its keeper long since furloughed, its light long since shaded.

Close your eyes.

"   "

I rounded the lighthouse and shut off the engine. I pulled Vera from the car by the hand, leaned against the hood of the car, and turned her northward out over the sound and the ocean beyond.

All right, open them.

"   "

On the edge of the horizon, Manhattan's glowing crystalline skyscrapers sat nestled in the velvety midnight waters, encircled by a glittering chain of light traced out by the Verrazano Narrows and the Brooklyn Bridge, Staten Island and Coney Island. Vera turned to me and smiled, her body resting against me, her face turned upward toward mine.

When she looked at me, everything—the sound of the waves washing along the shore, the trawlers idling in the marina, my own thoughts—slowed to silence. It was like coming to rest.

"   "
"   "

That was all I needed. All I ever wanted. From her. From anyone.

We lay on the hood of the car with our backs against the windshield and watched the moon trace its long slow course across the city as our breaths rose and fell in time together. Sometime around the time the moon passed over Newark, the sun broke over the edge of the Atlantic, its light, first red, then orange, then white, reaching toward us across the quietly shifting ocean.

As the sun warmed, I drove Vera home, perfectly silent, perfectly still, perfectly happy, adrift somewhere in the space between sleep and wakefulness from a night of open-eyed dreaming.

interlude

(EYE OF THE STORM)

The next morning, I lay on the sofa in the boatyard's break room, hiding out from the customers for a few hours. The Weather Channel played on the TV that was hung in the upper corner of the room. On-screen, a multicolored hurricane system hovered. Its longest tail touched Miami; its highest arm encircled Galveston. **HURRICANE JOYCE** The anchor traced her finger around the blue center of calm in the middle of the whole system, then set the whole system in motion, sending the rain and clouds spinning.

My phone buzzed. A message.

I didn't even hear it ring.

I rang up my voice mail.

Hey, Cincy. It's Vera. Can we talk? Call me.

I dialed back. The phone rang through to her messages.
I tried her a few more times over the next few days. Nothing.
That was the last I heard from her for a while.

side B

streets are watching

I cranked the air-conditioning in my office up a notch.

At the beginning of July, the Yanks are closing in on the Sox for the lead in the ****************

I swung the radio antenna around, trying to get it to rest on one of the exposed pipes that ran down the wall. The radio was an old seventies model, silver-faced, analog-dialed, bound with some kind of fake leather material, like a high-tech lunchbox. The sound was terrible, tinny and screechy, but it would do. Anything to occupy my mind, to fill out my time.

As of late, there was more time to fill, more room to fill. Up until recently, on slow days or quiet evenings when I had the apartment to myself, I'd pull out my notebooks and highlighted secondhand treatises and try to get started again on what was supposed to be my dissertation. The problems didn't go away, though, they just changed: it was easy, at first, to jump back into the same lines of thought, their details still clear in my mind, begging, seemingly, to be played out. Pushing the questions didn't lead to answers, though, just more questions, and, before I knew it, I was right back where I started. As the weeks crawled by, even the questions became less clear to me, the prospect of answering them now just a distant hope. It wasn't a question of being unable to answer the questions anymore; it was a question of being unable to ask the questions in the first place, to even understand why I was asking what I was asking.

One day, sitting on the beach at sunset, sheltered from the breeze in the crook of a dune by the mesh wire garbage cans where gulls poked at shreds of plastic shopping bags or plucked at sun-rotted banana peels, the dim desire to even want to question these things anymore sputtered, sparked, and died. When I got home that night, I dumped the frayed-edged and water-swollen notebooks, dog-eared paperbacks and jacketless hardcovers into a cardboard box. Then I bound it all up with masking tape and shoved it into the back corner of my closet.

I'm not going back.

All well and good, but all this thinking was hydraulic: the space I freed up filled up again with different thoughts.

I called. No answer. I called. No answer. "Aimi, where's Vera?" "I don't know."

What did I do?

Was I doing too much?

Was I doing enough?

Did I do anything?

My foot tapped on the linoleum, my whole leg joggled.

A knock on the doorjamb. Oz and Deuce stood in the doorway: they were dressed like a crew of skittish beekeepers, wearing long-sleeved coveralls and big hats I got for them early in the season after they picked up mild cases of sun poisoning. Since then, they'd been doing most of their work inside or in the shadows of the warehouses.

As far as I know,

I zipped the cover back: the storm

had filled the boat bench-high with

yellowed rainwater turned brackish

in the hold. One pump, two pumps

one hundred and eighty. I earned

all five bucks my parents paid me.

by the fence?

You know that old sailboat out there   What's the deal with that?

it's for sale.   Let me make a few phone calls and find out. I'll let you know.

Oz sat where my mother used to sit, hand on the tiller.

How much they want?

"   "

I spun back around to the phone.
Oz's and Deuce's reflections were still visible on the plate glass.

This might take a while.

Cool. We'll just go back outside again.

Oh, sure.

They disappeared down the hall as I picked up the phone.

Hey, Mom, I was hoping you'd be home.   Good. I think I have good

You were right. How are you?

news.   Someone here at the yard wants to buy your catboat. How much do you want

Oh, really?

for it?   That's it?

We tumbled into the living

room, sunburnt, exhausted

from a full day on the bay.

  She spent hundreds of

  hours on it, in it, prepping,

  sailing, cleaning from first

  light to last ray.

            "Five thousand."

    Let's see   Fifteen hundred?   It's an old boat. It's prob-

                                                  I'm on the phone,

ably not even seaworthy.   Well, maybe with some work.

                                          Hey, Cincy

Corey. So I can sell it for fifteen hundred and you'd be fine with that?   I'm on the phone.

  "   "

                                          Cincy!   Can I

    I'm sorry, Mom. Can you hold on?   You couldn't ask

  "   "

leave   Can I leave early? I got a train to catch.

me this earlier today?   What do you have to do?   Yeah, sure, what-

  "   "

        Something came up.   Catch a train.

ever. Do this ahead of time next time,

  "   "

  "   "

        I looked at the clock—a quarter to four.

all right?

"   "

SURE! THANKS!

Corey jetted off.

Sorry, Mom. I didn't catch that.   Sounds good. Talk to
                    I said I'd be happy with fifteen hundred.

"   "

Cincy, your father and I are coming up next week to clean some things out of the house. Will

            Yeah, sure, just let me know when you get in.
you be around?   Will do. I'll be so happy if you sell

        You loved that boat.
that boat.   We're old, Cincy. We live a thousand miles away now. That boat's

                                All right. Fifteen hundred it is. See you soon, Mom.
                        They settled in at the edge of the
                        cul-de-sac, their house backed up to a
                        shallow lake and a forest where cottonmouths
                        trespassed and hikers backpacked. Landlocked
                        for the first time.
                                My dad, just an infant, crawled by the tideline, grinning,
                                sand-covered, his trail traced out in tiny handprints and
                                knee-dug furrows, everything faded now with the film.
not doing us any good anymore.

        When I finally found Oz and Deuce, they were winching a Blue Jay out of the basin. The
boat swung wildly in the wind whipping off the bay.

I spoke to the owner of the boat. I can sell it to you for fifteen hundred. Sound good?

Yeah.

Definitely.

I'm just warning you: I think that thing's gonna take some work before you can put it out on the water.

"   "

"   "

"   "

We got a plan.

No prob.

I continued my circuit around the yard, along the docks and out into the back storage lot. We were deep into the summer season now, most of the boats out on the water somewhere, tied up to docks or cutting across the bay.

My mom and dad, newly married, leaned back in their deck
chairs, smiling, her hand resting on his arm, a few empty
beer bottles on the table in front of them. A pile of Uncle
Packy's ashed-out Lucky Strikes smoldered in an ashtray.

The party burned bright.
We floated above it all.
Her voice cloudy, her hair
perfumed. I breathed her in.

OOOO~oooo~~Oo~O

Just one more breath.

As I neared the main building, the locker room's outside door opened. Corey shuffled out, holding a bulky paper bag in his left hand. He placed the bag in the rear seat of his car, then climbed into the driver's seat and sped away, his tires skipping on the gravel and kicking up eddies of dust in their wake.

"   "

Ay, ay, boss man.

Tone was standing with Mike and the deflated hull of one of the yard's inflatable boats.

What happened to the Zodiac?   Mike, what the

Uh-hmmm

We   I mean, I popped it.   I got too close

You smoked up at lunch, didn't

"   "

to the channel marker and then it just popped! I didn't mean to!

you?   You smoked up at lunch! And then you went and drove a BOAT?!

"   "

I

Mike, look. You're a good worker when you're

"   "

I didn't think it would be a problem! Don't fire me!

straight, but you're high like A L L T H E T I M E. It's embarrassing to me, J.D., the rest of the team.

"   "

"   "

It's even embarrassing to YOU!   Tell you what. If you can promise to be straight

"   "

It won't happen again!

at work for the rest of the summer, I don't even care if you blaze up right after you leave the yard, you're

"   "

"   "

welcome back. Otherwise, no dice. Deal?

"   "

Deal.

Tone lost it as Mike shuffled off.

Cut him some slack, huh?

Ohhhhhhhhhhhhhhhhhh shitttttttttttttttttttttttttttttt   **You should talk, Cince,**

He'll be all right.   He'll be back even-

you basically just fired his ass.   **Yo, that kid smokes every day.**

tually.

You've got way more faith than me.

■ ■ ■

I spent the rest of the afternoon and the evening on the marina's floating dock repairing the
Zodiac: wet-vaccing the water out of the inner tube, cutting and heat-sealing a patch onto the
hole.

Footsteps crackled on the gravel behind me. J.D. approached with a folder in hand.

"   "

I was just looking over the pay stubs from the first month. We only paid Corey half of what he was

How'd that happen?

owed.   I must have mixed his rate up with Mike's when I cut the checks. Has

No.   Damn.

I handed Corey the envelope with his check.

He stuffed it in his front pocket. "Thanks, man."

he said anything to you?   That's odd. We shorted him a good two thousand dollars.

Sure. I'll call

So, I cut another check to make up the difference. Just make sure he gets it, okay?

him about it now.

"   "

No go—Corey's phone went through to the voice mail.

I turned back to the boat, pinching its side periodically to make sure it was still taking on air. Another good fifteen minutes of pumping and it was seaworthy again.

Just as I was getting ready to slide the Zodiac into the water, my phone rang.

"   "

What's up with this guy in the car at the surf shop?

The surfer had settled in across the street again. Not doing much of anything, just sitting, looking, staring, it seemed, from behind his shades.

The white car?   I'm not sure.

          Yeah.   He's out there almost every day. I just saw him as I was pulling

    Maybe the police detailed a guy to make sure there's not another break-in?

out.   They'd probably tell

                                                        Something Tone said.

us if they were going to do that. What makes you think he's a cop?   How

                            I don't know. He seemed pretty convinced of it, though.

would Tone know one way or the other?

"   "

Hmmm, I'm going to put a call in to the police. Lock up tight tonight, okay? And make sure there's

The car was still there when I returned from winching the Zodiac back into the basin. Gone when I emerged from the locker room, free of bay grime and sunblock residue. I padlocked the locker room entrance, double-checked the front door, and headed down the beachfront for Jimmy Byrnes's bar.

knife

Byrnes's didn't have the Tides's impulses toward the refined—it was the deepest of the boards' dive bars, submerged in the chaos of the midway and a shallow drunken swim from the city's seediest motels, a joint that dated back to our fathers' postcollege years downing beers and rocking out to the E Street Band while Bruce's boys were still on the D list, the kind of place that had had more knife fights than owners. I wasn't in the best mood after the day in the lot, or the weeks of Vera's silence, but I needed to move around, couldn't bear sitting still, spending another night at home with the record cabinet spinning away, checking my cell phone for missed calls or texts.

From the bar's rickety balcony, Tom and I watched the beachgoers coursing through the midway's narrow canyon of flashing lights and solid text: Pokereno Brooklyn Style Pizza 5 Pool Tables Pop One Balloon You Win Old Time Photos Lucky Leo's Proud to be American Fresh Fruit Orangeade ATM Waffles 'n' Ice Cream Frozen Custard Summer's Here Ice Cream Making Memories for Over 50 Years Meatballs Cheese Fries Hamburgers Hot Dogs Cold Drinks Lemonade Cheese Steaks Coin Castle 100,000 Prizes Free Drink w/ Slice Pints of Bud Bud Lite Family Fun Clams Oysters Shrimp Since 1968 Arcade Water Gun Fun Tub Game ATM Balloon Game Beer Pong Play Basketball Ping-Pong Air Hockey Shoot the Paintballs Tornado Moby Dick Bar Bathers Welcome Gourmet Coffee Calzone Fresh Cut Fries Grilled Chicken Breast Fried Calamari Stromboli Corn on the Cob Roast Pork Sandwich Super Subs Sausage Open Til 3 AM Welcome Back Fun Bar.

Patching a Zodiac, and then I had to shower, and

What was keeping you? **Patching a Zodiac? Some-**

WHOOOOOOOOOOOOOOOOOOOOOOOOOOOOOOOOOOOOOOOOOOOOOOOOSHHHHHHHH

Hnnnnnmmmmmthwapspsssssssssssssh

Pingping *Ping Ping*

SHUFFLE

Ping ping ping

SHUFFLE

I'm not going to say. Accidents

one popped a Zodiac?! Who? **What kinda idiot pops a Zodiac?**

happen. C'mon, man.

To idiots. Holy shit. **You work with some real characters, dude. I'd**

Let's change the subject.

probably kill myself if I had to put up with that kinda shit every day.

You end up going out with Aimi last night? How'd it go? Where'd you go?

Okay, fine. **Yeah.** **Good.**

What did you do?

Who cares? There's only so many places to go down here. **Walked around,**

You don't really sound all that

got drinks, went to her place. The usual routine, nothing special.

into it. What do you like about her?

She's just a girl. **Um, she's pretty hot. She's fun. She's easy**

"   "

to talk to. I think she likes me. You know, she's pretty much got the total package as far as

I guess that sounds good.

I'm concerned. **I'm sorry, man. It's just hard for me to get intense**

"   "

about things. Not like you and Vera. Speaking of which

Tom laughed and took a swig of beer.

I don't know.   No.

Good question.

Maybe she's sick.

"I get moody." Maybe she's been

having a hard time at work.

"Can we talk?"

Where's your girl?   **She never returned your calls?**   **She traveling or some-**

I don't know, I don't know. It's just been complete radio silence on her end.

thing?   **That's weird.**

"   "

Sounded like it'd gotten pretty heavy between you two. Maybe your swag is just so intense

"   "

she's paralyzed with some combination of lust and fear. Maybe she'll throw herself on you

I'm not holding my breath.   Three weeks? Four?

the next time you see her.   **How long's it been?**

Tom paused for a second and looked me in the eye.

Yeah.

Yeah.

Yeah.

Do you like this girl?   **Don't let her get away.**

I leaned back from the railing.

Let's go inside. It's a little too noisy out here.

Agreed.

"You have the option of the lion, the parachute parrot, or the wet tiger."

pifffffft ppiffffffft pifffffftpffftpiffffffftpiffffffft   slapPOP pifffffft pifffffft

pifffffft POP POP POPslapPOP pifffffft pifffffft pifffffft ppifffffffft

WAAAAAAAAAAAHNWAAAAAAAAAAHN

poppoppoppifffftpifftpopPUNKTPUNKTRING

pifft   pifft   pifft   POP

We ducked down the stairs to the ground floor. Quieter but no less confusing.

The inside of Byrnes's was like the under deck of a ship, its ceilings low and crossed with beams bowing with age, the walls and tables the same dark wood, dulled and scarred with knifed-in initials and symbols like some kind of wall-to-wall Shore cuneiform. The sounds of all the different isolated conversations melted into a white noise that seemed to cancel out any words that weren't spoken directly mouth-to-ear. Maybe that's why there were always so many shady types there—people went to Byrnes's to be alone in public, everyone too apprehensive to ask what anyone else was doing there, huddling in the corners conversing low under the sounds of the jukebox or the noise of the crowds passing outside, sitting side-by-side at the bar side-of-the-mouth talking with eyes fixed on the game playing on the rickety analog set above the shelves of liquor. The windows on the far side of the first floor looked out over Kingsley toward the parking lots, packed even at twenty dollars a night. The bar's boardwalk wall was a set of garage doors, rolled up now, the inside crowd merging with the passersby. The thick haze of tobacco and clove smoke that hung over the space dulled the light from the rustic lanterns and stained-glass shaded lamps that hung on tarnished chains from the ceiling.

girll |||||||||||||| *girll* ||||||||||||||

"   "

"She traveling or something?" "I don't know."

You see anywhere to sit?

                    Hey, man.

A stranger tapped me on the shoulder.

tried to get

        Hmmm?

"   "

Hey.

He had a skullcap hanging off the side of his shaved head and a week's worth of whiskers
that blended at the edges with the stark black lines of a tattoo that crept up the side of his neck
from under his collar.

a hold of you, girl   *But it's hard, 'cause* ||||||| *girlIIIII* ||||||||||||

        I'm sorry. Do I know you?

"   "

You got   Oh, my bad, I thought you were someone else. You got

"   "

    Take two for the road.

a match?

Tom tossed a half-empty matchbook to him. The stranger struck one to a Marlboro, waved
out the flame, and walked away.

    You know him?

Dirt bag.   **I don't like the looks of him. That's all I need to know.**

We posted up against the wall across the room from the bar. A row of used glasses, full of partially melted ice cubes and wrung-out limes, rested on a shelf about waist high. A group of painters having postjob drinks were throwing darts by the bar. The dartboard was gouged out, the only clean space the bull's-eye. A dart whistled into the wall beside the board.

Um, yeah, I think.   Let

Can you see the drink board from here?   **They have well drinks tonight?**

me see.   It looks like

"   "

I spotted Vera leaning against one of the columns on the boardwalk-facing side. She was in full view for only a second, before the ebb and flow of the crowds closed in around her.

I mean we   we ahhh   we

What's up?

The crowds parted again. She was dressed way too nicely for Byrnes's, nicer than she was on our date. She pulled her phone out of her bag, checked the screen, and then stashed it again. She looked up. Our sight lines crossed.

Did she catch my eye?   Did I catch hers?

Sorry. Vera's outside there. Hold on for a second.

Maybe she didn't get them in the first place.

Phone's not broken. Why's she ignoring my calls?

Cincy, yo.

Vera!

It's fine. It's fine. Things happen.

Is she meeting someone else? A girls' night out or something?

"   "

I waved at her and took a few steps toward the front of the bar. She looked up in my direction. Looked down. And walked away. I turned back to Tom.

Beats me.   I don't know.

What's with that?   **What did you do to her, dude?**

I mean,

You just going to let her walk away?

Tom widened his eyes at me.

Hold my drink?

Atta boy.

Outside. I looked up and down the boards, headed southward, around Byrnes's far corner. No Vera. Again to the north. No sign. Out oceanward, the water opened up, sheeted and ink-stained. Nothing. She was gone.

I leaned against the oceanside railings. The metal was cold, glowing softly purple in the twilight. A Coast Guard cutter skipped northward beyond the breakers. Something flared to my right. A silhouette sat on the ground, legs dangling out over the sand, head resting against one of the uprights. The tip of a cigarette glowed. A woman, wearing a black Byrnes's apron with a wad of tip money bulging out of the front pocket. She gazed out oceanward. The Ferris wheel shone and spun behind her off-center.

April?

I know her. *She smiled. Her hair thick and*
golden like the reeds that tossed alongside
the tracks with the passing freight trains.

She turned to look at me. Her eyes were glassy, ringed with gray turning almost black at the base of her nose, her hair thin, overbleached, faint crow's-feet visible beneath her cracking concealer. She seemed tired, way older than she should be.

April, hey.

She blew two plumes of smoke from her nose, then turned away.

She doesn't even remember who I am.

She closed the door behind her, didn't answer when I
knocked. Two days before I left for school, ready to go.
She beat me to it. "April, hey." She left for good.

I wended through the crowd, back to Byrnes's.

I'm fine.　　I'm fine.　　　　　Listen, man, let's
She blew two plumes of smoke from her nose.
You look like you've seen a ghost.　　　　　**Where's Vera?**

bounce.
She looked away.
"　　　　"

We inched around the perimeter, hugging the walls opposite the bar. The floor was sticky
with something vaguely sweet-smelling. A sort of resiny odor cut through the yeasty stale beer
fog. A round of laughter from the door.

Is that　　　　no　　that's Corey.

Corey stood near the back entrance. He was in hushed conversation with the same stranger
who bummed the matches from Tom. I brushed Corey with my elbow as I walked by.

I thought you had a train to catch?
"　　　　　"

Corey rubbed the back of his neck and pulled a toothpick out of his mouth.

But
I did. I caught it, and now I'm here.   I didn't say I was taking the train. I just needed to catch

You get my message?
a friend before she took off.   About the check? Yeah. Sounds good. I'll come

Right. See you tomorrow.
by tomorrow or whenever.

I could feel Corey and the other guy's eyes on us as we elbowed our way out the back entrance and onto Kingsley. I resisted the urge to look back. Instead, Tom and I continued upshore, along the backs of the arcades and pizzerias as the power lines hummed overhead with brownout levels of electricity. Puddles of water from overtaxed ACs trickled across the sidewalk, running together into a small stream in the gutters. Crowds spilled out of the latenight diners, lines formed up and down the block at the rear entrances to the bars. Police officers sat curbside in their cruisers.

That's one of the guys that works the yard with me, Corey. He came into the
What was up with that?

office earlier today, in a big rush saying he had to leave early to catch a train.   So, he's here now,
And?

like four hours later.   That he was just trying to see a friend before she left.
What did he say just then?

I don't know. Something about
Sounds fine to me. Why would he lie about something like that?

him's just rubbing me the wrong way.
"   "

It wasn't until we hit the new White Pearl Hotel a quarter-mile away that I caught sight of Vera. She was perched on the edge of a chair on the hotel's street-facing balcony, about half a story off the sidewalk.

Tall glasses sat on the table between her and her companion. Her face was framed over his shoulder. He leaned forward, his arm moving back and forth in a lazy swirl over his drink. Her chair was tilted forward, her legs crossed and resting up against his. She pressed her left palm against her cheek. Her eyes widened and her head dropped forward. He leaned back and placed his arms behind his head. Her chair fell back level as she laughed, clapping her hands together in front of her mouth. She bit her lip and looked down.

It was too loud and she was too far away.

"
Is there another guy?   What did all that mean, then?
"
                                 She kissed me, long and
                                 slow. We laid back in the
                                 hammock, as music

                                                        Can't be. What else could
"   "

"   "

Cincy, yo! Get in the car, man.

Tom was on Daniels, leaning out the driver's-side window of his car. Afraid he'd honk again, afraid Vera would turn and see me standing there in the middle of the sidewalk, I rushed over to the Chevy and sank low into the passenger seat.

              I don't know *what* I've been seeing tonight. Let's get out of here.
What's up with you, man?

As we drove, I leaned my head against the window, reeling, weightless with the first flash of a distance that I hadn't felt previously, that maybe had been there the whole time, that I didn't see, that I didn't want to see, wondering if she'd even miss me if I just drifted away, wondering, for the first time, whether I'd even been that close to begin with.

She bit her lip and looked down. He reached across
the table, taking her hand in his. He leaned
forward and kissed her.

I held her close and kissed her. "Call me." She leaped
up from the table when she saw me.

"Cincy!" He looked defeated.

It's been weeks. She reached for him and

[   ]

Faint crow's-feet visible beneath her cracking concealer. This is all so fragile.

Give it up. That guy did me a
favor. He held her close. "Vera"
she smiled like it meant nothing.

We lay back on the hood of the car. I lay
awake that night, thrilling. I pushed through
the crowd. "Vera"

"April?" She didn't even remember me.

The doors closed behind her.

"I'll keep you on your toes." She didn't make any promises.

Reel it back in.

Springwood was still as we approached our apartment, soundless except for the skittering
of a few dead leaves in the gutters. A black van passed us, heading in the opposite direction,
its front windshield blanked out by pools of lamplight. Farther up the block, across the street
from our place, a head peeked out of a Dumpster—a drifter picking through the construction
waste. He ducked as our headlights panned across the Dumpster.

I gave the street-level door an extra tug to make sure it was locked and trudged upstairs. Inside the apartment, Tom tossed his keys onto a pile of magazines heaped on the coffee table and
then lumbered off to his bedroom.

"A girl has to have some secrets." "I don't think I have to let everyone know everything that's on my mind." "Can we talk?"

So what am I missing?

Something clattered on the street. I picked across my bedroom to the window and parted the blinds. The drifter was still rooting around in the Dumpster, tossing scrap metal and spare piping onto the street. A lot of scrap metal. Maybe there was more than one person out there. I stepped away from the window and turned on the AC, listening as its churn drowned out the street noise.

The bedside lamp cast a pale glow over the record cabinet. An album lay motionless on the turntable. I reached for the dust jacket sitting on the top of the pile of records lying nearby and tucked my thumb and index finger inside—there was already a record in there. I looked at the cover.

Midnight Marauders.

I was listening to *Supreme Clientele.*

I checked the album lying on the turntable again. *Supreme Clientele.*
I grabbed the stack of albums.

Mecca & the Soul Brother. Illmatic. ATLiens. Cuban Linx. Fantastic, Vol. 2. Supreme Clientele. Why is this at the bottom?

I scanned the room. J.D.'s map was lying on the floor next to my dresser. My duffel bag was unzipped. The papers on my desk, the papers I had shuffled into a straight stack the last time I worked on them, fanned out slightly at the bottom.

A shadow crouched by the window, sifting through my desk, flashlight between its teeth. Spotted lights jumped across the walls of the apartment, the floorboards groaned with furtive steps.

Forget it. I'm overreacting.

I lay down on my bed, eyes to the ceiling.

The padlock lay broken. The dog lurched forward. Click, shutter, capture. The surfer tore through my desk. his drink. Her chair was tilted forward, her legs crossed and resting up against his. She pressed her left palm against her cheek.

Another clatter outside. The drifter again. A black van idled across the street from our apartment. A red dot blipped in the backseat.

A black van passed us, its front windshield blanked out by pools of lamplight.

The window at the top of the hallway stairwell opened out onto a fire escape. I popped it and climbed out, clattering down to the alley that ran behind the buildings on our block.

The moon hung like a broken plate. I picked along a warren of shuttered garages and barking dogs, out onto Ventnor. I peered around the edge of the corner store. The van was still there, idling, rear windows hearse-tinted.

This is a bad idea. As I approached, two figures leaped out of the van. Before I could turn and run, they were on me, fists raining

I crept along the far side of Springwood, back toward the apartment, toward the van, one foot after the other. Our building loomed to the right; the van's engine shuddered and purred. A form slowly resolved in the van's passenger's-side rearview, a dark blue sleeve, a whiskered jaw.

A length of piping clattered out of the Dumpster. The arm in the rearview shifted. Shadowed heads in the van turned. The engine revved. The van pulled away from the curb. I quickened my steps. The van sped up, audibly kicking into a higher gear. It wasn't until it reached the end of the block and turned onto East Main that the van's headlights flipped on. And then it was gone.

The doorbell glowed orange at our door; I looked up to our apartment.

I retraced my steps, vaulting back onto the fire escape, clambering up the thin ladder past the drainpipes and bootleg cable drops, the spaghetti-tangled power lines and copper-stained transformers, back into the apartment, into the bathroom, to wash off the rust and chipped paint, to calm my hands down.

I reached for the mirror's frame and tilted it . . . too quickly. My hands jumped, knocked the mirror off the wall. I picked it up and tried to hang it again, notched the wire into the wall hook and lowered it with trembling hands. Jagged cracks ran along its face, fracturing my own face, fragmenting the bathroom into a floating toilet and sunken shower, diffracting the regular grid of wall tiles. I leaned from side to side, trying to find a clean vantage point. No chance: the cracks too many, too sharp, too fine.

It'd have to do.

It hung there for the rest of the summer.

where i'm from

(ICEBERG)

I didn't sleep that night. I just stared at the ceiling, hovering in the feverish shoals just above sleep, waiting for morning to come, waiting for the day to be over before it even started. I dragged myself to work that morning, tried to keep my head down. I dragged through most of the rest of the week, really . . .

Thursday. The yard's ACs throbbed in the still, humid air. I lay on the floor of the warehouse, my face to the cool concrete, my eyes looking out over the storage lot.

"Did you try calling her again, dude?"

I fidgeted with my phone.

"Not until I figure this out, until I know where she's coming from." "You're crazy." "I don't want to be wrong."

The van pulled away from the curb. I quickened my steps.

The van sped up, audibly kicking into a higher gear.

What were they looking for?

A kicked pebble skipped by my head.

So, this is what you do all day, huh?

I rolled over to see my father and mother looking down at me. I stood up, brushing off loose pieces of gravel that had clung to my face and shirt.

It's, um, very hot out, you know. Just trying to keep cool.

"   "

"   "

I embraced my parents awkwardly. Despite our weekly conversations, I hadn't seen them in a few years.

Let me give you a quick tour.

The yard looks good!

"   "

I looked around the warehouse.

Let's go this way.

"   "

"   "

We crossed the warehouse floor and turned past the soda machines. Corey was leaning back on a metal folding chair by the propane filling station with a rolled⁄up towel around his neck and a Coke in his right hand.

That's Corey Montvale. He's one of the yard attendants.

"   "

Hmmm. He looks like he could be your

That's what some people say.

"   "

cousin.   No, seriously, he could be. What's his last name again?

Montvale.

Bob and Joanne's son?

Montvale, Montvale.   No, his mother is probably Joanne's sis-

"   "

The reunion buzzed with cousins, baby and elder, uncles and
aunts straight from mass, remote-controlled cars and baseball
broadcasts. A kid my age tugged up clumps of teary-scented
onion grass like a Mario brother. "Corey!" His mother plucked
him up with two hands.

"   "

ter, Linda. And she's married to Martin. They moved to Connecticut probably twenty years

Weird.

So I guess that would make Corey your second cousin, once removed.

ago.   Not so

"   "

"   "

much. Our family's pretty big.

We continued past the bobbing rows of blindingly white powerboats and racks of jet skis.
In the basin, a couple was lowering a Laser into the water.

Oh, hey, two of the guys bought your boat, Mom, and they've been doing a lot of work on it. Check

"   "

"   "

it out.

Lord knows what they've been doing to this thing.

" "

" "

Oz and Deuce *had* been doing a lot of work, coming early and staying late most days. They'd chipped the flaking lacquer off the mast and boom and refinished the seats and rails to a rich shine, stripped and replaced the metal fittings, debarnacled the hull, patched up a few hairline fractures on the bow. They even had Tone specially fit an old 35-horsepower outboard for traveling without sail.

See?

" "

It looks better than I remember.

A high-pitched grind erupted from the hold. A triangular section of fiberglass dropped from the boat's underbody. A second later, Deuce climbed out of the hold.

What're you doing, man? The boat was looking good.   Why don't we, ah, head back

" "

" "

It's a surprise!

to the front office?

" "

" "

" "

I dragged my mother behind me, her head turned back toward the boat, her fingers knitting together. As we approached the office, Tone's Caprice rumbled into the lot. He was out of the car before the engine had even wound down.

Cince! Cince! You wouldn't believe what this cop just did to my damn car!

Tone, these are my

I'm riding up the Boulevard, right, and this cracker Oh, hi.

Hello.

parents.

Tone's our marine tech. Would you excuse us for

How are you doing? So lovely to meet you.

a minute?

" "

" "

" "

Tone and I circled around the rear of his car, out of earshot of my parents.

What happened?

This cop pulled me over on the way back from lunch. I *know* I wasn't speeding. So

when he comes up to the window, I'm like, "How can I help you, officer?" And he just leans down in

About what?

the window and starts going in, like "You ready to talk?"   **EXACTLY! I *don't know*. So**

What did you do?

I say, "About what?" And then real slicklike, he says, "We know everything."   **I**

                    And?

told him to go fuck himself.   He just laughed and walked off. And then, *then* when he's walk-

"   "

ing away? He pulls out one of those little flashlights that they got, you know those metal ones, and

"   "

smashes out my taillight!

A collar of jagged red glass surrounded a bare bulb on the driver's side of his car.

What'd he look

Now, I'm probably gonna get pulled over for the taillight, and it starts all over again.

like?

Here's the thing: it was the same dude who's been up in that Impala the last few weeks, scop-

"   "

ing the yard out.

I looked over to where my parents were waiting.

Give me some time to think about this, all right?

Click, shutter, capture. He just sat there. Just sitting, looking, staring.

                    Don't wait too long.

Tone walked off, leaving me alone with my parents again.

I'm   I'm sorry about that. Tone had some issue this afternoon.

Are the van guys

with the cop? Focus.

"   "

Is everything okay?

About as good as it's going to be.

"   "

"   "

Gravel rattled behind us.

"   "

Is that who I think it is? J.D.!   The yard looks

"   "

Well if it isn't Jim and Renee. Good to see you.

"   "

like it's doing well.   Still getting used to

"   "

It's a bit different, but the better for it. How's Carolina?

"   "

the place.

"   "

It's broiling out here. Why don't we go up to my office to chat?

J.D. and my parents strolled off. Back in my office, catalogs from local alarm installers lay
on my desk, business cards stapled or paper-clipped to their inside covers.

COMMERCIAL SECURITY SOLUTIONS *"You ready to talk?" The flashlight butted through Tone's taillight.*

What's Tone's role in all of this? *"I think he's a narc."*

"Lock up tonight, okay?" "What makes you think he's a cop?"

"I think he's a narc."

"I don't trust cops." Why not? *"I beat that"* Framed?

The surfer just watched. But

The van glided along the curb. Who are they? Are they with the surfer? *I vaulted the fence.* What do they want from me?

By the time my parents meandered back downstairs, it was well past four.

"   "

The van tore off, headlights off, squealing onto East Main on two tires.

Scraped, and scraped, and scraped,

peeling back the layers.

It'll be just like old times.   Cince?

Want to go by the house with us, Cincy?

My father was looking at me as I stared off somewhere past him.

Huh?   Oh, yeah, why not?

I tilted the can over. Nothing fell out.

I shook the can. Nothing. Maybe I can

finally get inside.

"   "

"   "

We piled into my parents' rental car and drove off. The car's exterior was immaculate, its paint job fresh, its windows spotless. The same inside: there was none of the atmosphere of its owner, just new-car perfume, its floor mats and upholstery smooth and evenly colored, unclut-tered with the random runnels of sand and loose gravel, dried leaf detritus, and food crumbs that gathered in the crevices of my parents' own cars. I fiddled with the glove box and seatside compartments, the storage space in the arm rest: a rental agreement, a registration card, smooth open and smooth closed, free from crumpled and refolded road maps, cracked cassette tapes and jewel cases, hair-riddled combs and half-used shoe polish cans.

"   "

Maybe they'll be waiting when we get there.
There she is.

"   "

Nothing stirred along our old street. We parked in the driveway and clambered out. We headed down the driveway and along the front sidewalk.

"Go ahead, press your hands down."
My mother held me by the waist as I
leaned over the freshly poured cement.
It was like Play-Doh, but wetter, grittier.
"Press hard." I pulled my hands away,
leaving two starlike impressions on the
sidewalk. "Hold on." My mother picked
up a twig lying along the curb and traced
an '88 into the clean space underneath.

The sidewalk was blindingly white, fresh cement combed and ridged.
Up the front steps. The brass lamps outside the door were the same I grew up with, long since greened and salt-fogged, their stems snapped off.

Lights everywhere, three-foot floor lamps towering over me. In dense rows along the floor, hanging nested from the ceilings. "This? This'll cost ya one seventy-five a fixture." "Let's go, Dad," I said, tugging at my father's sleeve, "We can get a better deal at Ace's." "Did I say one seventy-five? I meant one twenty-five." "We're wasting our time, Dad." "If you buy three, I'll give you the fourth free." "Deal." We sat down for ice cream. "Good job, Cincy. I should take you shopping with me all the time."

My father pulled a heavy keychain out of his pocket and slipped a key into the front door. The lock snapped open. The door was warped, catching the jamb on the lower corner, leaving a triangle of open air at its top corner.

My father leaned in with his shoulder and stumbled into the vestibule. The air was dry, odorless.

I dropped my bag
in the vestibule.
I breathed in. The
mingled scents of the
yellowing books in
the study, dried cran-
berries, sticks of
incense over the fire-
place, and some mys-
terious perfume that
my mom and all the
women in the neigh-
borhood wore.

The granite tabletops in the kitchen were buffed to a high polish. Like the outside, the kitchen's walls were painted a fresh white. I circled around the island that housed the stove.

"Just keep looking forward. We won't get a good measure-
ment unless your head's straight." My father slid a ruler
across the peak of my head until it bumped against the
kitchen wall. He made a small mark with a pencil, then
drew the measuring tape out of its silver case. I stepped
back and looked up. Higher than last time! "I'm getting
taller!" "Soon you'll be taller than me."

I climbed up the staircase, straightening the pictures that hung crookedly from their hooks
like they'd been sliding down the banister.

My sister and I watched as our shadows played across the walls, expanding and shrinking in the flashlight beam.

Daylight flooded the second floor, the walls and ceiling painted the same blinding white. I
turned down the hallway to my room. The evening sun slanted through the highest pane of the
window. Most of the furniture had been cleared out. The only thing left was my surfboard,
propped against the wall near the window.

The shock lingered longer than the pain, the memories longer than the shock. I watched from the beach as my friends ripped
along the waves, my arm in a sling, my headphones pulsing out a loping swing, my sweatshirt heavy with ocean air and the
keening autumn cold. There wasn't anything to do but watch, study, observe. My physics textbook lay in the hollow between
my crossed legs. Forces and vectors, equations and axioms spiraled out across my notepad. My pencil traced answers, eraser
backtracked, marks layered over marks in a dusty gray graphite cloud. A flurry of white erupted offshore: an early breaker
taking down two of my friends in a tangle of arms and legs.
O~oOooooO~~o~oo~OOOOoooO~OO~oo~OOO~Oo~o~OOOOXOOoooooooooooo~o~OO~OOooOoooooOooOoO~~OOooOoO
O oOooooO~~o~oo~OOOOoooO~OO~oo~OOO~Oo~o~OOOOXXXOOoooooooooooo~o~OO~OOooOoooooOooOoO~~OOooOo
~OOO~OOooo~oo~OOooOO~oooOOOoo~OOooOO~OOOXXXXXooo~~OOOOOoooOOO~~~OOOO~~~OOOOoooOOOooooo
I turned the music in my headphones higher, until the churn of the waves drowned in the sound, voices covered voices, eyes
focused back on the page, problem after problem. Figure it out, figure it out, clean it up, make it perfect.

My father leaned into the room.

Those boxes are yours to keep if you want them.

Inside, a book of photographs, some soccer trophies, and a glossy brown folder full of loose-leaf paper covered with my swirly second-grade handwriting. A long tree branch threw an unfamiliar shadow across the bedroom floor.

"You kids sit still." My brother, sister, and I sat along the stacked slate barrier that surrounded the base of a sycamore sapling my father had planted. My mother snapped photos, one after the other, turning her camera on its side, righting it, turning it again, walking a slow arc, trying to get just the right light. When I stood up, the tree wasn't much taller than me.

Down the far end of the hallway, to my mom's studio, where she spent days staring out the bay window at the street below, musing about her new synesthetic children's book or collage.

The walls were covered with heavy brown paper, like shopping bag paper in sheets, the paper covered with impressionistic chalk drawings of neighborhood kids, pets, the bay. Her main subjects were the letters of the alphabet, some large and building-like, others tiny and petal-like, in fonts familiar and unrecognizable, the only constant being their colors: every letter had a color and never appeared in any other. Something about C and J didn't let her draw them in any other way, like she was being untrue to red U by painting it blue.

Hey, Cincy, can you help me move these chairs downstairs?

The stairs to the third floor creaked underfoot. We stooped into the crawl spaces, heavy with the scent of mothballs and dust, and dragged out chairs my parents had stashed up here twenty years ago. Once we had arranged the chairs downstairs, the living room looked more like it did before I moved in than it did when I had lived there. Over the fireplace at the base of the stairs, an old mirror hung, exhumed from somewhere in the basement, its face nicked here and there with brownish blotches, its frame dusty and tarnished.

I don't know. A few weeks?

You look pale, Cincy. When was the last time you went to the beach?

"   "

Working, thinking.   I'll be

Too much, by the looks of it.

What have you been doing this summer?

fine.

Renee, why don't we take one more walk through?

"   "

I watched my parents climb the stairs, my dad reaching over to hold my mother's hand, my
mom looking at him and smiling.

They walked side-by-side in the soft
pink evening, passing under the Belmar
arch, my dad holding my sister, my
mom holding me.

They sat in wing chairs on opposite sides of the
coffee table, heads down in their books, while my
brother and sister pawed through the pile of
magazines that lay between them, leaving
sticky handprints on the covers.

Dad and Mom disappeared around a
bend in the trail, his hands in his pockets,
hers turning over a leaf. I tagged along
in exaggerated strides, following my dad's
footsteps in the baking-powder-fine sand.

"   "

Grab your surfboard and we'll throw it on the roof of the car. Unless you just want to junk it.
"   "

No, I'll keep it.

I cut back on the wave, feeling
the board rumble beneath my feet,
my heart race. This was summer.
"   "

"   "

I held the board against the roof, skegs up, while my father lashed it down. Board secure, trunk full, we got back in the car.

"   "

Why don't we get dinner before we drop you off?
"   "

I sat in the passenger seat paging through the photo album, shot after shot of my siblings and me, relatives, kids from the neighborhood, baseball games, pool parties, beach days. I moved from the back forward, the way my parents always read their newspapers.

Why'd you guys decide to sell the house?

My brother and I lounged on the porch in
nylon replica jerseys, basketballs at our feet.
"   "

The market's gotten too good to turn it down. Do you

"   "

Remember, I didn't think we'd be in that house

know how long we waited for prices to go up?

I thought you loved the house.

Bridget's graduation. We were
decked out: Bridget with a
boulder-size college ring, me in
a blazer, tie, and shoulder sling.

for more than five years.   We did, but this city wasn't where we

"   "

"   "

wanted to raise you kids. And staying in the same place forever is tough.

Things just seem to

"   "

An early birthday, hands outstretched
for a piece of cake, adults with glasses
the size of dinner plates.

"   "

pile up here.

I focused back on the album.

First Communion, church carpet thick and smooth as moss.

We grew and played by the lot's edge, under the church's rosetta eye.

The custodian had a desk in the boiler room.
Double-fisted Italian mascot, that Irishman. Fight. The floors were mauve.
They sold fabric and Nintendo games. We saw many marriages, sometimes twenty dollars would come in an
envelope. Sometimes nothing.
The cheap bastards.

The car jerked forward. I started awake, then dozed off again just as quickly, waking, sleeping, waking, sleeping until my father eased the rental car into a parking spot at Red's Lobster
Pot. The lot was nearly full, cars packed door-to-door up to the wharf's edge. The masts of
trawlers bobbed in the water beyond, tissuey clouds of purple diesel exhaust floated through
the spotlights that dotted the wharfside. Deckhands scrambled to offload the trawler holds,
winches dipping belowdecks and resurfacing with nets loaded down with black-streaked
bluefish. After my naps, everything seemed a bit clearer, cleaner.

The waitress ushered us through the restaurant, all red walls and tilted dark wood floors,
out the rear door and onto the back porch, pulling out seats at a table overlooking the *River
Queen*'s slip. My parents sat with their backs to the water; behind them, the riverboat idled,
slowly taking on passengers, its twin decks and indoor bars rousing to life. The only things
missing from the Mississippi riverboat feel were a few blackjack tables and some one-arm
bandits.

So what's next for you guys?

Has Tom lined

Don't worry about us, Cincy. What's next for you?

What do you mean?

up a roommate for the fall yet?

You're going back to school in the fall,

I don't think so.

Next spring?

right?

I swallowed a lump of crab cake and coughed.

I don't think I'm ever going back.

"   "

"   "

My mother looked down at her lap. My dad stopped chewing.

"					"

"					"

"					"

The stuff I was doing doesn't mean anything to me anymore. I have to do some-

"					"

Over writer's block?

thing else.					Too much. I should've jumped ship a year ago.

Have you thought this out enough?

"					"

I'll keep working with J.D. until that runs out, and then we'll see.

Isn't

What are you going to do?

It might be, but so was the program. I can at least feed myself with this gig until I

that a dead end?

"					"

figure out my next move.

They're

But you like working down here? With that crew at the yard?

We get along really well.

an, um, interesting set of characters.

It's very different from the pro-

Yeah, I'm aware of that.

"I think he's a narc."

The van idled.

Is everything really fine with you?

gram.

Uh-huh.

She sat across from him, her legs resting
up against him. She turned her back on
me and walked out of Byrnes's.

"   "

"   "

It felt strange to keep these things from them; even stranger because I wasn't sure if these were things to keep. My head had begun to swim again; maybe it was the food mixing with the fatigue; maybe it was the deck shifting ever so slightly beneath us as the water ebbed and flowed in the wharf, audibly slapping against the pilings underfoot.

It's taken some time to get used to living down here again. Things aren't quite how I remembered them. Steady.

"   "

"   "

"   "

Things that I thought were gone forever are back.

A lot's changed down here since we moved.

"   "

"   "

And things that I thought would be here forever are gone.

Behind us, the *River Queen*'s paddle wheel spun to life, red, white, red, white. With a few lurches and blasts of its air horn, it pulled away from the dock and headed out to the bay. We dug into the softshell crabs that the waiter slid across the checked tablecloth, our conversation broken up by long spells of silence as we ate.

"   "

You remember Spencer Wilkins, your first Little League coach? The police officer?

"   "

Yeah.

I forgot about him. Maybe he can help me.

> *I was half my father's*
> *size, lying by his side*
> *as the afternoon sunlight*
> *poured through the*
> *open blinds.*
>
> > *We propped the comforter*
> > *up, crawling inside,*
> > *flashlights glowing at*
> > *my parents' bedside.*
> >
> > > *My mom held my brother,*
> > > *newly born, face smooth,*
> > > *hands relaxed.*

He was promoted to chief around the time you left for college. He's gone now, though.

"   "

"   "

The new mayor sent the whole department packing right after the last election. Replaced

"   "

You're telling me.

them all with a bunch of thugs.   You seeing anyone

It's a shame. Such a good group of guys.

No.

Too much. *She laughed.*

Not enough.

Her hand on

my shoulder.

right now?

That's probably better. You should take some time for

"   "

"   "

yourself.

Eventually, the check materialized. We paid the bill, slid out of Reds, and headed down-shore toward Springwood. The wharfside, the motel district, the Boulevard slipped past, our progress marked by the rhythmic skipping of the rental car's tires over the seams in 35's con-crete deck.

I continued paging through the photo album, catching glimpses of my trip home from the hospital and my first days here in the light of the streetlamps that ranged overhead. We slowed to a stop in front of my apartment.

No, I think I'm good. Do you guys want to

Do you need any help getting those boxes upstairs?

"   "

come up?   Yeah.

We're flying out on Saturday

Would we be appalled?   We'll pass, this time.

"   "

around five. Want to get an early lunch at the Atlantic Bay? I haven't had a good chicken
"   "

                        What time?   Sounds good.
parm sandwich in years.   Around eleven thirty?

                                                    We'll call you if any-

"   "
"   "

thing comes up.

    The rental car pulled off the curb. Instead of merging onto the road, though, it stalled for a second. Its taillights lit up and it reversed. My father rolled down the window.

                Yeah.
Hey, Cincy?   We understand.   Be safe, all right?

    The window slipped back into place before I could say anything more. Two blinkers and my parents were gone. I looked up and down the street. A few doors down, a set of new vinyl-clad Victorian facades leaned against a bank of half-finished townhomes, waiting to be craned into place. My surfboard rested against the telephone pole outside the apartment door. My childhood sat in two boxes at my feet.

byrd lives!

(DIGGIN' IN THE CRATES/

ICE CREAM REMIX)

The first place I would go on payday—after the bank—was the used record store on East Main. An hour in a sweltering, un-air-conditioned storefront might not seem like the most refreshing break after a day in the yard, but it was soothing to me—for an hour, it was just me and a room-ful of dusty cast-off vinyl, sifting around in the fragments of the city's listening history.

My fingers passed over a worn Charlie Parker LP jammed into the back of an overstuffed bin in the jazz section. The edges of its dust jacket were frayed and veined with white; a live session from some club I'd never heard of, sometime late in his career, Parker pictured in mid-note on the front, his cheeks puffed out, silent, skin and sax dappled with green and purple. I pulled out the record and angled it against the fluorescent lights, better to see cracks and scratches.

He could blow.

You a Charlie Parker fan?   **He blew himself right out of this world. Spin**

What do you mean?

that with caution. **His music was better for his listeners than it was**

A lot of people got hooked on it. Still

for him. They could take the needle out. He couldn't.

are.

I still think it's the realest shit I ever heard. But, at some point, it's like you get so

I think I'll take my chances.

deep into it, it becomes sort of a lie.

I slid the record back into its dust jacket, tucked it under my arm, and kept browsing, head down. My eyes blurred as I flicked through the albums.

Hey, stranger.

I turned.

Oh, hey.

Vera?   I thought I was the

It's been a while. Where've you been?   Chill, chill.

You're the last person I would have expected to see here.

Great to see you.

WHERE HAVE YOU BEEN?

Hey.   I thought I was the

I thought the same.   The pickings've been

only one who shopped here.

only one who shopped here.   Found anything good?

kind of slim lately. Maybe you've been taking all the good stuff.

"Hey, stranger." Like it's my fault?

Maybe

Maybe you just have to dig a little

Want to help me out? I'll give you a finder's fee.

I missed something.

deeper to find it. Sure.

     She strolled up the aisle and started flipping through the bins. Occasionally, she'd pull an album out and check its song listings, or skim its liner notes. She'd hold an album for a few minutes while she continued to browse, then look at it again, frown, and return it to the bin where she found it. After twenty minutes, she had a short stack of records. She carried them in her crossed arms.

"   "

That was easy.

That was too easy.

That was   easy.

"   "

That'll be twelve dollars.

     She reached for her purse.

I got it.

    Thanks.

"   "

We stepped out onto East Main. The late-afternoon silence was disturbed only by the pounding of hammers on nails somewhere in a gutted storefront in the distance. The old elms that lined the street were mottled with green and brown splotches, covered root to tip with peel-ing bark and creeping moss.

What do you listen to your records on?

Say something.

I have a little

She held the bag of records close to her chest.

My apartment came with this old record cabinet.

turntable at home. It used to be my parents'. You?

The sound is amazing.

She doesn't seem nervous at all.

Cool.

We walked a few paces down East Main.

You should   you should come over and   and listen to   We should listen to some

We slipped away for a while, I ran my hands along the sides of her face, tilted her chin up to me, kissed her. Her cheeks flushed, her eyes

"You should come over. We can listen to the

stuff you just picked out and" The record cabinet

leaked out something slow and sinuous as I pulled

her closer to me.

Her chair was tilted forward, her legs crossed and resting up against his.

"I'm sorry, I'm seeing someone and" *The doors closed behind*

her. "I can't, I've got something else I've got to go to."

"   "

music, at my place.   That's right. You haven't been to my place yet.

           Sure. Where do you live?

Four   four-oh-four Springwood. It's above a Laundromat. Very luxurious.

                                   I'll see you there then at

Nine

          Where's she been?

               Don't worry. She's back.

     at nine.   Bye.

       She turned up the block, walking away with a slight switch.

       The acrid traces of last night's massive fireworks displays wafted by on the east wind. A few children, standing up lock-legged on their bike pedals, zigzagged oceanward, hopping on and off the sidewalk with quick wheelies, pressing up closer to the buildings or swinging wide into the middle of the road to clear a tan Caprice parked curbside. There were two men sitting in the car, drinking Cokes and wiping their brows. A flock of dusky gulls wheeled soundlessly overhead. A line of newspaper kiosks leaned along the sidewalk:

**WILT THE STILT GOES FOR 100   YES, WE DID!   MAN WALKS ON MOON
ANIMAL HOUSE CRACKDOWNS CONTINUE**

"   "

The doorbell rang. The clock read
8:25. "I wanted to make sure I
wasn't late, so I left an hour early."

              Why didn't I stop her?

           "Vera, wait   Where"

                       Better that I didn't.

                       "What do you mean?"

Loose scraps of paper stirred in the vestibule of an abandoned barbershop. A figure slouched against the shop's door on a pile of dead leaves, his head cradled in his right hand, his left palm extended outward, his body reflected three times in the dusty display windows and the door's lower panel. It was Byrd; the same rumpled suit and tie, the same film of sweat across his face and hands.

"   "

Can I borrow a dollar?   Brother please, can I borrow a dollar?

His words echoed in the vestibule and his reflections moved in synch, as though four Byrds, real and reflected, were talking at once.

I'm sorry, but
                    Please, brother. I need it bad.

My fingers clenched and unclenched around the loose bills in my pocket. He looked up, his eyes glassy and twitching.

"   "

I shouldn't. Look at the track marks on his arm.
                              It's just a dollar.
"   "

I panned up and down the street, then pressed a single into his left palm.

"   "

God bless you, brother.

He clasped my hand. His eyes were still staring out at some point beyond me.

"   "

                              "He just talks in these endless circles. Kind of
Did you know Li'l Phil? Li'l Phil and me, we used to go to the Hi-Hat, the Reno with some

"   "

the same five or six topics. If you don't stop him, he can go on forever."

                                                          It's like I'm not even here.
mezzirolls. KC was hopping back then, we'd watch those cats cut, light up a mezziroll and watch

"   "

those cats cut because   you see   Since Since   He wanted it and

        I stared at my reflection in the upper panel of the door.

"   "

        Look at the track marks on his arms.   I gotta get out of here.
it could be, since   I mean, when you really look at it   because, you know   Maybe, because I

"   "

can read minds, you see, maybe

        I backed out of the vestibule and hurried along the street, faster now, trying to put distance
between myself and Byrd.
        A hand closed around the back of my neck. I took another step. It tightened.

        What?
Where is it?

The hand slammed me up against the wall of an apartment building. My palms grated on the brick.

"   "

What's that? A badge? A gun?

Where is it?

He shook me by the collar.

Where's what?   What drugs?

WHERE ARE THEY?   The drugs!   We know he's a junkie. Where are you

There are no drugs!

getting the drugs?

He lifted me off the wall by the neck and turned my face toward him. His hair was shorter, but he was unmistakable: the same surfer Tone had pointed out, the one who was staking out the yard a few weeks back. The police shield dangling from his neck glinted in the slanting sun.

"   "

Empty your pockets.

I turned my pockets inside out. The dollars landed on the sidewalk with a muffled pop.

"   "

The bag, too.

I dumped the records out. He bent down and sifted through them with one hand, the other hand on his hip. The outline of a gun bulged through his shirt and board shorts. Back in the direction I had come from, the two men from the sedan had Byrd pinned to the ground. The undercover rose from the pile of records and exchanged short "no" nods with his colleagues. A fourth figure stirred across the street from me. My shoulders unbunched and my fists unballed. The officer snatched his sunglasses off and cocked his head. His eyes were gray and bloodshot.

You won't.

Don't let me catch you.

The undercover hooked his glasses back on and stalked toward the sedan. He and the others climbed in and glided away. A tiny cyclone of dead leaves spiraled down the street in their wake.

"That same dude that was scoping out the yard."

I hit Tone on speed dial.

Yo, that guy that broke your taillight? He just shook me down, in broad day.   This is crazy. We

Really?

gotta do something.   I don't know   we could   we could file a complaint.

Like what?

"   "

No no no no. I'm not going anywhere near the cops. Especially not to complain about another cop.

What else are we gonna do? Just let him keep doing this?   If we

What else can we do? It's the *cops*.

can just find the right person at headquarters, I bet we can get to the bottom of this.

There's no bottom

There's gotta be someone that can give us an an‑

to get to. Cops are cops; they do what they want.

swer, right?   Then I'll go by myself.

An answer isn't gonna fix my taillight.   **Pssssssssssssssh**

Seriously.   Could you meet me

Look, if it'll make you feel better.   **All right, all right. You need a ride?**

at Atlantic Bay tomorrow, around two? We're doing the evening shift anyway.   Tone?

Why'd I doubt him? He wouldn't do this if he were caught up in it.

"   "

This'll work, I'm sure.

Sure. Peace.   **Keep the faith.**

The sound of rapping hammers grew louder as I closed up my phone. The only indication that the police had been there a few seconds ago were the abrasions that jagged across the heels of my palms.

Abrasions and the creeping sense that, in some office in another part of town, amid piles of photographs and testimonies and carbon paper slips, someone might be writing a story about me with a degree of authority that I couldn't even muster over the fragments of my own self.

■　■　■

8:25 came and went. 8:30 too. I lay on the couch in the living room, running my fingers across the abrasions on my palms, cross‑hatched and red, but clean now of gravel and dirt. As the adrenaline from the run‑in wore off, my nerves started humming, vibrating like a bass string pulled by the undercover when his fingers first tightened around my neck.

"Where are the drugs?" "Where are they?!" The red light blinked. Click, shutter, capture. *"What're we gonna do?"*

I was sweating again, despite the AC cranking in the window.

I wish they could tell us.   The complaints'll do it. We can get some answers that way.

I turned back to the TV.

Where is she? She wandered down Springwood
along the rows of Dumpsters and gutted
storefronts. I hope she's okay.

"I'll see you at nine."

She's not coming.

She took two steps out her door. Her
phone rang. "Oh   hey." She settled
onto the rail on her porch. "Nothing I
can't get out of. What's up?"

The doorbell rang.

Ten thirty.

I rose from the couch and shuffled to the call box.

I'll be down in a sec.

I'm sorry.

She was standing outside the front door in a circle of yellow light thrown down by the street-lamp. Her hair was different from just a few hours ago, wavier, fuller.

Hey, Vera.   No,   no problem.

  Where have you been? Are you all right?

  Where have you *been*? Are you serious?

  You're here.

  You're here?

  ARRRRRRRRGGGGGGGGGGGGHHHHHHHH!

  I'm sorry I'm late. Something came up.

The stairs groaned underfoot as we climbed up to the second floor. The squealing of the apartment door on its hinges drowned out our last few steps.

"   "

Something came up. "Hold on   yes?" *She looked in my direction. Then looked away, and walked out of the bar.*
So noisy.

"   "

We walked into the apartment.

So this

  "   "

I swept my hand across the living room with an exaggerated flourish.

,

is my place.

Where's she *been* the last few weeks?

                              Forget it. She's here now.

"   "

One of Tom's socks lay across the back of an armchair. I whipped it away in hopes that she wouldn't see it.

You want something to drink?

"   "

I leaned down to look into the fridge.

I've got a couple Stellas, some red wine.

I'm thinking this is a wine night.

I pulled the bottle out for a better look.

Oh, I can tell this is the good stuff. It's got a screw-top.   Looks fine.

That's the best kind!   Let's try it.

"   "

Ooh, what happened to your hands?

She took the bottle from me and rested it on the counter. I winced as she traced her fingers across my palms.

I tripped on a root or something on my way home to

"Where are the drugs!" He slammed me up against the wall. Watching

from across the street. "That same dude scoping out the lot!" "Cince!"

The chain-link bent in, a swatch of white T-shirt caught on a ragged edge.

Where'd you get that?

day. I fell hard on my hands.   I'll be fine.

Does she know I lied to her? Did she see all that

go down? She turned when she reached the

corner, watched me lean toward Byrd,

watched me fall to the ground.

Looks bad.

I turned back to the counter and filled a glass for her.

It's in my room.

Show me this record player you were telling me about?

I led her into the bedroom. The black starry shadows of sycamore leaves flowed across her face as she leaned over the cabinet, running her hands along the sides.

"   "

Now, this is cool.

She flicked the turntable on and watched the needle swing down onto the rotating vinyl.

If only somebodyyyyyyy-ayy, ooooooooohhhhhhhh, if only somebodyyyy-ayyyyy

"   "

You're right! The sound is amazing. So warm.

I threw the Charlie Parker album on low and sat down on the bed next to her. Her feet brushed up against one of the photo albums my parents had left with me.

"   "

What's this?

She pulled the album onto her lap and opened it up in the middle. She rearranged my story with a few flicks of her wrist, flipping from my birth to high school graduation to preschool to college move-in day at whim.

Yeah, when I was four.   My brother and sister.
The photographer pulled the points of my shirt
collar out and over my sweater. "Smile."

Is that you?   Who are these other kids?   Where are

Bridget my sister she's a risk analyst. She works in Manhattan.

they now, what do they do?   And

Eddie's an engineer. He works in disaster planning, like building sea walls and reten-

your brother?

tion basins for floodwater for the military. He's stationed in Virginia, at Norfolk.

How much can you

You'd be surprised. Eddie claims you can model anything.

really plan for disasters?

Modeling? Like

Yeah, it's very specialized engineering. Very physics-heavy.

mathematical models for floods?

It looks

I was at one point.

*It was my sixth hour in that chair, staring at a crack
running down the dorm wall that was big enough to
let in light from the room next door. I didn't know
where to begin. I wouldn't know where to stop. I
didn't even know what it was. I punched a few keys
on my graphing calculator. One thirty a.m. I opened
my third bottle of Coke and slouched farther down.*

like you're the only sibling who wasn't a numbers person.

And then?

At some point, I found other things to get into.

*The professor began translating the statements, p's and q's,
signs and primes swallowing up words, phrases, sentences. I
looked out the window, my eyes following a pair of students
as they crossed the yard, talking, books under arms, as they
climbed the steps of the library, eight stories high, windows
looking into the stacks, low-ceilinged, piled high. The professor
kept milling through the syntactical chaos, dispensing with
one thought after another. I closed the physics book I had
propped up on my knee under the desk. I could get into this.*

"

"

I lay back on the bed and put my other arm around her. Her right hand rested on the album; she held her wineglass with her free hand.

"   "

How did we end up here?

"   "

This was where I wanted her, where I had wanted to be, where I didn't think I'd ever be again after what happened at Byrnes's. But, her just reappearing? It was like there was a scratch on the record we'd been playing, some slack in the tape. She could sit here and run her fingers across me, and try to reel it all back in, but she wasn't playing right to me.

"   "

Wh wh wh Crap. I pulled the disc out of the changer—
a hairline crack arched around the edge. I rubbed turtle
wax across the surface, buffing, buffing, trying to smooth
it out.
Do I want what I'm getting?   Yeah.   Do I know what I'm getting?
          Her body pressed
          close to mine.
                    She looked up in my direction.
                    Looked down. And walked away.

"   "

I shifted my weight on the bed.

"   "

Where's she been?   "What do you mean, 'Where?'" I don't want her to think I'm crazy.
          Why don't I just ask?

"   "

Can't let her think I'm too deep into this.

> She smiled, her eyes lighting up, glistening, warming the
> afternoon, the room, me. So close to me, my heart leaped
> toward her. "..." Her smile dropped, the light in her
> eyes doused. I ruined it, killed it. She left the scene as
> quickly as she had come, while I searched the ground for
> the spent shells and a gun to match. I don't want to say the
> wrong thing.

"   "

Sure.

"Why don't you pick out some things you think I should hear?"

Why don't you play something else?

The night drifted by like that, she and I trading off on the record player, the seconds, minutes, hours melting away. We didn't speak, just let the records spin. She played what she wanted, why I can't say. I played what I couldn't say, grasping for something to cut through the noise, waiting for her to tell me where to take this.

If you only knew how many times / That I think of you / Quite surely you'll find I'm going out of my mind

I won't believe not a word you speak / Just make it sweet for me to hear

Let the music take your mind / Just release and you will find

I've said too much in trying to speak up

The hour hand crawled across the one.

"   "

I think I should go. It's getting pretty late.

She squeezed my hand and smiled.

Did you drive here?   Should I call a cab?   Really?
            I took a bus.   It's okay, I'd rather take the bus.   Have

                        Then I'll walk you to the stop.
            Don't go.
            Go.
you seen the cabbies here?

It was still warm outside, even this late, the air heavy and humid.

                    Sure will. How long does it take you to get back to your place?
It's going to be hot tomorrow.   Twenty

"   "

minutes or so.

The bus shelter's translucent white dome shone ahead. No bus in sight. She sat down on
the perforated metal bench. I sat down next to her, our bodies not even touching.

"   "

I can't just let her drift off like this.
"   "

I slid over slowly. She was still looking ahead, out to the street.

Relax, last time it all worked out. Don't push it. The bus pulled to a stop in front of the shelter. She reached for my bandaged hand again. "Be safe." Our faces drew close. This time I could feel the kiss, its edge and its depth, all its warmth. She smiled and stepped off.

//   //

The bus cleared the corner and rumbled up the block toward us.

"   "

[   ]

The bus pulled to a stop in front of the shelter. I stood and held my hand out to her. She pulled me down and kissed me, warm as the night. The driver shut the doors and continued on. She was still there. We were still together.

//   //

The bus pulled to a stop in front of the shelter.

"   "

[   ]

Vera grabbed me and kissed me, long and slow, her body pressed up against mine.

//   //

I held my hand out to her. Still looking forward, she stood up. My hand hung there, waiting for hers. She didn't take it.

She stepped onto the bus.

"   "

No no no.

Go go go.

See you soon, Cincy.

The doors closed behind her. She walked along the aisle and took a seat midway down the empty bus. I waved halfheartedly, watching my arm trace a weak quarter circle in the window. She didn't smile back. The engine throbbed, and she was gone.

My hand hung there. "See you soon, Cincy."

I stared out into the darkness.

Maybe she's looking to move on,
and doesn't want to start something
with someone here.
      Maybe she spent the bus ride home texting the other
      guy. Maybe she doesn't want to start anything with me
      here. Maybe I'm her second option.
            She leaned against a column in front of Byrnes's,
            like she did every weekend. Maybe she
            doesn't want to start anything with anyone.
            Maybe she just wanted a few hook-ups.

I ran my hands through my hair. Whatever I'd had with her was gone, a smile, a frown, a turn-away enough to remix it into something else, less happy, less certain, less mine.

When I finally got back to the apartment, it was nearly two. Tom had come home and was already out for the night, lying facedown on the couch with a milk carton empty and crumpled on the floor near his head.

In my bedroom, the LPs lay scattered across the desk. Near where Vera had placed her bag, a book sat.

Her journal.

I picked it up and turned it over in my hands.

"So it all goes in there?" "Most of it." Should I read it?

The cover was cracked, the pages bloated and rippled, as if she'd dropped it in a puddle. Inside was even worse, months' worth of pages stuck together and streaked with smudgy blue ink. A life in watercolors, illegible.

What happened to this thing?

> She stood on the curbside, waiting for her cab. A city bus rumbled down the strip, its tires sinking into a puddle, sending a wave of dirty rainwater rising toward her. She stepped back, startled, in time to avoid the water. Too fast, though, to save her journal. It flew out of her hands, hanging in the air for a second before it nose-dived into the puddle.

I flipped to the last sheet with writing, halfway through.

"July 8—when it comes to him, I" Nothing else but smudges.

> I could only be so lucky.

I tossed the journal on my bed and picked up my phone.
It rang through to her voice mail.

Hey,   hey Vera, it's Cincy. I think you left your journal here. I can bring it to you. Just let

Figures.

me know.

I lay back on the bed, listening to the turntable spinning away, still gliding despite the record being beyond over. I lay in bed, awake for hours, the same thoughts scrolling out and over to the pops and crackles of vinyl static, until—sometime around daybreak, when birdcalls began to drown out the static—I finally slipped queasily beneath the surface of a restless, fevered sleep, the kind of sleep that solved nothing, just gave me a little more energy the next day to keep questioning, keep thinking, keep burrowing deeper into the depths.

georgia

I woke up with a start a few hours later. The moment my eyes opened, my mind was off pause.

Maybe

I swung around in bed and let my legs rest on the floor. The warmth I had felt every morning earlier in the summer when I first woke, the feeling of Vera here, close to me, was long gone, just some sort of ghost floating in its place; even the anxious, spiky thoughts that had grown up in the presence of her silence, gone.

Maybe   she could

Maybe   I could

The flame petered to a blue nub, dancing on the tip of the wick. The smoke began to slip between my fingers.

I stumbled into the living room.

I gotta forget this. Let her go.

The moon hung over Manhattan.

Tuck it away. Save it. That's back there.

What do I have to do today?

"Want to get an early lunch at the Atlantic Bay?" "Eleven thirty?"

It was eleven o'clock. I hopped in and out of the shower and clattered down the stairs, hop-ing I wouldn't leave my parents waiting too long.

The air was heavy with the scent of rain as I stepped onto Springwood. I craned my neck upward and spun around once, staring up at the storm clouds cresting over the rooftops to the west. Growing up at the Shore, surrounded by water on all sides, you learned early the pat-terns that defined the days, months, and years. The steady rhythmic beat of the ocean against the sand, once a minute. The sun's blazing sinking into the bay, once a night. Even the bad weather was something you could count on: every summer, usually late in July or early in Au-gust, a traffic-stopping storm would tear across the island. Thunderheads gathered over the Pine Barrens out beyond the bay and crept slowly eastward, the wind whipped westerly until the flags went slack, the air tightened, the sky paled a queasy green, and then the wind switched suddenly easterly, the pines disappeared behind an advancing wall of water, the whole sky pitched into black and rained down. Even those days were mild in comparison with the nor'easters that descended every five years or so, cold, raging storms that sent leaden waves storm-surging over the sea walls as they dragged the Atlantic and the Barnegat together to min-gle in basements and backyards like two distant quarreling cousins at a family get-together, leaving layers of sand across the roads and sidewalks as a lingering reminder of their brief re-union.

You could mark the slow passage of your life in major storms, or you could mark it in burning-downs of the Atlantic Bay, which managed to find itself reduced to a pile of ashes and charred crossbeams with an uncanny, nor'easter-like regularity. By my own guesswork, I was three burnings-down old; the last one happened right around the time I left for college. No sign of an intervening fire as I rounded the corner onto St. Clair: the diner's facade was just as I remembered it, glittering over the tops of the pharmacies and auto parts stores, capturing and reflecting some light that was ambient in the air even on this sunless day. I cut beneath the canopy of the Sunoco station and rounded a row of parked cars into the diner's parking lot. As I climbed the long shallow ramp that led up to the front entrance, my reflection followed me in a blurry puddle on the diner's silvery outside walls until I came face-to-face with a faded green-tinted image of myself in the glass door at the top. I grabbed the giant filigreed chrome door handle and gave it a tug; the door budged off the frame then fell back heavily in place. A second tug, with two hands now, and the door swung outward with a puff of cold air.

"We'll meet you in the lobby."

Empty. I parted the doors into the dining area and looked up and down the booths, scanned the stools lining the counter. My parents hadn't beaten me there.

I took a seat in the lobby on a bench sandwiched between an old Ms. Pac-Man machine and a sad dusty fern. The floors were covered in fake marble; the walls in photographs of the diner in its past iterations, lined up like a rogues' gallery in sepia tones and black frames: a tiny shingled bungalow in a sandy unpaved lot, a dining car surrounded by fishtailed Cadillacs, the two-winged behemoth I was sitting in. It hadn't just gotten bigger with time; it had gotten shinier—chrome spreading across the facade, wrapping the whole exterior, plating the booths, counters, and doors. More reflective: the walls of the lobby were covered with some sort of reflective siding, like a boardwalk turned vertical, slatted mirrors pressed flush together, their surface run through with tiny parallel seams. As cars rounded the bend out beyond the diner's massive front window, their reflections leaped across the walls, elongated, distorted, skipping from slat to slat against a background of blurry green, brown, and black streaks.

The clock hanging over the door nudged past 11:30. I watched Ms. Pac-Man dart around her maze in a haze of blue light, until the room began to ripple and undulate with sleepless-ness and hunger. I stared down at the floor until the nausea passed, until I started to drift off.

My head jerked up as my phone rang.

Hey, Dad.   Ehhh. I'm good. Where are you?

You sound like you had a rough night.   We're on our

Wait, I didn't think your flight was leaving 'til like five?

way to Newark.   It turns out it's touching

                                        So
down at five. I must have read the tickets wrong.   We just had to get up and go. We would've

                                                No   no problem.
called earlier, but we were already so late. We're sorry.   It was good to see

                You too, Dad.   It's no problem.
you, Cince.   We wish we could have spent more time with you.

I understand.   Yeah.   Um, yeah.
                                                                        "When was

                Hey, Cince?   Have you really not been for a swim this summer?

I'm not even sure I remember how to swim anymore.
the last time you went swimming?"

                                        There isn't anything to remember. You just

                Just kidding, Dad.
dive in.   I know, I know. Be safe.

        I looked around the lobby. The smell of waffles and pancakes wafted by.

Well, I might as well eat.

As I lowered into a seat at the counter, the waitress slid a sweating yellow glass of water in front of me and pointed to the menus jammed into brackets along the counter's edge. The interior walls of the diner were clouded with the ghostly smoky reflections of people crammed into the booths or walking along the aisles, dozens of silent meals hovering behind real-life tables loaded down with bacon and eggs, pancakes and omelets, burgers and gyros. A set of fake crystal chandeliers hung above it all, reflecting the diners below in hundreds of tiny faceted snatches with sharp rainbowed edges.

Oh, double stack of pancakes and an orange juice.

Huh-loooo! What'll ya have?   Gotcha.

The Phillies game beamed out of the TV in the corner.

"   "

Maybe she

The plate of pancakes slid in front of me. I poured syrup across the top and watched it drip down the sides of the stack as I grabbed my fork and knife.

"   "

Or maybe she

I ate unconsciously, shoving the pancakes down while my mind spun off elsewhere. After a few minutes of eating, though, my momentum slowed.

"   "

Man, I do not feel well.

A half a plate of pancakes stared back at me. I pushed the plate away from me and leaned back on the stool. Twelve thirty.

Yeah.   Yeah.   I'm fine, I'm fine.

You finished with that?   You sure?   You look ill, honey.

A check with a black bar code at the bottom replaced my plate of half-finished pancakes. I reached into my back pocket for my wallet and placed a ten on the counter.

"   "

You haven't been here in a while, have you? You pay up at the register now.

My reflection stretched and shrank across the walls as I made my way to the front door. I slid the check and the money across the countertop, stopping only long enough to grab a toothpick from the dispenser that rested between the racks of chewing gum and peppermint patties. Back out onto Sinclair: over the course of lunch, the whole ceiling of the sky had lowered until the storm clouds seemed to be brushing along the rooftops.

"   "

It's probably better that they weren't able to make it.

Tone's Caprice wheeled into the parking lot. Its trunk imploded and exploded with the bass drops on his stereo. "Where are you going again?" "To file police misconduct grievances." "Right . . ."

"   "

A yo, Cince! What it is?

Tone's Caprice was creeping along close to the curb.

You eat lunch?   You want to get something at the diner before we go?

Not yet.   **Nah, man. I don't eat**

Why not? The food's good, they've got all those mirrors

there.   **So you can feel everyone giving you**

"   "

the screwface five times over? I'm straight.

We headed northward up the Boulevard, bound for police headquarters through the heart of the motel district. The tourists were playing it safe today, staked out at motel pools and hotel decks rather than risk a rain-out at the beach. Children in bathing suits and bare feet skidded around corners and up and down staircases, screaming in parallel lines two, three, four stories off the ground along exposed hallways dotted with doors that opened onto darkened rooms where manic Saturday-morning cartoons bounced bluely off the walls.

Police headquarters took up two whole city blocks, one for a parking lot, marked off from the sidewalk by Jersey barricades and lined with furrows of sun-browned grass that had forced its way through the blacktop, the other for the station itself.

"   "

The fuck?

Each era needed a monument, and I guess police headquarters was it, for every era. The building was a messy amalgam of tacked-on Italianate turrets and carpenter Gothic towers, neo-Egyptian archways and Art Deco doorways. A black-glassed cube rose out of the center of the building, like a meteorite that had recently fallen out of the sky. On either side of headquarters, minimalist annexes of some sort were in progress, huge panes of glass in weatherproofed sheathes stacked alongside the thin steel skeletons that curved over bare concrete floors.

We took a full lap around the headquarters, looking for an entrance. We eventually found a single-leaved steel door marked VISITORS on the building's northern face. We pulled curbside and climbed out. Two strong tugs and the door opened onto a tiny lobby, no more than five paces long, bare of objects beyond its polished gray linoleum floors, a few rusty folding chairs, a heavy door, and a window of inch-thick bulletproof Lucite covered by a shade. A bell sat on a stainless steel shelf beneath the window. I gave it a tentative tap. Nothing. I smacked it with the heel of my hand.

The shade snapped up to reveal a harried-looking desk sergeant, his face all jowls and eye bags, bent and sworled like a fingerprint.

My friend and I would like to file complaints.

"   "

Yeah?

He sighed, a whoosh of air sending static out of the speaker mounted into the glass.

"   "

"   "

Wait there.

The walls were papered with WANTED posters, several layers thick in places, the whole mass of them hanging in a glyphic tableau of bold letters and agency seals, police sketches, serial numbers, print blocks, biostats, and mug shots. Tone exhaled, then leaned against the wall, one foot planted on the ground, the other pressed against the posters, head cocked to the side, right fist balled up to check out his fingernails. The clock on the wall ticked off five minutes.

A buzzer sounded on the far side of the door. The lock clicked and the door opened, unleashing a torrent of sound into the lobby, a flood of clattering keyboards and howling walkietalkies, modem chirps and fax screeches, ringing phones and beeping phones, yells and shouts, laughs and barks. The desk sergeant leaned into the lobby. Tone backed away from the wall.

%(*(&Michaels! Where's Michaels?T*(HJHVGP*(*^*&$##hey hey!&(*^%&^$#*(&))!

"   "

What's going on back there?

An officer sat before a bank of CCTVs, images from eyes everywhere flickering across the screens, every alley, every car, every entrance, every home. Every second, every minute, every hour, every day.

"   "

Fill these out.

The desk sergeant passed us two clipboards and two pens, then stepped back inside, letting the door thunk behind him.

Silence again. There wasn't anything else to do but sit down in the folding chairs and begin working through the forms.

"This is wild. You see the "Officer Description" section? All white people look the same to me."

"License plate number? Do I remember that? The Chevy pulled up the block and hung a right. Nope."

"

The room was silent save for the fluorescent lights overhead oscillating out an even, cycling measure for our writing.

"

Badge number? Something glinted in the sun. A gun? A badge? No idea.

Pushpins marking out the clusters and outliers, patterning it all.

"

Tone finished before me. He stood up and dropped the clipboard on the chair where he'd been sitting. He clasped his hands behind his head and started scanning the wall of WANTED posters again, more carefully this time, seeming to take in each and every face.

Yeah.

Codes postered and framed on the wall, a perfect structure, detailed down to the minut-

Bobby Seale? **H. Rap Brown?** **Didn't they catch these dudes years ago?**

Seale's trial was like forty years ago.

est offense.

" "

Tone began prying at the posters, snapping off staples and thumbtacks to get to the under-lying layers. While Tone dug, I kept writing. Two sheets front and back seemed to do the job.

I turned my account over in my hands, skimming it to make sure I hadn't missed anything important, half-hoping I could remember some key detail that would tie the incident back to someone specific.

"   "

"Please, brother, can you spare a dollar?" "Where are they?" "The drugs!" Nothing.

I stood up with my clipboard.

I guess we turn it in to that guy.

So what do we do now?   **You mean, we're giving this to some crooked**

I don't know what else to do. We've got it all down on

cop's boy and asking him to look into it for us?

paper. That's gotta count for something, right?

"   "

"   "

The computer whirred as it parsed every signal speeding through the air, every bit and byte darting across the fiber optics.

"'s three number twos, one six, five turkeys with no tomatoes, and five liters of Pepsi for 1115 Broad?" "Yeah. How much will

"Don't you hang up on me!" "I didn't hang up! My celly dropped the call. Shit!" "Every time we get into an argument, your celly

Detroit (MI)—Federal regulators today announced the official discontinuation of their active supervision of the American auto

*   *   *   *   * Thank you for calling PSE&G. All lines are presently busy. A PSE&G representative will take your call shortly

"to this conference call music? It sounds like some kinda porno soundtrack.Like, right here, this is where the guy shows up at

I am a distinguished professor of economics at the University of Abuja. In order to claim the money that is rightfully mine, all

Byrnes's." "At Byrnes's, really?" "You got a problem with Byrnes's?" "Nah, it's just that   I mean   well, you know." "Don't

"lo?   Hello?   Anyone there?   Must be a wrong number."

"what to tell you. Like, what do you want me to say?" "That's your problem!" "What problem? Just tell me what you want." "I

"So, would you say you strongly support President Obama?" "I'm voting for Biden." "So, you're voting for President Obama."

Whatever.

Tone lumbered over to the bell and gave it a pound. The shade didn't rise. The desk sergeant's voice crackled through the speaker.

"   "

Yeah.   **Just out here in the lobby?**   **No thanks.**

You done?   Okay, you can leave them there.   Yeah.

"   "

I want to hand it to someone.

                          Fine.

The desk sergeant cracked the door and stuck his hand out.

Here goes.

His hand drew back, taking the clipboards with it. The door shut again.

(*&%%^*(**)_(*&%^$#@()_*($#!RT&)()(%$%#^&*()_)_(*^%*&^#%$^%*&())(*&^%^$%^#@$!@#$%*&^&^%%$@^^^(**)(**&^%#$@#$!%^%*()(*(&^%$&^%$@HAHAHAHAHAHAHA
                                                                                          That's it?
Instant coffee and microwaves, anything to keep from catching a cold case.
"   "
Someone from the force will be in touch with you to follow up on the investigation.

"   "

                    An explanation, an apology, *something*.
What else do you want?

The sound of shuffling papers crackled over the speaker.

"   "

                                                        I mean
We can't apologize for something until we verify that it happened.   We'll look into this

How long will that

" "

and when we've completed our investigation, we'll be in contact with you.

take?

" "

Could take two weeks, or two months. Sometimes the investigations never close. It's

So

" "

hard to tell beforehand.   When we've completed our investigation, we'll be in contact with

" "

" "

you. Have a nice day.

Tone drifted back to the wall. I rang the bell again.
Nothing.

Let's go, man.

Nah, hold up.

I followed Tone's gaze to a patch on the far end of the wall. The crown of a shaved head peeked out from behind a layer of fades and caesars.

" "

Gotcha.

Tone peeled the overlapping posters away to reveal a leering white suspect—the only one on the wall.

" **"**

You're going to the top of the list.

He tacked the poster onto the blank stretch of wall next to the window.

" **"**

Let's go.

For all of the desk sergeant's evasiveness, all of Tone's frustration, I walked out lighter, sat easier in the Caprice as we headed northward toward the yard. The burden of my story was off me; it was all down on paper, memorialized, something investigators could get to work on.

I've been meaning to ask, What's up with

"Sometimes the investigations never close." They'll find something.

the tattoos?

These?

Tone lifted his right arm off the steering wheel and extended it out to me for a closer look. The script was sharp, dark; someone had inked those tattoos in with a long needle.

All over?

They've

My favorite verses. **You cut me? I'd probably bleed these. They're a part of me.**

" **"**

gotta find something.

" **"**

We crept through the amusement area, the Tower of Terror, the Palace Casino, the five-story Water Works slides looming in the windshield then shrinking in the rearview. North of the amusements, where the Boulevard swung westward to the Bay Bridge, crowds of people gathered on the sidewalks, parents and kids holding balloons or makeshift construction paper and poster board signs, scrawled with the outlines of elephants or LUCY in big block letters, everyone clustered behind vinyl banners that lined the roadway: THE SHORE WELCOMES LUCY, JERSEY'S FIRST ELEPHANT. Clowns danced through the crowd, blowing horns and twisting up balloon animals. Around the bend in the Boulevard, a pair of eyes, big as manholes, peered over the rooflines and treetops, drawing closer to us like some sort of movie monster, until a convoy of pickups emerged in the southbound lanes, straddling the lane lines, yellow caution lights flashing; in their wake, an elephant-shaped building glided, three stories high, gray-skinned and smiling, a big rig with a flatbed under each foot. The crowd cheered; kids reached their hands out, mouths open, eyes glowing.

"   "

You people up here are crazy.

The Caprice's tires skipped along 35 until we hit a red light just a few blocks south of the yard. Tone cranked up the volume on his stereo. The sides of the car rattled as the vocals leaked out through the sunroof and open windows.

As we idled, an old rusty Bronco on mud-spitter tires pulled up alongside us.

No more pullin' capers / Onto stackin' papers / Plenty mansions and skyscrapers

"   "

"   "

HEY HEY   HEY! HEY! YOU HEAR ME?

We looked over at the Bronco; its driver was sneering down at us, so high off the ground he was almost staring through the sunroof.

I want the kind of life I dreamed of / Mink coats, fly boats / Lex Coupe and Bim'd

"   "

Is he talking to me?

HEY, BOY!   **LOOK OVER HERE! WE DON'T NEED ANY OF YOUR COON MUSIC UP HERE!**

The driver sent a Styrofoam cup flying out of the Bronco and onto the windshield of Tone's car. A slick of coffee splashed across the glass, hiding the Bronco from view as it sped off. Tone stared forward. His hands were gripping the wheel so tightly his fingers were three shades lighter at the knuckles.

up / Lord

You okay, man?

"   "

He looked down at his hands and loosened his grip on the wheel. He clicked the stereo off.

"   "

I swear to God, Cince. I thought I left this bullshit behind when I left the South.

He flicked on the wipers. The blades popped the cup onto the pavement and carved out a wedge of sky on the windshield.

"   "

Fuck.   **Damn it, man, for real. No matter how far I go, I can't get away from this shit.**

HONK!

Tone eased off the brake and the car lurched forward. He was slumped in his seat now, one hand on the wheel, the other hand cupping his chin. We drove the rest of the way to the yard in silence.

When we finally got to work, the parking lot was empty. Tone eased the Caprice into a spot near the front door and shut the engine off.

Want me to get a hose or something for the windshield?

Don't worry about it, man. I'm just gonna chill

Yeah, sure, whatever you gotta do.

right here for a while, okay?

From my office, I watched as the coffee puddled in the wiper wells and dried on the wind⁄ shield. Tone stared off somewhere in the distance out over the bay, the side of his face lying against the window, his hands resting in his lap. By the time he finally climbed out of the car, it had begun to rain; the droplets sent the water sliding across the windshield, dragging coffee in ragged rivulets down the sides of the car. Tone disappeared into his workshop.

Tone came out a few minutes later with a bottle of
Armor-All and a handful of rags. He sprayed down
the sides of the Caprice and began buffing the finish.

He drew the garage door down behind him. It stayed that way until he left at midnight, sliding back behind the wheel of the Caprice without so much as a second look at the coffee⁄ splattered paint job.

surf's up

The next day was an off-day, sunny, cloudless, an easterly blowing at a good clip. I sat on the living room couch, surrounded by the detritus of yesterday's recording session, eating cereal and reading the morning news: international affairs, business, dispatches from Trenton, the surf report—water temperatures in the mid-seventies, waves at eight to ten feet.

Tom stumbled out from his bedroom. He squinted from the sun pouring through the living room window and scratched his stomach.

I don't know.

We're going surfing, right? **C'mon, man! You got your board back, we don't**

" "

have anywhere to go. Let's go!

Remember what happened the last time I went out?   So

oOooooO~~o~oo~OOOOoooO~OO~oo~OOO~Oo~o~OOOOXOOoooooooooooo~o~OO~OOooOoooooOoooOoO~~OOoo

OoOOoOooooO~~o~oo~OOOOoooO~OO~oo~OOO~Oo~o~OOOOXXXOOoooooooooooo~o~OO~OOooOoooooOoooOoO

~~OOooOo~OOO~OOooo~oo~OOooOO~oooOOOoo~OOooOO~OOOXXXXXooo~~OOOOOoooOOO~~~OOOO~~

~OOOOoooOOoooooOo~oOOoOO~OoO~oOOoOOOoOO~O~o~oo~OOOoo~oXXXXXXXOOOo~~oOOOooOO~OOOoO

OoOOooooo~OoooOOOoooo

      XX   X   X   XXX   XXX   XX   X   XXXXX

      XX   X   X   X

                                  X

                                                                    X

                              Who could forget it?   You've been letting

      "   "

      OOOoo~OOOOoooO~OO~oo~OOO~Oo~o~OOOOXXXOOoooooooooooo~o~OO~OOooOoooooOoo

that stop you all these years? I'll tell you what. We go down to the beach. If you're still not

                                                                                    All right.
                                                              "You just dive in."

feeling it when we get there, you can sit out. How does that sound?

      "   "

Trust me. You can't stay out forever, man.

                              ■   ■   ■

Maybe I could. Thinking of going out and doing it were two different things: I had my wet-
suit on, I had my board in hand, but I couldn't bring myself to take that first step into the ocean,
couldn't follow Tom out to the break. Instead, I lay out on a beach towel, stomach-down,
hands crossed beneath my chin; my board stood up nearby, shoved tail-first into the sand.

Tom's technique hadn't changed over the years; he was still an angular and sharp surfer, carving breakers up with direct lines and precise turns, beelining down the waves' faces, climbing, slowing, dropping, accelerating, cutting back and back again, jumping ahead of the waves and then hopping back in, his arms out in straight lines the whole time, his fingers ripping through the wave face.

He waved me in. I waved him off.

Deep winter, home for Christmas break, two years since leaving for school, two years deep into theory, multivariables, integrals. My friends had bundled up their army blankets and half-broken twelve-packs and headed home to wrap presents or bed down before the holiday really began. I stirred the charred remains of the bonfire with the toe of my shoe, logs and coals, singed newspaper. The scent of the sycamore and elm scrub we'd burned still hung in the air. Snow flurried and fell like ashes. Clouds crawled fractally overhead, the ocean gray, slated and chalk dusted, waves smudgy and schematic, flows and volumes, fluid dynamic. I rattled the coins in my pocket; the air had the taste of copper. A supertanker stalked along the horizon line.

oOooooO~~o~oo~OOOOoooO~OO~oo~OOO~Oo~o~OOOOXOOoooooooooooooo~o~OO~OOooOooooooOooOoO~~O OooOoOOoOoooooO~~o~oo~OOOOoooO~OO~oo~OOO~Oo~o~OOOOXXXOOoooooooooooooo~o~OO~OOooOo

I pulled my parka close. I was warm. Safe.

By the time Tom barreled down his last break, the water closest to shore was covered in a foaming wash, marbled gray turning golden as the sun began its evening descent. The breakers pulsed and receded, sending fields of shattered shells wind-chiming and sparkling along the tideline. Tom cut down then climbed hard, racing toward the wave's peak, then launched himself airborne, reaching down and grabbing the bottom of the board with one hand before diving into the back of the wave.

"   "

So, did you learn anything new watching the master at work?

Tom lay back on his towel, his breath slowly shallowing, his hands crossed behind him cradling his head.

"   "

Look out there!

Tom pointed to a school of kids slugging their way through the surf out toward the break.

"   "

You can pick out the beginners before they even ride their first wave.   Look at these rubes.

As a breaker swept toward them, they pulled their boards close and tried to crest the wave by riding over the top. The wave broke and pushed them back toward the shore, toppling some of them as it caught their boards broadside.

The duck dive.

The rash guard hung floppy off my shoulders. "Nose down, Cincy, nose down and dive!"

What's the first trick you learn when you're just starting?   Exactly. The easiest

It's to dive right into it.

way to deal with a wave isn't to jump it, it's to dive right into it. There you go. See, you

That's a gift and a curse.

haven't forgotten everything.   You've got a lot of control over that,

" "

man.

Tom lumbered over to the outdoor shower at the foot of the boardwalk. The water ran off the tiny wooden platform at the faucet's base, carving out canyons in the darkening sand and flowing around the base of a nearby garbage can. The sudden rush of the water sent a flock of gulls scattering, plastic bags and rotten banana peels in their beaks. Along the tideline, a lone beachcomber paced, fanning a metal detector back and forth in front of him.

Speaking of finding things, do you think we could

I wonder if that guy could find me a new job.

go by the shelter to drop off some stuff Vera left at our place?

"   "

Tom stepped out of the shower and hunched down to towel off his feet before tiptoeing across the sand toward the boardwalk. I followed along behind him, watching his wet footprints dissolve on the planks.

A couple of records, her journal.

What are we talking about, exactly?

He stopped at the top of the stairs.

"   "

I did.

The pages were sodden and ink-stained. July 15. Smudged. I couldn't.

Her *journal*? You read it, right?

Nah, man, I didn't.   It's not that sim-

Dude, everything you want to know could be right there!

ple.

I think you make these things harder than they should be. Reading that shit's a no-brainer.

I don't really want to talk about it. Can we do this?

She stepped off. "See you soon, Cincy."

Fine, fine, we'll

" "

swing by.

I rolled the Chevy window up against the damp chill that had settled in along the beach-front as we cut our way westward toward the shelter. The businesses on East Main rolled steadily by: Marino's Deli Restaurant Pizzeria Real Estate Flannigan's House of Spirits Tabernacle of Resurrection Century 21 Bldg for Sale Blaze Bail Bonds MetroPCS H&R Block Sovereign Bank Office Pavilion Corbo Hotel Restaurant & Bar Equipment & Supplies Dunkin' Donuts Meat 'n More The Windmill Sales Rental Seasonal Real Estate Vote Greer for Congress Work-place Furnishings Panel Systems Computer Furniture New & Used Home Office Furniture Conference Room Tables Files & Storage Seating Reception Room Desk & Office Suites Modular Furniture Office Essentials Planning & Design Bail Bond Immediate Service Jew-elry We Buy Gold Jimmie's Convenience Deli-Food Store Johnson Fast Tax Service Bail Bonds Better Bail Bonds Golden Cheung Chinese Food Big League Hair Salon & Barber Or-der Express K.J. Fashion Men & Women The Hardware Store of Jersey Shore S&T Nails S&T Sneakers Shore County Awning Tires Tires New & Used Y&J Motors Used Tires Su-per Discount Kansas Fried Chicken Pizza and Gyros Pollo Camarones Pescado Costiyas Con Arroz $4.99 H&R Block Salon Azteca Unisex Shore County Prosecutor's Office AK Records & Electronics Country Drug Store Lowest Cig. Prices Super Pizza Fried Chicken Envio de Dinero Pasajes Taxes North Shore Medical Group Shore MMA The Loan Tree La Cosanita Main Liquors Caribbean Food MVP Sneakers Ramos Grocery Store Metropolitan Staffing Services MetroPCS Taste of Italy King Check Cashing Weichert for Sale 2,000 sq. ft. Lot for SALE Diane Turton WILL DEVELOP TO SUIT NEEDS Lot for SALE Zoned for Commercial Uses Motel Tropicalia FOR SALE BY OWNER 10,000 sq. ft. PRIME REAL ESTATE Flava Records LLC FOR SALE FOR SALE

We rounded the corner of Heck into a full-fledged traffic jam: cars extending in an unbro-ken line down the avenue, the shoulder blocked up with rows of double- and triple-parked cars.

Must be some kind of classic-car conven-

Did you see that old fishtailed sixty-four back there?

"   "

tion or something.
"   "

A full neon METROPOLITAN peeked out from behind the elm tops; the whole hotel was ablaze: light pouring from every window, the vines stripped away, the holes in the foundation patched, the graffiti murals replaced by fresh white stuccoed walls. Cars sidled up through the porte cochere, their passengers alighting in ball gowns and tuxedos, the men all behatted, the women in pillboxes and blocky high heels.

This place was a dump just three weeks ago!   I thought they were

Whoa.   **Were they renovating?**

getting ready to demolish it.

Maybe someone changed their mind.

I gazed off across the square, following the lit walkways out to the far side of the park. The hoods and roofs of cars—bumper-to-bumper, rearview-to-rearview—shone in the street-lights.

We're not going to find a parking space here. Can you just idle while I drop this stuff off?

"   "

Tom's eyes were fixed on the procession of cars snaking along the Metropolitan's circular front drive.

"   "

What? Yeah, sure.

I set off across the square, Vera's records under one arm, her journal peeking out of the pouch in my hooded sweatshirt. The streetlamps overhead sparked as I passed through the park; the air was heavy with the smell of dead leaves and the perfume of cheap smokes—menthols, slims, and lites, Backwoods and Swisha Sweets. In the shadows beyond the walk, people lay out on bedrolls and newspapers, smoking and staring up at the stars, shopping carts and backpacks, plastic bags and garbage bags full of their possessions nested by their heads.

Johnnie was posted by the entrance to the shelter.

Could you let Vera know I'm here?   Remember I came to visit her a few weeks ago?
                                                Times like this, I'm not sure if I'm moving forward,
                        You a guest?   Oh,

            Are you sure?   Do you know if she's coming
backward, or standing still. "Oh, yeeah." That doesn't sound like the right kind of recognition.
yeeah. She's not in, man.   I haven't seen her yet today.

in?   I've got some things for her. Could I leave them with you?
      I'm just the doorman here.   For sure,

                        Nah, just the stuff in this bag.
man, whatever. Not too much, I hope.

I stuffed the journal into the paper bag with the records and handed it all to Johnnie.

Please promise me you'll give these to her. It's really important.
                                        Don't worry. I got you.

As I backed down the sidewalk, I looked along the length of the building, hoping to catch a glimpse of her, maybe, sitting in one of the rooms, talking to a guest or working at her desk. No Vera. But the light in her office was on.

"   "

I turn it off whenever I'm not there. Did she tell Johnnie not to let me in?

"The security people want me to leave

"   "

it on."

"   "

If I could just get inside, talk to her.   Get some answers.

And what? Get some heartbreak.

A dog howled somewhere off in the square.

"   "

Keep moving. Don't look back.

Tom was half a block up, still caught in traffic.

She wasn't there.   With the guard. It should be fine.

What'd she say?   **So you just left the stuff?**   **Bum-**

"   "

mer, man.

We swung around the far side of the square, headed for home now.

No.

You didn't happen to hear the music coming out of the Metro, did you?   They were play-

"   "

ing a jitterbug. Total time warp.

knife

(MOVIE SCENES REMIX)

Frisco stubbed a Camel out in the semidarkness and leaned his chair back until his head was resting on the cinder-block wall behind him.

No clue.

So what's the big news?

While Frisco drummed his fingers on the table, I looked around the Diver's Bell for Tom. It was hard to see much of anything down here, all the way in the dankest corner of a window-less basement bar with three functioning lights: one over the cash register, throwing cloudy brown and green shadows of old Maker's Mark and Cutty Sark on the dirty wall-mounted mirror behind the bar; one over the pool table, where bald patches on the faded green velvet and on the stooped heads around it bounced some shine back; and one over the jukebox, an old chrome behemoth with a crateload of vinyl in its clear display case. Squares of blue and white from cell phones glowed like spelunkers' headlamps around the edges of the room.

The door to the kitchen swung open behind Frisco. Tom slid into the empty chair beside me; he had a sweaty T-shirt draped around his neck and a wad of dollars in his hand.

"   "

"   "

What a night, what a night.

Tom licked the tip of his index finger and began counting out the singles.

"   "

So this is where you work, huh?   This place looks like it's been in
The Bell's an institution, man.

"   "

mothballs for forty years.   And it looks like the moths have devel-
This is classic Shore right here.

"   "

oped a taste for plaster.
"   "

Frisco peeled a flaky white scale off the cinder block and flicked it at Tom.

I'm not gonna lie.   This place is a hole.
"   "
Cince, back me up here, man.   **Fuck you.**

Tom turned to Frisco.

"   "

"   "

And the fuck is up with your suit? You look like you were mugged on your way home from work.

Frisco was wearing dress slacks and brogues; his shirt was untucked and his tie hung loose from his collar.

"   "

My manager kept me late, asshole.   Not you, him. If I stopped at the apartment to ditch the

Hey, now.

"   "

monkey suit, I woulda missed the ferry.

Well, at least you got half out of costume. I'd take off

"   "

And risk losing it? No way, dude. This cost one-fifty.   So did you invite me out just to make

the tie.

"   "

fun of me? What are we doing here?

You know I had been working on that project with my band?

"   "

Yeah.

Well   wait

Tom held his finger up.

"   "

What

Shut the fuck up for a second, would ya?

"   "

What the fuck are you on, chief?   What?!

Awesome!   **We did it! We fuckin' did it!**   **That was the last**

record! We replaced every single record in that box and not a single person noticed. Not

I didn't even realize any music was playing.

Don't you want people to notice your

even you guys.

"   "

stuff?   I don't wanna

If you nail the cover right, people shouldn't be able to tell the difference.

"   "

rain on your parade, but I think people are too busy messing around with their phones to even care about

"   "

"   "

your music.

No way, people come here for the music. Where else are you gonna hear this

"   "

For this place? That music is just background noise. Congratulations on making the sonic equiv-

stuff?

Whoa, Frisco, I

alent of wallpaper.   Fuck it. It looks like

Fuck you and the boat you came in on.

"   "

this place needed it anyway.

"   "

Frisco extended his jaw out like a cartoon gangster and blew out a stream of smoke.

"   "

Are we going out tonight, or what?   Ah, c'mon, Tommy, you know I love you.   Who

Fuck you.   **Right.**

"   "

got you all those frat gigs in college to play shit people up in fuckin' Vermont had never even *heard of*?

"   "

"   "

          Who lent you the money to buy that discontinued Kramer?   Who said, "Great, do this crazy

You.   **You.**

"   "

ass project! It might help you perfect your craft"? Who   All I'm trying to say is that

I get it, I get it.

"   "

you owe it to yourself to develop your own style. Don't spend all your whole life trying to redo shit

"   "

"   "

people have already done a million times. You deserve better, man.   We're cool?

Yeah, whatever.

"   "

You see that, Cince? Perfect people skills.

"   "

Frisco slammed his palm down on the table.

The Mayfair's reopening tonight.

So what's the plan?

Really? That place's been closed for years.

We could hit up a movie there.

Whatever, you guys are like MC Jersey. I'm just along for the ride, as

"
                                                                                    "

Let me hit the bathroom first?

long as we're going somewhere.

Let's do it. I can even afford it now.

"   "

I'll catch you outside. This place depresses me.

"   "

Exposed piping ran along the ceiling of the bathroom, dripping water that lay in tiny pud-dles on the redbrick floor. Old newspapers hung behind a plexiglass panel on the wall above the urinals: March 2, 1943 The Estate of Jacob Ruppert announced today that the New York Yankees will hold their spring training sessions for the upcoming 1943 season at Asbury Park's Bradley Field.

When I got out of the bathroom, Tom was crouched in front of the jukebox, watching the record spin.

You good to go?

What? Yeah. We'll show Frisco next week when we tear it down at the Grove.

"   "

We're really coming together.

Tom dialed up the volume on the jukebox as we headed out.

Fuck these people.

HEY! HEY! TURN THAT DOWN!

Frisco was finishing off another Camel by the curb. There were no streetlamps on this section of East Main, the whole block nothing but boarded-up duplexes and empty sandy lots.
The Chevy sat in the shadow of a condemned motel; old bedding, linen, busted chairs, and
broken desks crowded out on the balconies. Tom and I rounded the front of the car. A figure
rose from a crouch by the Chevy door. He was wearing a baseball cap pulled low. His hair
curled out from underneath.

Nerf footballs and Tecmo Super
Bowl, plastic pistols and BB guns.

Poised at the top of the hill on his bike, the seat
about three inches too high. "C'mon, push!"

"He's my friend. I want to be just like
him when I grow up."

"I want a pit bull, mom!" "No!"

The first to talk to a
girl on the phone.

"Why noooot?" "They're beasts."

A fake football stadium under lights,
smiling with a front tooth missing,
holding his helmet under his arm.

"You gotta keep your thumb on
top of your fist, like this."

"It's called street hockey."

The same flannel shirt, Monday, Tuesday, Wednesday

"You shouldn't be hanging out with those boys."

He picked the brown speckled butt of a Marlboro
out of the gutter and held it to his mouth. Flick,
flick, one puff and it was gone.

"He can't come out today. He's grounded."

"Has anyone ever offered you any of these things?"

The first to get a job.

"Where's Joey?" "He doesn't work here anymore." "Why not?"

Fighting with McDermot   fighting with Kelly

He'd show up at the courts, glassy-eyed; his jumper
Wasn't falling quite the way it used to.

He got one punch in, but not a second. Mr. Dillard grabbed
him by the collar and threw him against the locker.

Driving past the cop cars and their flashing lights, past him sitting in the back,
cuffed-up after breaking into the house on his little brother's birthday.

"We told him he wasn't welcome
here anymore. We had to."

"We don't know where he's living now."

I grabbed him around his forearm. Sinews and bone were all there was left.

Hey, Joey   Joey

"   "

"   "

He shook free and ran for it, darting off through the motel parking lot. Somewhere in the darkness, the sound of rattling chain-link.

A jimmy stuck out of the driver's-side lock.

"   "

"   "

What dumbass is trying to break into *my* car? He must really be desperate.

Tom plucked the jimmy out and pitched it into the gutter.

"   "

"   "

A man's out here tryna make a respectable living, and this is what he gets. Some junkie tryna

"   "

"   "

jack him for a buck twenty-six in pennies.

A hail of jackhammers met us as we rounded onto Daniels.

You know who that was, right?   Joey Schibell. How could you not remember Joey?

"   "

Nah, who?   **Well,**

                                                                He was one of our best friends
"   "
by the looks of it, he didn't remember who we were, either.

growing up.
"   "
        You need two minds to be friends, dude.

    A bank of bright halogen lamps tossed their purple beams down onto a construction site
where crews were busy mixing and pouring cement for a foundation.

XXXXXXX   XXXXXXX   XXXXXXX   XXXXXXX   XXXXXXX   XXXXXXX   XXXXXXX

 XXXXXXX   XXXXXXX XXXXXXX XXXXXXX   XXXXXXX   XXXXXXX   XXXXXXX

XXXXXX   XXXXXX   XXXXXX XXXXXX   XXXXXX   XXXXXX XXXXXX X X
                                                                    Damn.
sinews and bone   "Joey   Joey"
                        Shore Ford, coming Fall 2012, is what happened to it.
Yo, what happened to the Palace?

    The developers had salvaged one piece from the Palace: in the neighboring lot, its carou-
sel tilted and whirled, illuminated with hundreds of bulbs. Children and parents screamed
and laughed, the horses galloped, frozen wide-eyed and open-mouthed, moving at speeds I'd
never seen before, the lot laced with saturnine rings of noise and light. Farther downshore,
the whole island in the middle of the Boulevard had been reconstructed, the steel skeletons of
abandoned condo projects replaced with several blocks' worth of rough-hewn five-story bed-
and-breakfasts in a turn-of-the-century style, all weatherworn cedar shakes and white window
borders, their lights on, laundry fluttering from the sills—striped full-body swimsuits and long
socks, beach blankets and heavy navy bathing gowns.

"   "

The carousel spun. "They were playing a foxtrot." *Wilt Scores* 100.
The hull of the Morro rose past the breakline.
It's always something new with the people down here.

"   "

    By the time we got in the neighborhood of the Mayfair, right in the heart of downtown, the line from the theater's front doors wound for blocks, looping past the freshly pasteled town-houses that surrounded the theater's gleaming chrome facade like sheets of tissue paper giddily ripped from a polished heirloom. We parked the car in a metered space outside a Doo Wop–windowed all-night diner and joined the line.

    By whatever trick of the Hollywood calendar, the Mayfair was redebuting with the fifth se-quel to the last film it showed, a remake of a spy film set around the same time the theater last closed its doors twenty years ago.

Yeah, man.

Freedom was unsticking your feet from a movie theater
floor on a Tuesday night in June.

"   "

Cheer up, dude. Remember when we used to go here as kids?   **Sneaking into**

Or, or remember when we saw *Terminator* when we were like six?

"   "

movies?   **I felt like such a badass**

"   "

"   "

when I got my dad to take us to that. We were like the first kids at Saint Vitus to see an R

"   "

I hear this one's pretty good. Some guys were talking about it at work today.

movie.   **As long as there**

With standards like that

"   "

are some explosions and some hot chicks, I am good.   **Look, I don't**

"   "

Damn, Cincy, what

go to a theater to see people walking around thinking. Give me something!

A narc shook me down like a week ago. Had me up against a wall.
happened to your hands?   I love this
"   "

"   "

"I'll see you at nine. Bye." "Friend of a friend. I'll get her over here. Aimi!"
place. This shit is better than a movie.
"   "

The line lurched toward the doors.

Hey, you know anything about Aimi's friend Vera?   I guess you could
Ahhh, she's got her hooks in you.
"   "

say that.   What's her story?   Her story.
What do you want to know?   Her story, or my story of her?   Don't
"   "

Okay, what's your story of her?
know.   Pretty much whatever I want it to be. I've been hanging around
"   "

And?

her off and on for a while now.　　　I'd run into her and maybe I'd invite her somewhere. Most of the

"　　　　　　　　　　　　　　　　　　　　　　　　　　　　　　　　　　"

"　　　　　　　　　　　　　　　　　　　　　　　　　　　　　　　　　　"

time, she just didn't show up. If she ever did, she seemed totally uninterested and then would just let

"　　　　　　　　　　　　　　　　　　　　　　　　　　　　　　　　　　"

"　　　"

things drop.

"　　　"

He held his cigarette up for another drag. The tip flared. A wreath of smoke drifted off into the marquee's rows of flashing bulbs.

So you gave up on her?

　　　　　　　　I didn't have time for games. All that not-coming, not-speaking was disrespect-

"　　　　　　　　　　　　　　　　　　　　　　　　　　　　　　　　　　"

　　　　　　　Wait. Those are two really different things.

ful. Or cowardly.　　　　　　　　　　　　　　Results in the same thing, so what's the dif-

"　　　　　　　　　　　　　　　　　　　　　　　　　　　　　　　　　　"

　　　I mean

ference?　　　Look, if you want her, go for it. Just don't expect it to be easy.

"　　　　　　　　　　　　　　　　　　　　　　　　　　　　　　　　　　"

Frisco flicked his cigarette onto the sidewalk. We passed into the lobby and followed Tom up to the balcony. The audience, full of people chatting and pointing and gazing, buzzed beneath us.

How's work going?

        Ehhhh been better. Yesterday

        Hey HEY, you ladies here for a movie or a tea party?

"   "

"   "

Leave the gossip outside.

    The houselights lowered and the curtains drew back from the screen. I settled back in my seat as the projector hummed to life. The theater was an old‑school gem—an elaborate prosce‑ nium to hide the curtains; gilt work on the walls; a crystal chandelier hanging from the ceil‑ ing. Everything seemed like it hung together perfectly, until the first trailers slid across the screen: new‑model luxury cars rocketed around closed courses; shock troops dropped out of helicopters; offices overflowed with glowing monitors. Then the film's opening scenes—set sometime in the seventies—rolled. After a few minutes, it was hard to tell which was the anachronism: the theater, the film, or the audience. Maybe all three.

    Frisco slipped a flask‑size bottle of whiskey out of his pants pocket, took a quick swig, and passed it to Tom. I panned over the crowd as the theater lightened and darkened. Try as I might, I couldn't focus on the film. The screen flared white; I caught sight of Vera, or a woman who looked like Vera, slipping into a seat along the far aisle below. She pulsed dark, light, dark, light with the projector's flicker. Here one moment, gone the next.

    On‑screen, a man and a woman walked arm‑in‑arm across a bustling plaza. It was snow‑ ing. He . . . a white dot specked the screen. A swarm of people. A quick skip and a pop. A perforated black film border sped behind the couple's backs. Another white speck. He opened his mouth. Nothing. She laughed silently. He turned toward her and . . . the images on‑screen jumped. The man and the woman were

BOOOOOOOOOOOOOOOOOOOOOOOOOOO   *BOOOOOOOOOOOOOOOOOOOOOOOOOOOOOO*

Hᴇʏ, ғɪx ᴛʜᴇ ᴘʀᴏᴊᴇᴄᴛᴏʀ!

Someone lobbed a box of candy at the screen. It hit a building that should have been a mile away and fell to the floor. The image puddled.

HAHAHAHAHAHAHAHAHAHAHAHA
BOOOOOOOOOOOOOOOOOOOOOOOOOOOOOOOOOOOOOOOOOOOOOOOOOOOOOOOOOOOOOOOOO

The picture stabilized again in a flash of white. She lit up. She was still there, but not *right* there, layers of thoughts between me and her, flickering along with the images on-screen.

"She comes and she goes." The bus rumbled off.

She sat there, with my history in her hands, flipping back and forth,
first day of school, high school graduation, tenth birthday, junior prom,
the years circling through, image by paper-thin image.

Lying in bed, staring at the ceiling. I slid closer. She kept staring straight ahead.   I don't want to go through this again.
"My fav." "Mine too." Waking up beside her, every day, thrilling. We could go on like that forever.
I checked my phone. Nothing. I checked my phone.   We won't go through this again.

I don't much remember the rest of that movie.

■ ■ ■

I do remember the houselights rising and me trailing out behind Tom and Frisco, staring at the chevron pattern in the red-and-black theater carpeting, one foot in front of the other, down the crowded stairs. Somewhere in the flood of bodies passing through the front doors, Vera walked past us. She was with a group of guys and girls, all of them traveling through the lobby in a loose pack.

I took her by the hand, my other hand around her waist. The time signature was fluky though, something I'd never heard before. I stepped right, half a beat off, stepped left, half a beat off. The smile faded from her face. I was ruining her prom. Reach out to her.

She turned around, eyes wide. The guy

by her side turned, too. She could shoot

me down in front of all of these people.

She smiled. The rest of the group

kept walking. I turned to Tom and

Frisco. "See ya, guys."

    I couldn't bear, didn't even try, to catch her eye; my own wandered back to my feet as I eddied there, frozen, silent. As if speaking or not speaking, saying anything I could have said would have made a difference: she was focused somewhere off in the middle distance, seemingly oblivious to the crowds ebbing and flowing around her. Except for the times she tilted to let others pass by, it didn't even seem as if she was really there, like a hologram or a reflection, visible only from the right angles, intangible.

[   ]

Didn't she see me? She had to have.

Maybe she likes me too much. Maybe she's afraid to get wrapped

up with anyone.

Maybe she likes me less than she thought.

Uh, yeah, sure.

Ay, Frisco, you wanna ride home?

Huh?

We lay back on the hood of the car. The city glistened on the horizon. Maybe

She looked up. "I better go." "It's getting late." Maybe

I took her by the hand and led her out of the party. I ran my hands

along the sides of her face and kissed her. Her cheeks flushed, her eyes Maybe

What's up with

Hey, Cincy!   **Stop drag-assin' man. It's starting to rain. Let's go!**

It's cool.   I'm cool.

you?

"   "

Frisco took the front passenger's seat, resting his left leg on the bench seat and propping his right foot up on the dash. He pulled the bottle out again and held it up to the light. Empty. He dropped it to the floor and reached for the packet of cigarettes in his shirt pocket.

"   "

She reached for my hand. We lay back on the bed as

the record played, her fingers playing across my palms. I blew it right there.

She paused for a second,

her head tilting up and to

the side, her eyes wide, her

gaze on me. No, right there.

"I can't call it." Gone. *She paused*

before she said yes. "We should

listen to music at my place." "Sure."

No. *"at my place." "Sure."* Yes, *a*

pause. She was never mine to lose.

Maaaaaan.

No smoking in the ride.

The highway passed beside and beneath us in streaks of yellow and red light, water droplets coursing off the windshield, glowing, sparking momentarily before hurtling off into the night. The Shore slipped by in the rearview, couples in new sports cars and tourists in horse-drawn carriages from the Grove, the newest apartment blocks and antebellum banks. Frisco pulled one of his pens out of his pocket. He used Bic lighters, but his pens were fancier, clear canisters with wells of black ink, their retractable points on plungers, the whole thing like a hypodermic. *click click*   *clickclickclickclick*   *click   click*

"   "

Keep thinking, keep thinking. I can figure this out. I can figure her out.

Turn this shit up. Give me something I can feeeeeeel.

That's already annoying the shit out of me.

Frisco leaned forward and dialed up the knob on the stereo. The sides of the car began to beat in and out, the glass in the rearview and sideviews vibrated visibly, the road and cars behind us shook along their edges until they disappeared in a watery muddle of undulating lines.

Hold up / Roll up / Keep that drank po'd up / Life moving fast / So we keep our sound slowed up

Keep thinking.

triggerman

The late-July and early-August doldrums hit the yard hard, the regular midsummer spike in humidity and gas prices taking the wind out of our sails and the customers out of our parking lot. Each of the guys had his own way of coping with the downturn in business: Oz and Deuce kept themselves occupied with the catboat; the union guys played cards and continued to keep up their steely indifference to all of us; J.D. blew through stacks of travelogues, driving out to Princeton twice a week to pick up new reads; Mike was back,

"Hey, Cincy." "What's up, man?" "You were right." "About what?" "About the weed. I'm swearing it off."

staring out the window and rolling the tips of his hair into little mini joints. The only ones who didn't seem to be suffering much were Corey and Tone—Corey was still rushing out to help the boats coming in off the bay, Tone still had at least half a garage of engines to fiddle with. Me? I continued to poke through the more paranoid corners of the Internet, continued to think, pocket change jangling, toes tapping.

stay intrusion   vascular pattern recognition   private military company
crisis management

        licensed armed officer with patrol vehicle   *seemingly oblivious to the crowds ebbing and*
flowing around her

executive personal protection   antiterrorist security   surveillance detection and planning
armed chauffeurs

        special mission security teams   *like a hologram or a reflection, visible only from the right angles,*
intangible

I was glued to the floor. Did she see me?   risk assessment   security contractors
        tactical training facilities   tactical driving catastrophe planning
        political and security analysis   risk mitigation training   *She's gone.*

    I felt a sharp pain like a belt pulling around my stomach. I glanced at the clock: 2:23.

Man, I'm starving. How'd I forget to eat lunch *again*?

                  I watched the shadows lengthen

                  eastward, eastward, eastward.

                        We sat side by side on the

                        bench. "You eaten yet?"

    I reached into the drawer for a take-out menu. My hand brushed up against a folded en-
velope.

Corey's check from last month. *"Yeah, okay. Whatever."* He never picked it up.

    J.D. strolled into the office, holding a roll of papers in his hand.

"   "

Should I tell him about the check?
Just wanted to give you a heads-up. Some crews are going to be coming through here in a little

I'm sorry.   Why?

No, he'll probably be upset. I should've made sure he took it.

bit to start hauling things out of the graveyard.   Apparently they can't get their

"   "

cranes deep enough into the lot to grab the stuff they need. I told the owner they could cut across

Roger.

the yard. You know, trying to be a good neighbor and all.   You give any more thought to

I really appreciate it, but   I

the dive?   But what? A month overseas doesn't do anything for you?

"   "

Give it a little more thought. Don't wait too long, though.

He slapped the roll of papers against my desk and strolled out.

The crew arrived an hour later, a procession of pickups and big rigs with flatbeds ushering a crane toward the back of the yard like a captured giant or sacred totem. For the next few hours, the crane dipped and rose, cantilevering whole sections of scrapped steamers out across the graveyard and onto the waiting flatbeds while the guard dogs in the graveyard barked and bayed.

I winced as the ship parts swung out over our boats, completely lost it when the crane missed its target rig and sent a house-size steel panel crashing down in the gravel near the boat racks. I raced out to the back lot, where workers holding power saws and blow torches swarmed around the panel. Tone stood to the side, toweling his head off and sipping lemonade.

Careful, man!

Don't worry, don't worry. Everything's fine.

"   "

The crane rumbled and tugged again, lifting the panel edgewise off the ground. A couple yards of fence had been knocked over, the fence poles bent at their bases, flat to the ground. Workers scrambled under the panel, the whole team of them guiding it with their hands up onto the flatbed. Out beyond the confusion, the third guard dog glowered, chained to a metal stake. He must have driven himself crazy that morning darting after all the moving metal: his chain was wrapped almost entirely around the stake, forming a bed of rusted links for him to lie on.

What are you doing this for, anyway?

Guys! Get this fence back up, pronto!   **Sorry, kid.**

"   "

"   "

We need more scrap for the *Morro* job. We're gonna cut all this up into new panels and

"   "

You do this kind of stuff a lot?

weld 'em into the frame offshore.   **There's a bit of recycling in**

"   "

everything. There's so much stuff lying around, it's kinda hard not to.

I feel you. It's all

Is that your secret?   Repairs?

HEY! HEY! IDIOT! WATCH OUT! Sorry, guys, I gotta straighten

about repurposing.   **Secret to what?**   **Aw, shit. You found me out!**

"   "

something out.

"   "

My phone made the nebulous high-tech sound it made when texts arrived: So I'll be seeing you at the show tonight? xx V

Oh   uh   nothing. Just got a text from some girl.

How does she know I'm going to the show?   Probably guessing.

What's up, Cince?   **Oh, you got a little side piece**

I guess you could say that. I don't really know where we stand.

Why would she go?   She hates Tom.

She watched me watch her,

as I stood amid the rush of bodies,

nailed to the floor. What's his issue?

there?   **You put anything out there?**

Like?   I don't really know what I'd tell her.

Probably going with Aimi.

You tell her what you're thinking?   **Times like this, you**

What if you only have one bullet?

just gotta shoot your shot, playboy.   **Simple. Aim for the heart.**

shelter

(HELLO, GOODBYE REMIX)

I finally reached the band shell around nine that night, after a winding walk through the north side's litter of ratty motels and abandoned school buildings. The roads that jutted off from Main Street in the Grove were lined by parti-colored Victorian houses three times taller than they were wide, huddled so close together that a homeowner could reach through his kitchen window to shake his next door neighbor's hand while she cooked eggs on her own stove, or pick up a newspaper on the sidewalk and knock on his cross-street neighbor's door. The top of the Great Auditorium peeked out at points, until the Auditorium itself rounded into view, squat, hexagonal, coated with a shiny inch-thick shell of marigold paint and surrounded by clusters of bungalow-like tents, where summer pilgrims slept through summer nights under roofs of striped canvas sheets or even out under the stars when the Weather Channel said all clear.

The band shell sat a block farther along, at the head of the Green, which cut a straight swath bayward through rows of Victorians. The band shell's stage and wings were covered by a wooden canopy that stretched out far enough onto the Green to shelter a few hundred people. By the time I got there, the show—really more a showcase for local bands—was just warming up. People clustered around a temporary bar draped with vinyl banners from the area radio stations and beer distributors, holding Solo cups and conversing out the sides of their mouths with their eyes on the stage, where a woman with a honeyed voice cooed over a superamped bass and warm, welling guitar chords as the klieg lights pulsed a soft purple overhead. The singer was too modest for her own good, thanking the crowd like she couldn't believe they were still there and then slipping away into the wings without even giving her name.

WE LOOOOOOOOVE YOUUUUUUUUUUUUUUU! WHO ARE YOU?!

As the crew busied around the stage, a guy with a scraggly weeks'-old beard loped toward the frontmost mic stand. He carried a two-foot-long pedal board studded with a dozen stomp boxes on his shoulder. The crowd applauded; he placed the pedal board at the base of the mic and ran his hands through his hair with a look of quiet amusement. He pulled a bottle of water out of his back pocket and started poking around the stage, checking the dials on the amps while screwing and unscrewing the cap on his bottle. The keyboardist appeared stage right, hunched now over an old laptop that sat above a synth on a bilevel keyboard rack. His glasses shone white then blue as he fiddled with presets on the computer. By the time he had finished tweaking, the band shell was packed, the crowd loose, the air perfumed with liquor and weed.

Frisco tapped me on the elbow.

I think it's these guys I used to go to high school with.

Who's up next?

That's their name? That's awe-

Nah. They call themselves This Too Shall Pass.

They do gigs

some.

So you've heard them before?

down here pretty much every weekend.

They're pretty good.

They're good?

Great. 'Cuz I'm ready to

"

"

rock! WOOOOOOOOOOOOO!   WOOOOOOOOOOOOOOOOOOOOOOO!
WOOOOOOOOOOOOOOOOOOOOOOOO!

That guy knows what's up!

Frisco pulled out his flask.

Yeah, sure.
You want some?

The lights dimmed and the crowd erupted. As I passed the bottle back to Frisco, the band stabbed eight head-banging power chords that spiraled out into a whirring atmospheric hum, pulling the crowd up, pausing, then launching them into a frenzy with hard snare hits and hyperdistorted bass lines that laced through a driving industrial churn. The kliegs blinked in time with the music, cutting out conical beams of light in the smoke-filled air that color-changed with the music's shifting tempos, hard yellow to soft purple and back again, the bass player deep in the pocket, the crowd completely wrapped up, lurching one way, then the other, held up and dropped again, drum breaks rolling hard enough to give me an extra heartbeat every half-measure, each kick rattling from my stomach up into my chest. It was times like this— head nodding, pulse racing, body bounding—I could feel why the drug spiral was the classic rocker arc; this stuff hit you emotionally, it hit you chemically, it put your body at the mercy of the force picked out by someone's fingers and banged out by someone's hands, sound projecting out at you, coming out of an hour-long set with your hearing blown, your head spinning, your skin covered in sweat, your heart aching, and still a whole night to get through, impossible to sleep through, so high, anything to take you down and then gear you up for the next round. By the end of the second encore, the crowd was beyond beyond, milling around nervously, junkily looking for the next hit.

I'm gonna hit the bathroom, man. I'll be back.

Man, Tom's got a tough act to follow.
WOOOOOOOOOOOOOOOOOOOOOOOO!

I followed the reek of industrial-grade disinfectants that wafted off the wings to a bathroom floored with gray and black tiles, which were spread out in a pattern that didn't look like a pattern until I stared at four different sections of identical apparent randomness underfoot—the tile inside the door, by the urinal, at the sink, at the paper towel dispenser, all the same. Even when the pattern became clear, it wasn't clear whether it was the work of an architect's careful planning or a lucky accident. I tossed a water-darkened paper towel into the wastebasket and headed back outside.

Aimi passed by the door as I exited. I hooked her arm.

Can I talk to you for a second?   What's up with Vera?   Nothing?

          Sure.   I wish I knew.   I'm not trying to

                                                            Could

hold out on you, Cincy. I'm best friends with the girl, but she's kinda shut me out recently.

you

     I don't have any answers for you. Just questions. Take care of yourself, Cincy.

Aimi squeezed my hand and disappeared into the women's bathroom, leaving me alone in the welter of concertgoers.

When I found Frisco again, Tom and his crew were already up onstage, rolling through a brief soundcheck. Tom gave the thumbs-up to the soundman, nodded to Rico, and off they went, launching into a spirited cover of "Livin' on a Prayer." The crowd leaped up at the chorus, fists pumping, voices cracking, beer sloshing out of the tops of their cups.

It *was* a hard act to follow. For the next half-hour, the band spooled out classic after classic, but they couldn't hook the crowd again, no matter how many solos they killed or pitch-perfect choruses they delivered. The crowd came unglued, pulling back from the stage, spreading out beyond the canopy, its attention shifting to the bar, the walk home, the beach, anything but the stage, where Tom and his band continued to jam, their songs beating to slower and slower BPMs, their rhythms slipping, eyes shifting down to their own instruments as they picked and banged and keyed away, losing the moment.

By the time the first synth notes from "Dancing in the Dark" leaked out, the crowd had all but disappeared, wandering out of the band shell and down the Green, the last few stragglers just a bunch of older shirtless bums lurching around the floor with their arms in the air like acid-tripping scarecrows. Cutting off before they got to the sax solo for the sax player they didn't have, the band trudged off stage. Tom stared out slack-jawed and defeated, one hand on the mic stand, his guitar swinging from his neck. The bums clapped and waved.

ENCORE! ENCOOOOOOOORE!

"   "

He walked off to the wings, head down.

We should probably go talk to him.

Wow, that suuuuuuucked.

We found Tom sitting on a folding chair in the wings while his bandmates quietly packed away their instruments.

"   "

I love that song.

That was the worst show of my life. Who doesn't love "Dancing in the Dark"?

"   "

Best movie song ever.

"Highway to the Danger Zone"?   **"I Don't Wanna Go Home"? We played**

"   "

You're not supposed to go home during "I Don't Wanna Go

fuckin' "I Don't Wanna Go Home"!

Maybe people wanted to hear something new.

Home."

I mean, what-the-FUCK?   **C'mon, you know**

"   "

"   "

how this stuff works. Nobody dances to shit they don't recognize, even if the song's good.

"   "

"   "

You just wait for everyone to get all liquored up and play the old shit. It's the oldest formula

They loved This Too.

I loved those guys. They ROCKED.

in the book.   **Who knows This Too?**

"   "

"   "

They're just a bunch of dudes from around here that play a bunch of weird-sounding shit.

It's not like people don't know who they are. They gig hard, man, they figured out a way to make

"   "

"   "

people know their stuff.

I love those guys.

FUCK, MAN!

Tom threw an empty water bottle against the far wall and dropped his head into his hands. While the bottle bounced hollowly in the far corner of the room, Aimi walked through the door; Vera trailed behind her. Aimi sat down beside Tom and put her arm around him; he resisted, sitting stock‑still. Aimi leaned forward and whispered something in his ear. He looked up at her and smiled.

Hey.   He's a tough guy. He's been through waaaay worse.

She really is good for him.

Hey.   It's a shame he lost the crowd like that.

"   "

                                    I've got faith in him. He'll

But still, that was a really bad way to go out. He looked totally broken.

"   "

figure out what to do.   See

"   "

           Hey, everyone. I'm gonna take off. Looks like you've got this under control.

ya, Frisco.

"   "

"   "

He stumbled out onto the Green, looking once over his shoulder before the door closed behind him. Tom was still smiling as he and Aimi stood up. Tom pulled his keys out of his pocket.

You   you want a ride back?

                                Sure.

Tom picked up his guitar case by its strap in one hand; he wrapped his other arm around Aimi's waist and led her out the door. Vera and I followed them, walking with the ocean breeze between us. We strolled along streets that intersected at weird obtuse angles, wending slowly south then east, south then east toward Main Street.

I looked at my watch. 7:15: Outside, gridlock,
bumper-to-bumper through the Roman streets.
Departing 7:45. I'm not gonna make it.

I   sorry   Right before This Too went on.

I   I didn't see you at the show. When did you get there?

There was some woman with a piano. She was pretty good.

                                        "When did you get there?"

                                        Was she looking for me?

                                        Oh, you must have gotten there right

            She must not have been looking hard enough.

when I did.

Tom and Aimi walked faster and faster as they went; within minutes, they were a full block ahead, in danger of disappearing out of sight. Vera and I drifted in their wake, on through the shadows of the town's old monuments, each bent from years of trusts and secrets like old hungry men with empty stomachs—the First National Bank and its facade, run with green rivulets of rusted bronze, full of vaults of tiny drawers dead-bolted with tinier keys, the town hall, stacked with filing cabinets stuffed with old land-use maps and ordinances.

            Eleven.

What time do you have?

        She squinted at her watch.

Hmm, mine must be slow.

She pulled out the bezel and spun the hands forward an hour and change.

"   "

Should I take her hand?   Forget it. Let her

make a move.

She slid farther over on the bus shelter bench, her eyes straight ahead.

A broken watch is right at least twice a day, right?

A station signal sounded, piercing in its nearness. By the time we made it back to the gates, Tom and Aimi had already slipped into the backseat of the car. Their silhouettes merged under the Chevy's dome light.

"   "

"   "

Hey, man, could you do me a favor and drive home?

We headed downshore, Tom and Aimi in the back, Vera in the passenger seat beside me. She sat with her chin cupped in her hand, eyes window-ward, staring at the scenes passing by outside. Out beyond the glass, the marshes shuddered, the signs along the roadway flashed reflective then receded into the dark behind us. She picked my free hand up off the armrest and turned my palm over.

And that's one out in the top of the eighth, runners in scoring position for Jeter.
"   "

"What happened?" "A narc" "I tripped over a crack

Looks better. What did you say happened to you again?

First pitch for a ball.

I tripped over   I fell

in the sidewalk" No. "I fell while I was playing basketball" No. Think. "I tripped over a root"

"   "

Koufax checks the

" "

[   ]

// //

Tom and Aimi fell against the rear driver's-side door.

runner at first.

What's going on back there?

[   ]

//. //

Vera blushed and turned the radio dial.

What I've been lookin' been lookin' for

" "

Sing it, man.

// //

Ay, Cincy!   **Let us out here.**

" "

I pulled the car over in front of our apartment.

Wait   what

// //

Thanks, dude. See you tomorrow.   **Later, man, later.**

" "

Tom and Aimi stepped onto the sidewalk.

"   "

//   //

Don't get into too much trouble, you two.

"   "

They disappeared up the stairwell. So now it was just Vera and me, sitting in an idling bust-down Chevy with slow jams pulsing out.

Woah-oh-oh-oooooooooh Woah-oh-oh-oooh-oooooh Woah-oh-ooooo-ooooooh Woah-oh-oh-

I'd invite you up, but I don't think they want visitors.   You feel like going home?

I bet they set this up. Tom dialed Aimi. Aimi dialed Vera. They're smart.

                                                                                    Not

        So why don't we go for a drive and see if we can't find some trouble?

really.   Let's.

We crossed town, headed for the beachfront. Vera sat framed in the window, a motion pic-ture gallery of moon-vigiled seascapes flickering beyond her. Ocean Avenue was busier than usual for this time of night: people meandered hand-in-hand down the middle of the road, tak-ing in the stars that were beginning to disappear behind approaching cloud cover. I slalomed the car around the strollers.

                Yeah, but it's Ocean. The people around here treat it like a sidewalk. I don't

This is a street, right?

normally drive this way, but I'm a little distracted.

//   //

She smiled and looked out the window again.

The old-money Cape Cods that lined the western side of Ocean gradually gave way to the south side's squat cottages and sandy side lanes. Green signs pointed off to the bay bridge, the sole link in the Shore's chain of barrier islands. I banked right onto the on-ramp and joined the double line of cars heading bridgeward. As the front end of our car began to rise, the warning lights on the bridge gates started winking. Seconds later, the traffic signals flashed to red and the gates fell. Five car lengths ahead of us, the drawbridge's leaves slowly rose.

yeaahhhhhhhhhhhhhhhhhhhhhhuh   *huuuuuuuuuuuuuuuhhhhhhhhhhhh*

So what did you think of This Too Shall Pass? I used to go to high school and not speak to those guys,

"   "

yeaahhhhhhhhhhhhhhhhhhhhhhhuh   *huuuuuuuuuuuuuuuuhhhhhhhh*

you know.   No, but really

        So you're tight like that, huh?   They were great. I just wish I had someone

"   "

to dance with.

        She turned the volume up.
        She was grooving in her seat, ever so slightly. It was the first time I'd really seen her move.

yeaahhhhhhhhhhhh   *uh uh uh*

You want to go dancing?   Here.

            Sure. Where?

        I cranked the volume knob up more, sending a bass pulse shivering along the length of the car.

Never have I

"   "

Here?

In one motion I was out of the car, racing to her side and reaching through the window to take her hand.

Been so close, so far, can I

I don't care

How silly do I look?   Who cares?

I

I opened the door and pulled her out of the car. The deck of the bridge was a perfect dance floor, the concrete smooth, the lanes just wide enough to step and turn. After a few beats she loosened up, our hands intertwined, our bodies moving in time with the music that pumped out of the open doors and open windows. She moved so well, so smoothly. I felt closer to her, for those three minutes, than I'd ever felt, the layers and layers and thoughts peeled away, the beat moving forward, forward, forward, moving, moving with her without thinking. Perfectly timed, perfectly present.

Have a minute of your time, so I / Can slow this down

Look at this turkey!

Whatever

They

We keep spinnin' round and round / Baby, can we

"   "

"   "

The warning indicator on the gates began to toll.

Slow this down

Looks like we'll have to cut this a little short.

"   "

We ran back to the car and fired up the engine just as the gates lifted. We touched down on the far side of the bridge and cruised along the curve of the beach, wedding-cake houses on massive lawns to our right, towering dunes to our left, the moon edging out from behind the cloud cover, the night sky opening up over the water. Coasting down the avenue in the moon-light was like driving through a daguerreotype: shadows and mirrored silver, the details on the surrounding houses stark and magnified down to the fine black lines etched into the cedar-shake shingles, the air cool and metallic, the moment fragile.

I pulled into a parking spot near a beach entrance. The walkway to the beach was stark in the moonlight, sheer silver and solid black shadow. We left our shoes in the car and padded across the sand.

I watched from the base of the dunes as Vera danced along the tideline, her feet tracing a looping waltz in the wet sand. The Atlantic, shiny and shadowed like blue velvet, folded in; she tiptoed forward. The ocean rolled forward, she scampered back, a hairbreadth ahead of the water. She turned on the dry sand and faced the ocean. It rolled back once more. She ap-proached again. It paused at its farthest remove, then pressed forward. And again, she ran back, sand and shattered bits of shell clinging to the bottoms of her feet.

The storm closed in over us while she danced, onrushing clouds blanketing the moon be-hind a silver-lined patchwork. The first raindrops fell softly, barely noticeable, steadily build-ing, sweeping eastward until the sounds of the waves washed out beneath the steady static of a summer downpour.

We raced back to the car, shivering, soaked through. The only warmth I could find for her was an old Windbreaker crumpled up in the backseat. She pulled it close around her, lying back in the passenger seat with her head propped against the window, her eyes closed, her body tilted away from me.

"   "

I need to dry off. Can you take me home?

As we drove, the wipers swiped back and forth, each pass across the windshield tracing ridged crescents that caught and diffracted the light from passing traffic signals and streetlamps. Our pitched reflections hovered inverted in the windshield, Vera visible upside-down, layered beneath the vinyl-like rainwater ridges.

She held her records close to her chest, the last one in the stack covered by her crossed arms. Up on the counter, into the clerk's hands, off to the plastic bag. I didn't see anything more than a track name here or there, a UPC code, a big capital letter. What's she thinking?

"   "

I had to keep an eye on the speedometer; the car kept edging up past the speed limit. I eased off the accelerator.

“   ”

I'm right up here on the right.

A line of cars was parked in front of her house. I slid into a space farther up the block. I drew her out of the car, her hand in mine. Our steps fell in together as we walked down the sidewalk, the grass on either side gleaming with raindrops.

"I'm glad we could do this, Cincy. I'm sorry I kinda dropped off the radar."

"I guess I owe you an explanation." She paused for a breath.

A rock skidded from beneath my foot. Click click click it skipped three times before landing in a puddle at the base of a nearby driveway. I kicked another pebble. Click click click her image bent inward, collapsed in upon itself, refocused again, shook, then exploded in dozens of undulating rings. Bent into circular waves, the pieces of her layered then dissolved at the outer edges. She reappeared at the center of it all, still, shining, luminous.

“   ”

"Look, maybe I should go."

She lay back beside me. I pulled her closer to me.

"   "

I held her hand more tightly. We turned up the walk to her house. She paused as we reached the front porch.

So stay out with me.

I pulled her out of the party.

It's so beautiful. I feel like I could stay out forever.

Even here, under a canopy of elms, the rain reached through. Water coursed down our arms, pooling in the space where our fingers intertwined. Her hand fidgeted in mine.

It's Friday night or   um   Saturday morning. What's a few more hours?

"Umm   Something came up." "Look, maybe I should go." *She looked down. And walked away.* Just go.

She squeezed my hand and stepped off, looking once over her shoulder. She looked back up at me, smiling. Don't let her go.

I can't.   I've   I've got

"   "

work. I shouldn't.

I brushed a wet strand of hair away from her face, running the back of my hand down her cheek.

I ran my hands along the sides of her face, tilted her chin up to me, kissed her. Her cheeks flushed, her eyes

She lowered her eyes, her face turned away from me, toward the door.

With just a few words, she could make me see it all differently—the last few months, my memories, my thoughts, her; with a few words, she could take it all away, like it had never been there to begin with. I didn't have to say anything. I could let her go, and take it all back with me, tell myself my own stories about it, keep it from her, keep her from breaking it.

I turned it over in my hands   cradled it gingerly in my palms.

the cracked saucer

the wounded bird

the still-drying photo

So, I let her go.

I let her fingers work free of mine while her other hand grabbed the door handle, let her go as the door closed softly behind her, let her disappear without another word.

"   "

We lay back on the hood of the car.

She's not ready for me. I made her

too happy.

She stood by the pillar. It was just

another night to her, another

few weeks to her.

"Why would I go?" "Cincy will be there."

"I'm done with him." "Veeeera, c'mon."

She never wanted to come out in the first

place. She was just looking to work off her

high from the show.

I cupped my hands around the candle, blew softly

until the blue flame oranged again, until it licked

against my palms. I can keep this alive.

I could tell myself my own stories about it all, any story I wanted, anything that I thought could make me happy, anything that would make this make sense to me. Flushed with so much thought and hope and anxiety and regret and desire, I didn't even notice the rain falling, running down the back of my shirt, rolling down my arms. I didn't notice the chill as I fell asleep that night, tangled in my sheets, lost in thoughts. I didn't think twice when I woke up the next morning with a cold.

we bought yachts

As quickly as business at the yard bottomed out, it picked up again. Some things never change: calendars turned to August, back-to-school ads started rolling on the TV and radio, and the whole tristate rushed to us to save the summer for them. We need Jet-Skis! Fix it quick! Fuel up my yacht! Jangling pocket change and spinning keychains on ring fingers, watching the numbers on the gas pumps spinning like a countdown to fall.

The weekdays were brutal; the weekends worse. The kinds of days people quit over; the kinds of days we spent unwinding as much as we spent working. It was good for me, though, I guess: not enough time to think about Vera, at least not to myself.

and it was just   It was kind of funny. But not really

If ole girl is gonna front on you like that, you

"   "

"   "

I don't know, man, I don't know. I guess I still have hope. I guess.

should just cut her off.

Whatever

"   "

"   "

I agree.   **You**

you do, do   call her.   come to you.   That's a first.

NOT   Let her   You agree with us?

"   "

finally said somethin' smart, so yeah. One thing, though: When she comes back, you damn sure

"   "

"   "

"   "

I grabbed her by the hand.

I let her go.

better know what you're gonna do. You only get so many chances.

"   "

"   "

My phone rang.

On-screen: a restricted number. I let it ring through. A missed call registered. The phone rang again: another restricted number.

Hello?   Yeah.

Is this Mr. Stiles?   I'm calling from the Jersey Shore PD to follow up on your complaint.

Hold on   Hey, Tone! C'mere.

"   "

I clicked on the speakerphone and held it out toward Tone.

Hello?   Speaking.
      I'm calling from the JSPD for Mr. Stiles.   This is in regard to your complaint number
"   "

                        I filed that   That was a long time
twenty twelve dash one thirty.   Five weeks ago, on July 14, 2012.
"   "

ago.   Have the investigators found anything?
      Sometimes these things take a while.   Our investigation
"   "

"   "

has established no instances of misconduct. In fact, it hasn't turned up any sign of any conduct by a
"   "

                  Then you didn't look hard enough.
JSPD officer at all.   There were no JSPD officers within a mile of
BULLSHIT!

"   "

the area you identified at the time indicated in your complaint.
"   "

The room swam for a second, the table, chairs, floors sinking then rising.

How do you know that?   He had a badge.   He had a *badge*.
Something glinted. A badge? A gun?
                  How do you?   Was it a JSPD badge?   And?
"   "

Look, I *know* something happened.

So? How do you even know he was a police officer?   Are you

"   "

"   "

sure?

"   "

I looked at the scars on the heels of my palms.

Yeah, I'm certain.   Wait!

Well, we all have our beliefs. Have a nice day.

"   "

The line went dead.

            I

Awww, c'mon!

Tone's phone rang. Another restricted number.

Pick it up.

                              Uh-huh.

Is this Mr. Hawkins?   I'm calling from the Jersey Shore PD to follow up on your

"   "

What's your name?

complaint.   This is in regard to your complaint number twenty twelve dash one

"   "

"   "

thirty-one. Our investigation has established no instances of misconduct. In fact,

Tone clapped his phone shut and pitched it against the wall.

"   "

I guess you gotta get this shit on camera with a dozen witnesses to get anywhere up here. This is

I'm sorry, man.

bullshit.

Tone bent down to pick up his phone, brushing off an edge where the casing had scratched.

"   "

You know the saying, "All we got is us." I haven't seen anything up here to convince me otherwise.

A knock on the door.

Huh?

"   "

You two coming to the yacht club with the rest of us?   It's Saturday-night dinner. I'm going

"   "

"   "

over to meet with some clients. You want to come?

I glanced at Tone. He shrugged his shoulders.

Sure.

"   "

Oz and Deuce are going to take us over in their new boat.

J.D. led the way down to the docks.

I saw all that shit with my own two eyes.   Nah, nah. They covering up for someone. I'm telling you.

"

                                                                              "

Huh? Yeah.

Everything's cool, J.D.

Everything all right?

Oz and Deuce's boat was tied up in one of the yard's temporary slips, rocking gently back and forth on the swells churned up by the passing trawlers. We piled in and shoved off, Deuce jumping from the dock onto the prow, holding the mast in one hand and the bowline in the other. We crossed the bay under one of Tone's own rebuilt outboards.

Tone himself crouched on the bench in the stern. He gazed off in the distance, seemingly oblivious to the boat leaping and jumping over the chop in the bay. I slumped near the bow, exhausted.

"They covering up for someone." So some cop's going rogue? Is he cracking down? "Ready to talk?" "Where are the drugs?" Trying to shake us down? "No JSPD" something glinted Maybe he's not a cop. Maybe he's a dealer? Day after day, watching. They sat along the tops of the benches, hands in down jackets, heads down against the cold. "Blue tops, I got blue tops." "Say 'Hello,'" boarded-up Baltimore townhouses scrolled past *Shovel that snow G packs sellin'* Would a dealer even do that? The chief sat down with the review committee. "Call 'em back, and tell 'em that the investigation didn't turn up anything." "But" "Nothing more. Don't blow this." An officer leaned over his desk in some crowded work space, scrawling more notes in an open file. My name on the tab.

The prow slammed into a whitecap, jarring me back. The setting sun was beginning to orange as we reached the opposite shore, the water and sky pinkening as Oz and Deuce's boat slid into the club's western basin, gliding into an open slip amid a cluster of other cats and E-Scows that tilted and leaned with the slow pulse of the water past the bulkhead.

We passed through racks of Optimists and Lasers, canvas-hooded and triple-stacked, a fleet of Blue Jays and Lightnings, Sandbaggers and Flying Scots on old rusty trailers, on through a parking lot full of station wagons and sports cars with prep-school lacrosse and college crew stickers, along the decks to the clubhouse, a two-story whitewash of terraces and balconies, bay windows and bay views, ringed in on the inland side with hard-surfaced tennis courts in white lines and tonal greens, on the bay side by a forest of bobbing masts with fittings that chimed against their hollow aluminum surfaces in steady rhythm. The club was one of the bay's new-money clubs, mainly membered by transplants from the city to the northern bayshore. Unlike a lot of the older sailing set, J.D. didn't discriminate between the clubs, taking it upon himself to ingratiate himself with all the commodores—upbay and downbay, new money and old—if not for the business, then at least for invitations to the weekly dinners.

The buffet was set up in one of the clubhouse's downstairs galleries. Two lines of people flowed around a line of tables loaded down with foil trays of watery ziti and salad. We grabbed paper plates and got on line.

"   "

Man, I'm starving.

Buddy Woodbury was walking down the line toward us, a tall Solo cup in his hand. He passed too close to Deuce and they clipped elbows, sending his drink spilling out on Tone's shirt. A red stain spread across his chest. Buddy looked at us in disgust.

"   "

"   "

Shit. Now I have to get another drink.

He looked Tone up and down and walked away. Tone looked down at his shirt in dis-belief.

We continued along the buffet, Tone dabbing at his shirt with a fistful of napkins while we loaded food up for him. With our plates drooping with noodles and palm-size slices of bread, we passed through the French doors onto the patio. There was an empty bench at the crowd's edge that backed up to the docks.

Members and their guests stood along the rails or kicked back in wooden wing chairs, sipping light drinks out of clear cups or twiddling spare plastic ware. Older men clutched bottles of whiskey and dipped their cups into coolers full of ice while little kids in mini—madras shorts and wrinkle-collared polo shirts, ice cream stains on their hands, shirts, and faces, scampered along the porches in search of more dessert, waving tennis rackets with missing strings and Ping-Pong paddles with chewed-up ends and stripped-off padding. We watched J.D. work the crowd, shaking hands and thumping the backs of seemingly everyone he met.

I picked at the ziti on my plate. I couldn't seem to put any down, no matter how many swigs of Coke I took in between bites. My body was tensed, like it was trying to jump ahead to something, feet, legs, shoulders tightened.

" "

Every person here is white. Oh wait, hold on

" "

" "

" "

The guy Tone was watching pulled back his collar and rubbed his neck, revealing a nasty farmer's tan.

" "

"Where are the drugs?" Where are the drugs in all of this?

Nah, man, he's white, too. This is officially the whitest place in America.

" "

The epicenter of white-

" "

" "

" "

" "

ness.

The North Pole.

Buddy sauntered past us on the dock.

"   "

What? Excuse me?

"   "

"   "

Well, it's good to hear the help is having a good time.

Buddy didn't turn around. Tone walked up behind him.

"   "

A YO!   **What did you just say?**

"   "

"   "

Oh, you. What do you want?

We all craned our necks in their direction.

"   "

Buddy looked Tone up
and down. "You?"

"WE DON'T NEED ANY
OF YOUR COON MUSIC
UP HERE!"

"BULLSHIT!" Tone pitched
his phone against the wall.

This is not going to go well. Buddy got in Tone's
face. Tone took a step back. Buddy pushed
up again. Tone clenched his fists and
That's what I thought. Listen

I said, "It's good to see the help is having a good time."

"   "

[   ]

"   "

No, you listen.

A crowd began to form on the patio as diners edged toward the two men, almost tangibly straining toward a fight. Buddy pushed up in Tone's face. Tone took a step back and

"   "

Do something!

I stepped between them, wrapping my arms around Tone and pulling him down the dock toward the boat.

It's not worth it.

[   ]

Nah, son. This dude needs to get put in his place.

YEAH, THAT'S RIGHT!

Tone tried to push forward. The crowd looked on eagerly. Oz and Deuce came up behind me and helped drag Tone back to the boat, talking him down the whole way. As we stumbled toward the slip, Mike and J.D. overtook us, jumping into the catboat and starting up the engine. We cast off and shot out across the bay. It was all over in a blink.

Tone sat in the stern, sweating.

No problem, man.

Thanks for doing that, Cince. I was afraid I was gonna have to straighten him out.

"   "

"   "

"   "

"   "

You could win that fight any day, but you couldn't win that fight at the end of the day, you know?

"   "

"   "

Yeah, yeah, I know.

"   "

"   "

Tone exhaled and looked out over the bay. It was well past sundown now, the city lit up in warm yellows against the dark blue sky and tracing shaky reflections across the surface of the water. Yachts heading up- and downbay skimmed across our wake, tiny bow lights shining red or green. For all the chaos back at the club, it was calm out here, the air, the water still, the skies cloudless, the stars just beginning to emerge.

Hey, y'all, check this out! It really works!

Oz was crouched over and staring into the hold, his face illuminated a ghostly, pulsing blue. We crowded up behind him.

Look!

Oz and Deuce had cut out the floor of the hold and replaced it with some kind of thick plexiglass. The glow must have been coming from marine spotlights they had installed in the bottom of the boat. A week of wiring work, easily.

I doubled over and climbed down into the hold. In the space between my feet and the bay's bottom, a school of silvery spearing streamed by, more than I could count, all headed ocean-ward on a current that waved the bay grass northward.

We jumped off the bridge feet first,
legs crossed, eyes closed, noses pinched,
toes down to pierce the surface, cold
blackness rising up to envelop us.

                    I clapped the goggles over my
                    eyes and dove off the prow. Water
                    rushed in as my face broke the
                    waves, my eyes shutting reflexively.

This was the first time I'd ever seen beneath the surface, the first time I ever glimpsed all that might be down there in the depths. And down there, in the boat's hold, at least for a few minutes, I didn't even have to risk drowning to see it all.

animal house

(SILENT REMIX)

The moon was hanging above the inlet a week later when the Friday-evening ferry, lights ablaze, air horns sounding, chugged up to the landing. A few tidally synched bumps and scrapes against the bulkhead, a few metallic groans, and then the riders, fresh off their hour-long journey over the open ocean, tottered down the gangplank and into the parking lot, most—puffed out with overstuffed duffels and sandy canvas beach bags—heading out by foot into the city or toward the line of taxis idling just outside the lot's main gate. I was sitting with Tom in the Chevy, waiting for Frisco. I perched on the edge of my seat, my toes curled up, legs tight, tensed.

Ten days into August, the Bombers have a seven-game lead over the second-place Rays. **Soriano has

Who's this?   What's going on?

Stop worrying about this shit, man.

***   ***   ***Hey, Cincy.   It's Corey.   I'm gonna have

You sick?

"   "

to take a few days off.   Nah, I'm fine. My mom's in the hospital. I gotta go outta town

How long do you need?   Um, sure.

"
for a bit.   Probably like a week. It's not really bad.   Thanks, man.

Keep me posted.
                    The fuck is Frisco?
          Will do.

A lone straggler teetered down from the landing.

                    Frisco?
"   "

TOM! CINCY!   Just the guys I was looking for. You won't believe what happened

"   "

"   "

today!

Frisco was dressed about as casually as I'd ever seen him, wearing cargo shorts and an untucked, V-necked undershirt. He had liquor on his breath and a drained bottle of Jim Beam
in his hand.

What?   No, really, what did you do today?   Today? Just like that?
"   "
          I quit my job.   I QUIT MY JOB!

          Really?
"   "
Yeah.   I was sitting in this meeting today. All the top execs were there. And I was looking around

"   "

"   "

at these people, and their suits and their BlackBerrys and personal assistants and shit, 'n all I could think

"   "

"   "

was "I hate this shit." So, this afternoon, I served notice, they flipped out, gave me two weeks' pay, and

Just like that? Gone?

What are you going to

escorted me straight down the elevator.   Just like that.

What about your whole "Jeff, Ad Professional"

do now?

Get hammered and hit the beach. What else?

thing?
"   "

All bullshit. That person talking, I barely recognize him. Just forget everything you've heard

"   "
"   "

from me up to this point.

Frisco stumbled against the side of the car.

You drink all of that?   Why
"   "

Nah, not even half. Snagged it from the bar on the ferry after a few beers.

don't you sit down in the car?
"   "

Nah, I'm not drunk, honestly. I'm a hundred percent there.

Frisco half-fell, half-sat down on the curb. He settled in and pulled a Camel out of his pocket. Flick flick. One long, slow drag. He leaned back and blew smoke out of his nose. The black water of the inlet rippled behind him like vinyl spinning; the moon traced a ribbed band of white light across its surface.

Where's your stuff?   Did you just come with that bag?

"   "

          What stuff?   Wha oh, I musta left it on the ferry.

He hauled himself off the curb and stumbled back toward the bulkhead.

"   "

                              Wow, he's gone.

Just be a minute.

We watched Frisco ramble around the ferry, looking under the empty benches and opening up footlockers. The ferry was rocking left to right in the northerly wind, sending him caroming across the deck.

"   "

Oh shit   look at him

Frisco returned, glassy-eyed and slurring.

No bag?   You sure you're all right?

"   "

          Nah. Threw it overboard off Sandy Hook. I think. Who cares.   Yeah.

                              You're completely wasted.

"   "

I just see everything very clear now, very clear.   I might be wasted, but I'm

"   "

"   "

being honest. I've been letting other people tell me what to do for toooo long. Haven't been honest with

"   "

"   "

myself. You're not honest with yourself, people just wrap you around their finger. No more for me. I'm

"   "

"   "

being totally honest now.

Frisco wavered on his feet. I grabbed him by the arm and ushered him into the backseat.

"   "

First thing we're

So, let's get back to my place. It's a party there. You're gonna party with me, right?

"   "

gonna do is put you to bed.   **Calm down.**

I really appreciate it. You guys are some good guys.

We rumbled out of the parking lot and headed south.

Yeah.

"   "

No, really. Most people don't give a FUCK about other people, you know?   I'm serious, man, I'm

By what?

"   "

serious. You're good men, I just don't want to see you get hurt.   These women. She broke my

Who?   Vera?

Are you talking about Vera? Aimi?

heart, man, I tell you that?   Can't trust her.   Me?

"   "

"   "

Just trying to warn you about these women, that's all.

The car lurched forward. Frisco slumped sideways, disappearing behind the headrests.

"   "

"   "

What's in this bag, Tom?

Frisco held up a plastic Guitar Center bag.

"   "

What? That?   Just some new picks and shit.   I bought a lot of
                                    Seems kinda heavy for picks.

"   "

them. I got a lot of playing to do.
"   "

The bag dropped to the floor with a dull bump.

Hey, Frisco!
"   "

"   "

Frisco was slumped against the door, asleep. A thin line of drool hung cobwebby from the corner of his mouth.

Was Frisco seeing Vera?
          I have no idea what Frisco does when he's not directly in front of me.

You don't know anything? Aimi hasn't said anything?

I just assumed he worked all the time. What

He showed up at the ferry, wasted, and started talking about how she "broke

makes you think that?

his heart" and how he wanted to make sure we didn't get hurt. No.

Did he say that *she* was her?

He was drunk, though.

So maybe he was just talking about women in general. **He probably**

"   "

had no idea what he was talking about. I remember one night in college he grabbed me by

"   "

the face and said, "Tommy, you're a wonderful man. I hope you don't get caught in the

"   "

snares of the world." Then he started talking about how he got picked on in kindergarten.

I'm trying to put two

We ripped him for that one for months. You got anything else, Sherlock?

and two together. Well, when I first met him, he said that he knew Aimi as a

Try another four.

"friend of a friend." She's friends with Vera so

Aimi's friends with everyone in town. He could

Why don't you ask Aimi?

have met her a hundred different ways. **I don't think she's the best**

source of info right now. I had to break it off with her.   **It's just how it goes: Guy**

"   "

meets girl. Girl and guy sleep together. And then they keep sleeping together or they leave

That's it?

each other and find other people. Isn't that always the story?   **Yup, that's it.**

The orderly grid of the center city gradually gave way to the south side's sandy meandering lanes, half-asphalted roads that traced tangled paths through the city's old servant quarters, where the help and hired hands for the city's hotels used to retire after early mornings and late nights scrubbing, cooking, and tending. A giant neon lobster flashed red and dark, red and dark above the road, bright enough to bathe houses for a block in a rosy glow. Traffic slowed to a crawl, filing down to a single lane as it pushed deeper into the neighborhood.

"   "

Ten thirty.   **We're like blocks away from your place.**

What time is it?   Just park the car here.   Not

You can barely walk.

"   "

gonna be able to get a space any closer this time of night.   Don't worry about me,

"   "

"   "

mannnnn. I'm a fucking champ!

Frisco unlatched the door and stumbled out onto the shoulder.

Tom slid the Chevy alongside a pile of broken storm fencing at the top of a street that led down through a motor-home court. We followed Frisco as he stumbled homeward, guided by the music pulsing through the jumbles of bungalows and rickety Cape Cods that spilled like sugar cubes across the sands. We loped along pitted streets that wound through haphazard lots overflowing with their own microcosms of disorder: empty plastic pools, tangled piles of bikes, welters of rusted beach chairs, shattered bottles and crushed cans, nests of tar-streaked hoses. Behind the sunrooms and porches that crowded the street, dishes clattered, people stirred. Firecrackers exploded above the rooflines as packs of children ran along the lanes and alleys. There seemed to be more people than space. More people than air, even out under the stars. It was getting louder as we walked. Pounding from blocks away . . . smudgy crowd sounds at a block, with the deepening curb- and double-parking a dead giveaway . . . bottles, doors, laughter, yelling, clinking, rattling, slamming.

Frisco took a knee on a rounded mound of cement that marked off a storm drain, then fell into a seated position, hands dangling between his parted legs, head hanging below his shoulders.

                                                                                        You look

C'mon, we're almost at your place.

                                    I'm just gonna sit here and get my bearings, Tommy.

like you're about to lose it.

                                                                            You sure?

                        I'm fine, I'm fine. Go, go on to the party. I'll catch up.

"   "

"   "

I have spoken! Away with you!

Frisco flourished his right arm, then leaned back, hands at his sides, eyes to the sky.

"   "

Well, you heard the man.

"   "

We left Frisco by the drain side to a rising chorus of dog barks. His summer share was a half block on, a rickety two-story cedar-shake bungalow with a sagging porch halfway up a sun-grayed macadam lane that was dusted with white sand like three hours deep into a snowstorm. The house, one in a line of saggy Cape Cods, seemed half-buried, sitting higher on its west side than on the ocean side, the whole street on unsteady ground. There were no streetlights down here, the only glow coming from the moon overhead.

We elbowed our way across the gravel-covered front yard toward a warped porch overflow-ing with partygoers. A cloud of weed smoke wafted by from the far side of the front yard. The house's storm door hung ajar, its corroded hinges squeaking in time with a dull bass pulse from inside. Vera's face, reflected in the door's yellowed glass, wobbled over Aimi's shoulder.

What he doesn't know can't hurt him, right?

"   "

Aimi's eyes widened, her head jutted forward, her chin tilted toward us. Tom and I kept walking, approaching the door now, both of us glancing out of the corners of our eyes to see if they were still watching. Nothing. We stepped inside the house.

My guns stay nickel-plated / Rhymes forever top-rated / From cradle 'til the

A dining room without a table opened off to the left, a living room to the right, both rooms packed with people, paired off or in groups of four or five, leaning close to each other, their faces, shoulders, arms, and hands moving in exaggerated gestures as if to cut through the noise coming from the stereo, whose volume meter jumped into the red with each bass hit, the treble edging up through the high yellows, all of its pieces—CD carousel, equalizer, speakers, sub-woofers, antenna—scattered across the floor in front of a blocked-up chimney, sound ricochet-ing off the cracked and dirty linoleum floor. A raggedy couch sagged at the far end of the room. A few small seascapes in cheap frames hung crookedly off the walls.

"   "

Now I really need a drink.

We pushed through the crowd to a folding table littered with half-empty bottles and a sleeve of Solo cups. Tom palmed an amber-colored fifth of something and poured out two cups' worth.

"   "

I can't get drunk enough for this kinda shit, man.

Tom's eyes widened.

What?

Heads up, dude.

Tom nodded over his drink toward the front door. Vera stepped through, followed by Aimi. Her eyes met mine, then darted away.

"   "

We need to find some new women, brother. You down to prowl a little tonight?

I glanced around the room.

I'm not ready to give up on her.

"Hi, I'm" *and it starts all over again.*

You're a stronger man than me.

"   "

Let's get outta this room.

We worked around the edge of the room and back into the foyer, sweating already, taking a few deep breaths in the cooler air by the door. Vera was inching down the stairs, sidestepping around the clusters of people that leaned against the banisters and sat on the steps. Her eyes locked on mine.

I'm good.

You want a wingman on this?　　　　**I'm going thataway.**

Tom leaned into the front door and disappeared out onto the porch.
Vera clasped my wrist.

I'm good. How　　　　　　　　How

Hey. How are you?　　　　I can't hear you!　　Let's go out back.

We tightroped down a wood-paneled hall lined with upended mattresses—summertime
beds for the renters who probably slept there three or four to a room. Through the kitchen's mess
of cups and empty bottles to one of the back bedrooms, where another four mattresses littered
the floor, each separated from the others by clotheslines that ran the length of the space.

I leaned up against the threshold.

So, how you been?

That's a little better, I guess.

She looked into the bedroom. I followed her eyes. The last bed sheet in the line billowed toward us, puffed out by a breeze blowing through the open window. On the mattress beyond,
two sets of feet lay tangled. Vera pulled the bedroom door shut.

"   "

"Seeing someone else."

"Waiting for you."

"Getting tired of you."

I've been pretty busy. I've started

There you are!

Vera narrowed her eyes and turned toward Aimi.

Vera looked once at Aimi, once at me.

Hey, Aimi.

We turned across the bridge's deck, so smooth, so natural, perfectly timed, perfectly in sync.

She bit her lip and looked down. She smiled like it meant nothing.   *"I don't want"*

The tip flared amid wreathes of smoke. "Comes and goes." She scampered back.

Oh, hey

I thought   What's up, Cincy?   I thought we were going?

Aimi gestured to her watch. Vera looked back at me.

WHAT IS SHE DOING?!

She dropped my hand and stepped back. "Look, maybe I should go" Go, take her.

She pulsed dark, light, dark, light with the projector's flicker. Here one moment, gone

"   "

Don't make us late again.

Vera kneaded my hand in hers. Our eyes met. I held her hand more tightly.

"   "

I think I'd rather stay.

And make me go back alone?

Vera looked at me again, shrugged, and moved away. My hand trailed in hers. She dropped it. Aimi led her back up the hall.

I started up after them.

"   "

no no no

"Maybe she's a tease." She bit her lip and looked down. She placed her hand on his elbow. "Maybe I should go" Go.

She bent inward, collapsed in upon herself. Refocused again, shaking, then exploded.

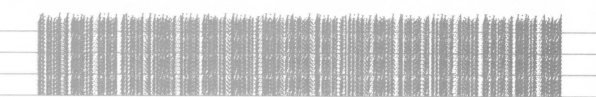

They were already halfway down the hallway.

VERA! VERA!

She reappeared at the center of it all, still, shining, luminous. I held her hand more tightly.

Give it up, give it up, give it up.

"I'm not a mystery." "I'll keep you on your toes."

She lingered behind Aimi. I pushed toward her.
My hand lighted on her wrist.

Vera.

Say it.   That I want her.   But she hesitated.

What?   Do I?

No way. She would have stayed if she wanted me.   But she left.   But I

I'll see you soon. Don't worry.

She turned. A smile lit across her face.

COPS!

The party exploded. Cans, bottles, plates dropped as people scrambled out of the house, doors and windows equally fair for exits. I stumbled backward as several people levered themselves off my shoulders in the rush for the front door. Red and blue flashing lights swept through the front windows.

"   "

"Plenty of time for them to find something on you, you know what I'm sayin'?" MOVE!

I grabbed Vera and ran for it. We tore out the back door and rocketed across the yard. Our strides shortened as we neared the rear fence. I kicked the gate open and we were clear into the neighboring lot. Some unexpected sand gave way underfoot. We leaned forward for more trac‑ tion, windmilling to get back up to running pace. A hard corner, then up a side alley. Trash cans fell clattering behind us. Porch lights flickered on, tracing our way from house to house as we sped down the block.

A patrol car, lights on, windows lowered, turned onto the lane. We dove behind a bank of double‑parked cars. We were both breathing heavily, our chests rising and falling in rhythm as we hugged the sand, our eyes on the space between the underbellies of the cars and the road, light, then dark, then light again, dark, then light to last.

I think it's safe.

"   "

I staggered up. She pulled me down again, her two hands on my shoulders, her eyes look‑ ing into mine.

"   "

Cincy, what do you think of me?

My mind raced.

"   "

oooooekwuhfnakeuwhfalksduhaelsdkfasdkjfhlhuaweehuealekwuhflakeuwhfalksduhalsdkf   I want you.

oooooolkwuhflnkluwhfalksduhalsdkfasivndkjfhlhuawlIhuIalIkwuhflakIuwhfalksduhalsdkf   Do you want me?

oooooookwuhfmakouwhfalksduhalsdkfasdkjfhlhuawoohuoalokwuhflakouwhfalksduhalsdkf   I don't want to be wrong.

oooooykwuhfpakyuwhfalksduhalsdkfasdkjfhlhuawyyhuyalykwuhflakyuwhfalksduhalsdkf   Tell me what you want.

ooooowuhfxapeuwhfalksdsdkfasdkjfhlhuawvevehuvealvekwuhflakveuwhfalksduhalsdkf   Let me go.

oooolakveuwhfalkxduhalsdkfasdkjfhlhuawvevehuvealvekwuhflakveuwhfalksduhalsdkf   I want you so badly.

"   "

She dropped her hands.

"   "

I see.

Then she stood up and walked away. She was gone. She didn't even stop to wipe the sand off her skin.

I slumped down against the cool metal of the car's side, spent.

The wick curled over, blackened, burnt. The smoke wafted through my fingers. Outside, the snow was already over the curbs.

Vera.

Heart sunk, I lay on the ground until the motion-sensored lights darkened again.

I gotta

I gotta

I gotta get out of here.

I tried dialing Tom.

Nothing. My watch showed 1:00. I straightened up and headed northward, picking along the side lanes, holding close to the cars on the shoulder, panning up and down each cross street before jogging to the opposite side. My skin cooled slowly, the sweat from the party and the pursuit wicking off my skin in the night air. By the time I reached the Chevy, I was shivering, my shirt clinging damply to my chest and shoulders.

Tom was sitting on the hood of the car, his face red with or without the glare from the lobster sign. The left leg of his jeans was torn.

What's   With Vera   for a little.   Gone.

angry fence. Where've you been?   **Where's she now?**

Two

Probably better that way. How many fingers am I holding up?

Tom counted each finger with his left hand.

"   "

You're in better shape than me. I thought it was three.

He tossed me the keys.

"   "

You gotta drive back, man.

Inside the car, the seat belt wouldn't pull out. I gave it another tug.

What's up with this?
                         It's jammed or something. Don't worry about it. It's just a couple of

"   "

minutes.

We drove north, back onto the Boulevard, the road empty now this late at night, only a few stray cars parked along the median, the houses all blackened.

"   "

"What do you think of me?" She brushed a loose strand of hair from her face and
Smooth sailing.

WOOP WOOP

A city police cruiser sat in the rearview, lights flashing.

I don't know. Maybe he's trying to get past?

WHAT?   Headlights are on.   My seat belt?

What's up?

I pulled over to the side of the road. The cruiser did the same. Tom sat up straight in his seat
as the cruiser's floodlight filled the car.

"   "

They're probably tryna hit quota.

The officer stepped out of the cruiser and ambled toward the Chevy. He motioned for me
to roll down my window, then flicked on a long-stemmed flashlight and shone it into the car,
sweeping its beam across the floor, the dash, our laps.

I'm sorry officer, I

                                                                    There
"   "

You know why I pulled you over?   You didn't stop at that sign back there.

            Which one?   I'm sorry, but
were four in a row.   Something's not right here. The officer leaned toward his radio.
"   "

                    The one back there.   License and registration, please.

"   "

The suspect is male, twenty to twenty-nine,
"   "

                    Thank you.

The officer turned back to his cruiser. He glanced over his shoulder several times as he walked, his hand floating over his holster. I sat with my hands on the wheel. Tom looked out the passenger's-side window.

"   "

End this. Just throw the cuffs on, lock me up, and finish me off. Stop playing games with me.
Don't sweat it. You're just going to get a seat-belt ticket or some other sort of bullshit.

Garbled voices leaked out of a walkie-talkie in the cruiser.

"   "

"Where are the drugs?" "Are you sure?" "I'm sure." "Well, we all have our beliefs."
COPS! *They slammed the dealer against the hood of the cruiser.*

"What do you think of me?" We ran and ran. All because of the cops. She was right there for me.

"   "

******** **** ****** ***** ** ****** *** *****_male_ ***

The cruiser's flashers continued to play red-purple-blue. In the rearview, I could see the officer looking up periodically from his dash-mounted laptop, as if he were afraid we were going to drive off.

"   "

"Two of my boys got hemmed up." "Shit's goin' down everywhere." We ran and ran and ran. Jumped the fence. Hit the alley.
Just get on with it, man. C'mon.

"   "

I ran. "Fuck it." I stumbled out onto the shoulder, hands up, drenched in the cruiser's spotlight. I screamed at the officer. "Here I am! Come and get me!" Tom yelled, "What are you doing?! Stop!" I took another step toward the cruiser. The officer opened his door and reached for his holster. "What are you waiting for!"

"   "

I reached for the door handle.

"   "

The fuck are you doing, man?! Are you *crazy?*

Tom batted my hand off the handle.

I just want answers.

                    All you're gonna do is get us shot!

I reached for the handle again.

"   "

The officer reached for his holster. A flame jumped from the tip of his gun.

I swear to God, Cincy.

I let my hand fall back into my lap.

"   "

Don't. Move.

********   *That's not the guy we're lookin' for.*****   ******   ****** **   ***

The officer hauled himself out of the cruiser and returned to the car. He had abandoned his flashlight. His hand was on his hip holster.

"   "

Shit shit shit

Get this over with.

"   "

I'm gonna let you go this time. Just make sure you drive safer the next time you come through.

Before I could even say, "Thank you, officer," he tossed my license back into the car and walked away. The cruiser revved up behind us and leaped off the shoulder, screaming up 35, siren dopplering off into the night.

"   "

That's not the guy.

Damnit.

What's the rush?

Star of the Show

The sun had barely cleared the eastern horizon the next morning when the gulls swooped across the clam shack's parking lot. A whole flock circled around an unfortunate blueclaw that had fallen out of the back of a crabber's truck, giant gulls, wings brown and mottled like they were carved out of wood, hammering at the crab's brown crackerlike shell while it waved its single remaining claw in halfhearted defense, to no avail. The gulls clouded around two black vans that were parked in the long shadow cast by the shack.

Mismemories of the night before rattled around as I trudged into work, as I texted her: Meet me at the inlet Thurs. nite? 7?

She dropped her hands. "I see." She walked away.

I jumped up and grabbed her. "I

I was walking down the hallway in the main building when I felt cold air streaming from beneath the break room door.

The AC is on already?

I opened the door. Mike was huddled on the far end of the sofa, his knees drawn up to his chest, his forehead resting on his knees.

What're you doing in so early?

"   "

He looked up. A thin film of sweat glistened on his forehead; his hair was matted. He ran
a hand across his face. His eyes were red, cracked, and cratered.

What happened?

My parents are gonna kill me.   They're gonna kill me. I'm gonna go home, and

"   "

they're gonna take one look at me, and they're gonna kill me. On my front lawn, in front of the

What did you do?

neighbors, they're gonna kill me.   I didn't come home last night, I didn't call

                                   Dude, what   For what?

them   Well, I couldn't call them   come home.   I got arrested last night.

Weed?

        No, not even for weed! Me and some of my friends were out at Jimmy Byrnes's last night.

How'd you even get in?   So you were at Byrnes's, and?

                Fake ID.   And I ran into Corey.

Oz, Deuce, and Tone strolled into the room, trailed by the scent of coffee and doughnuts.

I thought he left town.

                Really? That's weird. Anyway, we're talking and then he's like "I gotta take
What's popping?
Yo.
What it is?

Ssh

a piss."   So he disappears for a few minutes and we're all like drinking or

"   "

What's going on?

"   "

"   "

whatever and then all of a sudden Corey comes falling outta the bathroom with another dude on

"   "

"   "

"   "

"   "

top of him and they're fighting! And the guy goes to punch Corey so I   Yeah.

"   "

You jumped in?!

"   "

So the cops arrested you, huh?

I HAD to. The guy had him pinned against the floor like

Oh SHIT!

MY BOY!

"   "

And you got charged?

They arrested *all* of us.   Disorderly conduct. I think I got off easy because I

"   "

"   "

"   "

How much was bail?

didn't actually land any punches.   Don't laugh, guys, this is *serious.*   Noth-

"   "

"   "

"   "

"   "

ing, my brother knows the desk sergeant. But still I'm gonna have to go to court.

"   "

Where's Corey

"   "

"   "

They didn't catch him. A cop tried to grab him, but Corey hit him and ran for it.

But it's just

at?

"   "

Coke?

I think he was dealing. They found coke on the other guy.

fighting! Why would he run?   wow

wooo

"   "

"   "

The cops were yelling at him like, "Where'd you get it?" And he said he bought it off Corey.

Corey?

ooooow   Noooo

"   "

Oh, great.

"Shit, Corey, how'd you get so damn popular?"

When they were taking me out to the cop car, I saw them going through Corey's car with dogs.

"   "

oo way.

"   "

Maybe he just thought

"   "

"   "

"   "

That's probably why that cop was following us! He thinks we're in with Corey!

we had info? Or that we could get info for him?

"   "

"   "

"   "

Nah, nah. I know exactly what he was thinking.

Tone reached for the doorknob. The clock hit eight. Just then, the morning erupted with the sound of tumbling gravel and police sirens. I ran out to the front lobby. A dozen cars rumbled through the front gate, converging on the yard in a welter of skidding tires and squealing brakes. Out beyond the lobby's plate-glass window, a cloud of dust wreathed around a fleet of black vans and blue-paneled police cruisers. Lights flashed in blue-red quasars. Forms materialized from the dust clouds: blue-shirted police officers in bulletproof vests with pistols and rifles pointed at the office. Smaller teams scrambled in the distance behind the main phalanx, fanning out across the lot, low to the ground with guns drawn. Dog barks rattled out of the rear of one of the vans.

Everyone out of the building. Hands up! Hands up!

Get up here! These guys aren't playing around.

"

Oh SHIT!

What's going on out there, Cince?

"   "

      We stepped out into the lot, our hands above our heads. Officers rushed in from either side. Hands frantically patted up and down our bodies.

CLEAN!

Don't move!

      Half the phalanx broke ranks and scrambled around us into the lobby. They fanned out into the shop and down the hallway. In the distance, two police cruisers barricaded the entrance to the yard; bayward, a small flotilla of State Police Whalers cordoned off the docks.

CLEAR!

      The lead officer holstered his gun.

All right, guys. Keep your hands up. Back in the building.

      We about-faced and shuffled back into the lobby.

In there.

      Two officers took up positions in the hallway on either side of the office door.

Don't move.

Another two posted themselves inside the room, hands on their sidearms. J.D. was already seated on the couch, massaging his temples with a confused look on his face.

Good morning, everyone. Anyone have any idea what this is about?

QUIET!

No one dared move; no one dared look at one another. What else was there to do but think?

There wasn't much to go on. Just fragments of Corey rushing back and forth from the boats, stumbling out of the lot with his paper bags. After a summer of working with him, I knew even less about him than I did when we started.

Two more knocks.

I got a few more for you.

The cop from the street.

The undercover stood stock-still. The document he was holding in his right hand dropped to the floor.

"   "

How'd   Cuff this guy, get him out front!

The guards jerked my arms behind my back and tightened a pair of plastic cuffs around my wrists. One guard stayed behind with the rest of the group while the other prodded me outside. The undercover officer slammed his open palm against the threshold and stalked out behind us. As we walked down the hall toward the front entrance, he unholstered his walkie-talkie and started yelling at whoever was on the other end.

"   "

xx   xx   xx   xx   xx   xx   xx   xx   xx   xx   xx   xx

Guess who I found out here?   Montvale! How's fuckin' Montvale walkin' around

****   **Wh***

                                                                    I don't know

xx   xx   xx   xx   xx   xx   xx   xx   xx   xx   xx   xx

the yard without guards!? I'll ask you one more time: where're the drugs at?

what you're talking about.

xx   xx   xx   xx   xx   xx   xx   xx   xx   xx

Game's up, buddy. The only question now is whether you're going

                                    I don't know anything about drugs.

xx   xx   xx   xx   xx   xx   xx   xx   xx   xx

down hard or soft. Where are the drugs?   **Enough of this**

"   "

xx

bullshit.

By now, we were outside the front entrance to the main building, surrounded by a semicircle of police and drooling German shepherds. The undercover opened the trunk of his car and tossed a package down at my feet.

"   "

xx   xx   xx   xx   xx   xx

One brick, that's twenty years right there. Wanna up the ante?

He tossed another package at my feet.

I'm not Montvale!

This isn't happening. This isn't happening. This isn't happening.

"Where are the drugs?"

I ran. Until my lungs screamed,
until my legs gave out. I didn't
hear the bullets, didn't feel
the first one until it passed
through me. Surprise.

He thinks I'm Corey?

XX XX XX XX XX XX XX XX

I'm not too good at math. What's twenty times two, Montvale?

A State Police cruiser pulled into the lot. All heads swung around to watch as Corey, cuffed, head bowed, was ushered out of the backseat by a pair of state troopers.

"   "

XX XX XX XX XX XX XX XX XX XX XX

Who's this?

Montvale. We caught him driving a stolen on the Turnpike near Haddonfield. Didn't you

"   "

XX   XX

"   "

get the relay?

They placed Corey next to me. A day's worth of whiskers covered his cheeks. His sunglasses were gone; his eyes were bloodshot. The undercover's eyes darted from Corey to me and back again.

xx   xx   xx   xx   xx   xx   xx   xx   xx   xx   xx   xx   xx

If that's Montvale, who the fuck is this clown?   **Is he in on this?**

That's the yard manager, Stiles.

"   "

"   "

xx   xx   xx   xx   xx   xx   xx   xx   xx   xx   xx   xx   xx   xx

They look alike, don't they?

Chill, Desk Duty. He's clean.   I guess you could say that.

                                    You gotta do
"   "

"   "

xx   xx   xx   xx   xx   xx   xx   xx   xx   xx   xx   xx   xx   xx
"   "

Montvale said he'd cooperate and
your homework, Heisler. Stiles is a witness at best in all this.
"   "

"   "

xx   xx   xx   xx   xx   xx   xx   xx   xx   xx   xx   xx

So what are you waiting for? Go get the drugs.
show us the stash. Right?
\\   //

Whatever you want.

"   "

xx   xx   xx

You and you. Keep an eye on this one. I've got some other things to handle.
"   "
\\   //
"   "

The undercover walked back inside the main building, disappearing down the hallway. I slumped against the tire of one of the patrol cars.

I'm not Montvale! The brick landed at my feet. *"Where are the drugs?" "I don't know!" "He could be your cousin." "Montvale" "Hey, man, you got"* **I'm not Montvale!** *This isn't happening. This isn't happening.*

Through the entrance to the supply shop, I could see the undercover speaking with Tone. It seemed sedate enough until the undercover shoved him for the first time. Tone reeled back, slamming into the glass supply case. As he fell to the floor, the undercover drew closer to him.

"   "

He shoved me to the sidewalk. "I think someone searched this place." He watched from the lot outside the crab shack.

"Of course not! The police ain't never let the facts get in the way of a collar."

This stops now.

The guards' walkie-talkies sputtered out static. They raced off across the yard without so much as a second look at me. I stumbled up and grabbed the front door. The undercover had Tone by the neck up against the display case.

First you mistake me for someone else, now you're trying to intimidate a

WHAT DO YOU KNOW!

"   "

witness?   I'm just gonna ask you to smile for the camera.

And *what* are you going to do about it?

"   "

I pointed over the undercover's shoulder. The red light on the security camera blinked back. The undercover's face fell. He pulled away from Tone and yelled for the guards.

You have something you want to tell the judge, "Desk Duty"?

Get him back there!

"   "

As the guards led us back to the break room, the undercover kicked the front door open and trooped off toward the warehouse. I couldn't help but smile a little.

"   "

"You never know when it might come in handy."

■   ■   ■

The sounds of the agents and officers ripping through the boatyard continued well into the morning, until the clatter of paint cans and halyards falling from the shelves of the store drowned out the churn of the air conditioner.

Two knocks sounded on the door. One of the officers smirked and tilted his hat. And then we were alone.

The undercover's document still lay on the floor.

"   "

"I gotta take a few days off." "I gotta catch a train." "How'd you get so popular?" His check lay in the drawer.

"   "

Check this shit out.

"   "

"   "

"   "

Deuce pitched the document to me.

An affidavit for a warrant to search the yard. A DEA agent wrote it up.

What does it say?

"   "

"   "

"   "

What is it?

A lot.

"   "

"   "

"   "

Read it out.

"   "

I sat down on the desk and started skimming the affidavit.

Um, the DEA thought "significant" amounts of drugs were being trafficked through the yard.

Some buyers snitched on Corey and the feds started watching the yard. It says

they saw Corey moving coolers off boats with Maryland tags and then moving them later onto boats out

in the yard. The night they tried to arrest him, they found drugs he'd promised to sell in his car.

Damn   Coke, heroin, PCP.

"   "

His face was hidden beneath a mop of curly hair and blocky black wraparound shades.

"*I think he's a narc.*"   *The outside door to the locker room hung ajar.*

That piece of shit. How could he do that to us?

Doesn't surprise me at all. Something always

"   "

"   "

"   "

How could we miss all of this?

"*Where are the drugs!*"

He slammed me against the wall. "*That same dude from the lot!*"

"   "

seemed off about that guy.

He was slick with it. It's not like he did

"   "

"   "

"   "

"   "

"   "

anything crazy or anything like that. He just played his part, early in, early out.

Yeah, I just

"   "

"   "

"*Cince!*" "*Cince!*" *The chain-link bent in, a swatch of white T-shirt caught on a jag of fencing.*

He was moving *ki*'s through here, man. *Ki-los*. Fuck.

"   "

thought he was a really hard worker.

"   "

Calm

"

C'mon, J.D.! You know how this is gonna work. Even if they say we're innocent,

"

"

"

down, Tone.

"

they're gonna want us to go in to talk to the prosecutors. And then testify at trial. And the whole

"

"

"

"

"

time, they're gonna say, "Oh, you're just a witness." And while you're in that office and the court-

"

"

"

"

"

house and shit, there's gonna be some other investigators trying to see if they can tie you in to this

"

"

"

"

"   "

shit. I trust these feds about as far as I can throw them.   **You know damn**

"   "

"   "

"   "

That may be the case.

Aren't you worried at all?

well that's the case!   **But?**

"   "

"   "

"   "

Yes, but.   All we can do is stick to our story

"   "

You ever stare fed time in the eye?   So, how're you gonna play it

"   "

"   "

"   "

and ride this out until it ends.   No.

"   "

like there isn't anything to worry about?

"   "

"   "

"   "

Because, the fact of the matter is, we don't have any

"   "

"   "

"   "

"   "

"   "

other choice. I *will* say one thing with certainty, though.

       J.D. opened the door out onto the hallway. A file cabinet lay on its side, its innards spilt across the floor.

"   "

"   "

"   "

"   "

"   "

I'm pretty sure our story will hold up.   If you guys need to take the rest of the day off, you

"   "

"   "

"   "

"   "

"   "

can head home. I'm going to start cleaning up.

       J.D. walked out of the lounge, leaving the rest of us behind. I looked around at the guys. Something clattered in the lobby.

So what do we do? Deuce?   Oz?   Mike?   Tone?

"   "

       Let's help J.D.

       I'm down.

       Sure.

Tone ran a hand down his face.

"   "

I'm too tired to run anymore. So, yeah, I guess I'm down.

"   "

"   "

"   "

When we reached the lobby, J.D. was standing amid the mess, rubbing his temples again. The investigators had gone through everything: Money from the register and merchandise from the shelves were scattered across the floor; in the yard beyond, the shrink-wrap had been sliced crudely from the yachts; it hung in jagged strips of white and blue that twisted in the breeze. Sail bags had been rifled through. Sails lay plastered around the corners of the out-buildings. Life jackets, coils of rope, canned foods, hand pumps, power tools sat in heaps on the gravel. Even the tops of the in-ground fuel tanks had been unscrewed and plumbed. The locks on all the lockers were clipped. Paperwork fluttered and tumbled across the parking lot.

The text alert on my phone sounded: Sure. C u on Th.—V.

"   "

Phone calls later. Can you hand me that broom?

inlet/outlet

I waited for Vera atop the railing that ran along the south side of the inlet. It was hard to sit up; I was tired from the fifth straight day of cleaning up the yard: endless stacks of paper to reorganize and put back in drawers, new supplies to order to replace the items that had been damaged, long letters to write to customers to explain why their boats had been ransacked. Sorting through old invoices like I sorted through the feelings of relief and dread that bubbled up after the initial shock of the incident wore off, the weird attenuated nervous rush of coming so close to a disaster only to swerve clear of it at the last possible moment, mixed with the easing of some sort of inner tension when Corey got collared, taking my place in the center of whatever story I thought I had been the star of, the randomness, the stops, the searches, the endless watching, neatly described in a document prepared by someone else's hand.

Tired, too, from our first meeting with the prosecutors: the whole crew from the lot packed onto a rickety old commuter train to Newark, off for an endless day spent fifteen stories above the city, sitting in an undecorated conference room with buzzing fluorescent lights and dull green carpets, staring out across the brownstones, brown fields, and wetlands to the Empire State Building beyond, each of us waiting to get called to another conference room farther down the hall, where the prosecutors and their investigators worked slowly through each of our stories, bit by bit, backtracking, questioning and requestioning—What did you know?

What did you see? Forget what you thought, just give us the details. Realizing after an hour of this—ping-ponging back and forth across the table as I took questions from all sides, as they probed and refined and pushed, sleeves rolled up, fingers nervously tapping pens—I was playing a different game than the one that I had been playing in my head: they didn't want stories, they wanted facts; they didn't want ideas, they wanted events. An hour deep, knowing that, as I told all these things to them, they'd take bits of my story and mix it with bits of everyone else's, and go to trial with it.

So we talked, and the prosecutors got a case. What did we get out of all of this? Realizing that the answer, when it came, wasn't really an answer, something I was still trying to swing my head around to: The story I had been waiting a summer for the police to tell me had a beginning, and a middle, but no end; it named us, caught us up in it, but one man's affidavit wasn't going to resolve it. I wasn't a subject, anymore, it seemed; not an object either. I was free of the undercover trailing me, but not of the consequences of it. The only answer I really had was the possibility that someday, maybe a year from now, maybe two years, maybe never, I might have the chance to go to a courtroom, sit in the witness stand, and talk. And that the jurors, just some other people—after they listened to everything I said, and listened to my friends, and listened to who knows how many other people who didn't know us, who might not have even been there, and after they retired to their room and took in the truths and lies, the coincidences, consistencies, and contradictions—would decide for themselves what the end was going to be. And maybe it would turn out, when all was said and done, that the conspiracy wasn't all in one investigator's head, that we'd been caught up in something, someone else's scheme.

It was cold comfort, a cloud of ambiguity that hung more thickly than the fog creeping across the inlet. A few days into it, who knows how many days, months, and years until I was out of it.

It was getting colder outside.

All of this was enough to distract me from Vera until I left the yard for the evening, hair still wet from the locker room, a vague hope still struggling somewhere in me as I meandered along the bayfront to the inlet promenade.

She smiled, rising from her seat on the inlet bench. "I feel the same way."

Evenings along the inlet were like mornings elsewhere in the city. As the streetlamps sput-tered on, local fishermen roused themselves from their makeshift beds in their conversion vans and pickups to prepare for the night ahead, double- and triple-checking their departure times, shuffling lures and jigs around their equipment boxes, peeling double-thick sweatshirts and long pants off backseats or roofs where they hung to dry, testing rod belts and harnesses with short tugs. Prep work done, they ambled along the promenade, massaging their temples and nibbling on sandwiches wrapped in white deli paper. Here and there, straggling beachgoers returned to their cars. Doors slammed, trunks opened and closed.

Sure. C u on Th.—V.

An elderly fisherman crouched in the space between his car and the next. At his feet a stand-up rod, at its base a spool of tangled line. He turned the line over in his fingers; its filament glinted first white, then blue in the fading light. Sighing, he reached into his pocket and pulled out a knife; a quick cut severed the tangle from the rest of the line. He threaded fresh line through the rod's eyelets and tied on a sinker.

The inlet clock showed seven. Some of the fishermen, wearing jackets with pictures of swordfish or crabs on the back, meandered down to the docks to catch the night's cruises; oth-ers shouldered their rods and trudged toward the inlet jetty, a few flashlights and headlamps marking out their progress as their metal cleats scraped along the blacktop. Gulls picked at strings of shattered mussels and dark green seaweed that trailed across the pavement before swooping back to their roosts on the tops of the streetlights, heads into the breeze to keep their feathers flat to their bodies.

I spun around and let my feet dangle over the inlet. Ships' horns blasted in the basin around the bend. Beneath me, mingling ocean and bay water slapped against the concrete bulkhead. Mid-inlet, a green channel marker flickered in the whipping ocean fog. Seven thirty. No Vera.

"   "

Maybe she got held up at home.

Maybe she's on her way now.

The night's first trawler took shape to the west. The ship's mates scrambled across the deck, coiling loose lines into neat spirals and hosing down the detritus from the day's first trip. The ship's horn sounded again, echoed by a blast of the foghorn on top of the National Guard tower. The mid-inlet channel marker disappeared behind the trawler's blue-and-white prow.

"   "

Maybe she thought I meant a different day.

Maybe I should call.

Maybe it's better I not.

The ship continued to churn toward the ocean. Little by little, its features blurred beneath the fog's smudging thumb. In the ship's wake, the channel light was barely visible, a microscopic mint glow in the grayness thickening to black. Another blast from the foghorn. To the east, out over the open Atlantic, the horizon had dissolved—land, sky, air all the same gray-black flatness. Eight o'clock.

"   "

Maybe something came up.

She stood me up.

She smiled. "I'll see you soon." She wouldn't leave me hanging. If it happened earlier I'd write it off, but not after all this.

I rose from the railing and headed for home, my mind whirring with all the pieces piling up.

There must be something else.

Vera looked at me again, shrugged, and stood up. My hand trailed in hers.

"Maybe I'll stay here. dropped it. Aimi led her back into the house "I just can't" "Good nig
go somewhere else. I wouldn't go what? "I can see it on your face." **I want her.** Ma
She's not going to stick she sees something in me that I don't see in myself. "I could tell
She doesn't want to start something that She squeezed my hand. She traced her fingers across my palm.
she can't finish. didn't let go. pifftpifft her image bubbled and scattered across the slicked

"I like it here." She's dark, she's here, she sits up upon herself. "Call me."
He folded his hands behind his head. Not Frisco. That not Frisco away I front it about Your five muscles are bulging."
standing in his driveway, browned over with a screen that glows in the dark that it **Don't walk awa**
mirrored walls of the ice cream stand. He held another scoop She reappeared at
of ice cream from the tub in front of her. "I think I should I meant someth
saw him again over my shoulder, with the as I got closer. There isn't anything more to her, t
caught sight of Vera watching him. Vera "People see whatever they want to see." "Just eyes a
woman's hand. "What's wrong?" "Nothing." Vera **I can't stand her.** her image her doubles, tr
waiting on her phone. They sat on the Black Pearl's porch stand in the flas
game, in their game. Keep me away from all of that. lights. She light's dark, light with the projector's flicker. Here
moment, gone the next. The image puddled. Click click click she bent inw

R Ripping RRR Ping SHRUFFLE RingRRR ping SRUFF RRRRRRLE. Refocused again, sh
GHRGH RRRRRRRRRRRRRRGH ing, then exploded in dozens of undulating rings, traveling across the surfa
She got what she wanted. the puddle one after the other into circular waves, the pieces of her lay
"You should come over and" "Sure" She came over then dissolved at the outer edges. She watched me "You should come o
because she wanted me. and" "Sure" "I just can't" The doors closed behind her. **I ca**
So why I just **trust you.** A thrill? Control? Or is she worse than th
"I don't want a pack of rabid followers." She just doesn't trust Everything?" "Everything." played it by me there." "What do y
Why? Was she cheated on? Worse? Who? "She broke my heart." But Vera. the bed She didn't want. A smile flickering me too mu
"Whatever. *cough* Is there a place to buy cigarettes near here? She pulled closer She kept inching closer. "What do y
loose ones peeked out from the foil packet. "Can I get you something?" think of me." Everything, all Then stood outside. Nothing. She held
"No, I'm fine." I dialed her number, waiting to hear her voice in Her hands. She held my face in her I turned my face to her her fac
phone rang as she walked arm in arm with Frisco down Song after song played His folded his hands thrown against the
"Is it safe down here?" his head.

It was midnight before I finally made it home, footsore from hours wandering the city. I found Tom sitting at his desk, staring out the window, a blank sheet of staff paper in front of him, a pencil in his hand.

She stood me up.   I don't know what it is, man. Maybe.

After all this?   **Dude, this is endless. You**

How?   I can't.

gotta stop this.   Tell her what you're thinking.   You can't? Or you don't want to?

What if I'm wrong?   What she's thinking.

About what?   What do *you* feel? You won't know until

But what if she

you say something.   What do *you* want? Seriously, man! You want her to give

"   "

you an affidavit like the cops did, with everything spelled out for you? You're living in a

Where do I start?   What

dream. She's a person, not a theory.   What do you think about her?

don't I think about her?   They're all connected, the thoughts, the feelings. The

What do you *feel*?

longer this goes, the more complicated it gets.   HOW?! Anything I'd say

So just be honest with her.

will be a lie the moment it leaves my mouth.

So just put it all out there.   Yo, being who I am,

"   "

speaking for me? I don't have to consider these sorts of things, because I don't ever get to

"   "

this point. In fact, I've never *gotten* to this point. I'll tell you one thing, though. The how's

Maybe

the least complicated part of this.   Maybe she feels the same way! Maybe she's going

"   "

through the same stuff on the other end! Maybe she doesn't think about you at all! Maybe

"   "

she never wants to see you again! It could be anything! You'll never *know*; it's just some-

Or not figure out.

thing you're going to have to figure out between yourselves.   Trying's better

"   "

than thinking.

Easier said than done. My bed groaned beneath me as I crashed for the night.

She was dressed better than our
date, better than I'd seen her before.
A necklace? Pearls.

"Cincy said he'd be there."
"I'll tell Vera." "I. Don't. Want
to see him anymore." "Vera,
c'mon, he's a good guy. Plus,
you can help me with Tom."

I kicked off my sheets and rolled onto my back. The moon hung over the treetops outside my window, full and silver.

Maybe Maybe
Maybe Maybe
Maybe Maybe
Maybe Maybe
Maybe Maybe
Maybe Maybe
Maybe Maybe
Maybe Maybe

Keep climbing, keep ascending, from waves to wave motion, motion to "motion," eventually leaving even my calculator behind, no classes or classmates, dorm rooms or classrooms, just a pile of monographs and a carrel five stories below ground, a distant advisor I'd check in with from time to time, a bare-walled apartment with barely any furniture, food supply on the short side. Pure thought now, my mind and nothing else, rules for the most unruly, language, mind. Contradictions? Reel them all out, unify them, make it perfect. Epistemologies and truth values, factuals and histories, counter- and otherwise. An early New York evening, feet on the bulkhead, thumb in a broken-spined book and eyes straining out over the East River, the water somewhere out there beyond the fog. I ran my hand along my shoulder where the scar tissue lay glassed in deep in my skin. ☐~o☐ooooo☐~~o~oo~☐☐☐☐oooo☐~☐☐~o✗o~☐☐☐~☐o~o~ ☐☐☐☐☐☐ooooooooooo Keep thinking, keep thinking. You can leave it all behind.

I can't.

I shouldn't.

I won't.

A green digital 5:15 hung in the corner of the room. I rolled out of bed and crossed the apart⁄ment. Tom was sprawled across his bed, facedown. I clapped a hand on his shoulder and shook.

Yo!   Tom   Tom   Let's hit the waves.   Yeah.

zzzzzzzkkkk   **Wha' what?**   **What? Really?   Dude,**

I won't.

if you pussy out

We didn't need wetsuits this time of year, after a summer of the sun slow‑roasting the ocean. Just our boards and our leashes. We tipped our boards in through the Chevy's rear window and set off for the beachfront, letting the cool morning air slide through the windows, wake us up, keep us going.

The casino.   Yeah, let's do it.

Did you look at a surf report? Where are we gonna go?   You sure?

If I'm gonna ride, I want waves.

Man

I'm not sure Tom ever drove faster in his life. We pulled into a parking spot at the base of the south jetty, in the looming shadow of the old casino's gutted shell. The long knobby fingers of trees that had taken root in the broken‑up ground inside the casino reached through its bare steel skeleton, the ocean breezes rustled the leaves that canopied thirty‑five feet above the old gaming floors. A ribbon of pink along the eastern horizon separated the sky from the ocean, lively already with rolling waves. Out beyond the break, the *Morro* reared, free of the flocks of cranes that had surrounded it through the summer, fully rebuilt. It was sandblasted to look newly grounded, its windows blown out, white upperdecks smoke‑clouded, belowdecks fire‑scarred. A few Adirondack chairs sat open on the aft deck. Its side hatches hung open; white lines ran from the inside to moorings beneath the ocean's surface. A lifeboat dangled to port.

We hopped the promenade rail onto the beach below. Our boards jolted underarm as our feet touched the sand. The moon hung at our backs, precious, china‑smooth. I kicked my shoes off and pulled the board's leash tight around my ankle, giving the old cord a test pull, making sure it was still moored into the fiberglass after all these years.

Yeah, let's go.

Good to go?

The first breaker approached, rumbling slowly and cleanly shoreward. I nosed my board down and dove under the oncoming water.

"Jus' tryna
protect you."

"I've been waiting to   I want her so badly.

hear you say that."

I surfaced on the other side and dug in harder, trying to get past the break before the next wave came through. Arm over arm, straining against the water, until another breaker

"He probably had no idea what he was talking about."
"That person talking, I barely recognize him myself."
"Just forget everything you've heard from me up to this
point." Is Frisco more trustworthy when he's
drunk? Or is it more lying? What was he even
lying about? *"She's just just not the type of person*
I think you'd want around you. She's real unreliable."
So is she not unreliable? Or is she worse than
that? *"Everything?" "Everything."* Everything?
She turned back to me. What difference does he
make? She chose me.

"what he   I can't stand her.
doesn't know
can't hurt
him."

The ocean grew cooler out here as we bobbed beyond the break. Our boards rose and fell with the ocean as we waited for a rideable wave. The ocean was rhythmic, calm, soothing like a lullaby, lifting us beyond the rooftops, dropping us below the dune lines.

"   "

She nodded her head like   and grabbed my hand. She squeezed my hand.
"*I wouldn't take you anywhere I thought was dangerous.*" Maybe she thinks she can't have me. Because she thinks I don't want her. "*Is it safe?*" *She passed her fingers across the abrasions on my hands.* Because she shouldn't. *She clutched her cup and drew her arms closer across her body in a slow hug.*

TAKE THIS ONE MAN, GO FOR IT!

I lay forward on my board and began kicking and crawling, feeling the ocean pulling back from underneath me. I pulled and pulled and, with a momentary feeling of weightlessness, slid down the barrel of my first catch, steadying myself with my upper arms before swinging up in a standing position.

She lay down on the bed beside me. I wrapped my arm around her. I lifted her face to mine. "How long were you going

"*I'll see you guys later.*"
OOₒₒₒₒₒₒₒₒₒₒOOOOOOOOOOOOₒₒₒₒ~ₒₒₒₒₒₒXXXXXXXXXXXXXXXXXXXXXXXXXXXXₒₒₒₒₒₒ~ₒ

My foot slipped on the wave side of the board. As I fell forward, my right foot kicked out, sending the board rocketing off behind me. I hung for another second before crashing headfirst into the water.

"Just keep the pot warm, stir it up every once in a while."
She watched me as the bus receded, opened her phone, and gave him a call.
OOOOOOOOOOOₒₒₒₒ~ₒₒₒₒₒₒXXXXXXXXXXXXXXXXXXXXXXXXXₒₒₒₒₒₒ~ₒₒₒₒOOOOOOOOOO

The ocean closed in around me, twisting me as I headed down. I bottomed out in complete darkness, in complete silence.

I turned over, skyward, my eyes open despite the salt sting. The moon hung above, its edges clear and sharp despite the shifting water in the way. My lungs began to strain. I kicked and broke the surface. I tugged on my leash, drawing my board closer to me.

Yeah.

Yeah.

Yeah.

Yeah.

You all right, man?

I slid on top of my board and paddled back out, diving and rolling, falling and rising with the rollers, until I caught my next one, easier this time, a few butterfly strokes and I was in, dropping to the base before kicking and heading back up the wave, crouching then straightening as I zigzagged, leaning down hard, spinning and shooting back across the wave face, one more pivot, hand and body canted out over the water, zipping just ahead of the barrel as it chewed up the breaker behind me.

I wiped out a few yards offshore from the old skating pavilion, after a run that took me halfway down the promenade. My board and I floated in the tangled shadows of the pier. Safe, sound. I jogged back up the shoreline and headed out again, duck-diving and Eskimo-rolling back to the break, riding out until the moon passed behind the casino and the sun broke over the ocean. I was home. A little late. Right on time.

in the music

There was no time to sleep before work started, only enough time to jet by the 7-Eleven, slosh some coffee into a mug, and roll into the yard, shirtless, still soaked with ocean water, buzzing. It was Friday, the beginning of the weekend, the evening only a few hours away. I knew what I was going to do that night; I just had to get there, helped on my way by the music blaring from my headphones, the office radio, the computer, anywhere and everywhere, moving forward, forward. The clock spun for eight hours, but the day seemed only three bars long. By the time I got back home that evening, I had hit some sort of second wind, sleeping as far from my mind as possible.

Tom was seated on the edge of the living room sofa, hunched over his guitar, a small sea of staff paper spread around his feet.

You going out tonight?   I'm going to find Vera.

     Wasn't planning on it. You?   **Great plan, man.**

    It's not a big city. I figured I'd hit the boards and

Where exactly?   **Not a big city, but you still**

       What does that mean?

don't know shit about it, newbie.   **The last five years or so? Chambers**

"   "

has been throwing an amazing year-end party. Four DJs, crazy drink specials, all that shit.

You down?   What's up?

If she's around, she'll be there. I guarantee it.   Not really.   I just don't

"   "

feel like going.

I raised my eyebrow.

You *always* feel like going.   Aren't you always?

Can I be honest with you, Cince?   Usually, yeah,

You didn't break up?

but recently, no. I kinda lied about me and Aimi.   No, I lied when I said *I*

Did she say why?

broke it off with *her*. Really, *she* dumped *me*. And I'm pissed.   Actually, yeah,

He looked back down at his guitar and picked out a few notes.

"   "

she did. She said I was too predictable, too boring. Like she could read me like an open book

That's cold. She really said that to you?

and she was always a couple of chapters ahead.   It's true.

But, you

She deserves better than me.   **Look, I don't need any Oprah-ass esteem-building**

from you. I'm happy she kept it real with me, I'm just pissed at myself.

for you.

Her dumping me and the band flaming out at the show were even better for my mu-

"   "

sic. You see this shit?

He pointed to the staff paper laying across the floor.

"   "

This is the first original shit I've written since I picked up a guitar. I'm not tryna get up from

"   "

this couch anytime soon.

His right foot fidgeted around a brick-size green box with metallic plungers and tiny black dials.

What's that?   I didn't

This? It's a delay pedal. I picked it up at Guitar Center a few days ago.

think you went in for effects like that.

I thought it was time to try something new.

He pressed his foot down and picked out a few silent notes, then rolled his foot back onto his heel. As the plunger rose, the sequence played out in full volume. Tom leaned down and turned a knob; the sequence spun back on itself. Tom began to play again, tracing out a spindly countermelody. The sound had a crystalline feel, totally different from the classic ragers he normally played.

I like it.   Maybe you *should* stay in.

I do too.   If you want to take the car, go for it, man. I even

"   "

got the transmission fixed. It can go forward *and* backward now. Pretty novel idea, right?

A quick shave, a change of clothes, and I was out the door, grabbing the keys from the counter as I ducked off. The Chevy sat silently at the curb outside the front door. I cranked down the windows and cranked up the volume. The car's floors and seats pulsed and sang as I headed oceanward.

Trunk blowin' screens showin' neon lights glowin' / Bangin' on screw

What was the idea? To find her, to let her know what was on my mind, to let it all spill out, however it spilt out. I didn't want to be right, not anymore. I just wanted her.

I parked a few blocks from the beachfront and walked toward Chambers. The pink smoke of the weekly fireworks drifted off the beach, carried inland by a faint breath of North Atlantic cool. The late-night crowd at Chambers was spilling out the front doors and welling onto the Boulevard. A team of police officers with sweat-soaked POLICE polo shirts and glowing red hand lamps waved the passing traffic by. I cut across the club's parking lot and pushed my way inside.

It was darker in Chambers's warren of galleries and hallways than it was outside. Every inch of the main space was packed; partygoers with plastic bracelets on their wrists tiptoed through the crowds with drinks and wide-eyed looks; rowdier crews jostled their way through the tangles of partiers, pushing them onto the balls of their feet and sending their arms flailing for balance. The club rattled with the sound of a single DJ playing somewhere below.

If you trill and you rowdy and you rep yo set proudly get on up and clap yo hands

A head lunged across the crowd; a few partiers stumbled against the club's cinder-block wall. Two men came crashing back to the left, cutting a narrow clearing out of the crowd. A fight? A fight. Flurried fists and frenzied voices. Necks craned for a better look, mouths opened in silent excitement. Heads bobbed, arms windmilled. The taller of the two had the shorter— stooped, pale, baldheaded—in a horse collar, whipping him back toward the far wall. The sickening sound of a skull striking against the bare concrete floor. A knot of onlookers formed around the taller, talking him down as he shouted over their shoulders to the shorter. The shorter glared back, swaying and trembling, a drained tumbler in his right hand, his chest rising and falling as he inched away from the clearing, his face twisted and eyes empty. I crept farther into the club, anywhere to get away.

To the left, a single set of steps led down to the lower gallery, where a thick slow stream of R&B churned away. In the dim light below, hazy red forms and dark moving bodies faded and resolved. A row of glasses rested on the bar's edge, deep-toned prisms bending, bunching, trembling in rhythm. Packed dancers swayed and dipped. Smoke was in the air. The clock struck midnight.

One, two. One, two. I don't know about y'all, but I ain't come here to play the wall tonight.

A single bass line roared through the club.

Well e'ery girl wanna *scratch* e'ery girl wanna *scratch*

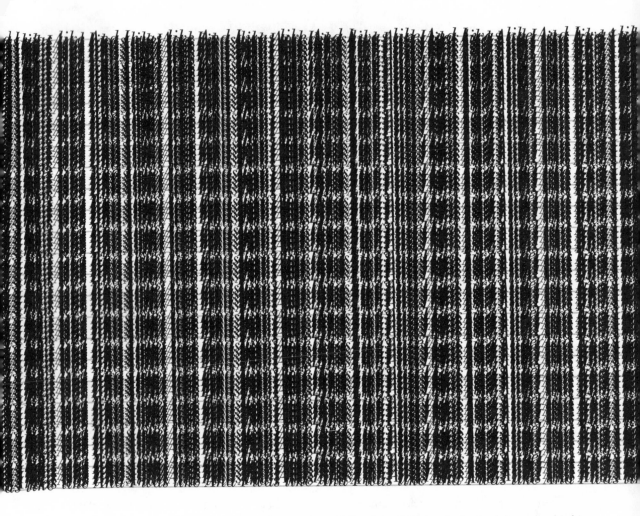

My second wind died somewhere in the middle of the DJ's set, the lack of sleep, the thinking, the music, the pulses bottoming out into some sort of hyperreality, the walls of the place seemingly contracting and expanding with each bass hit.

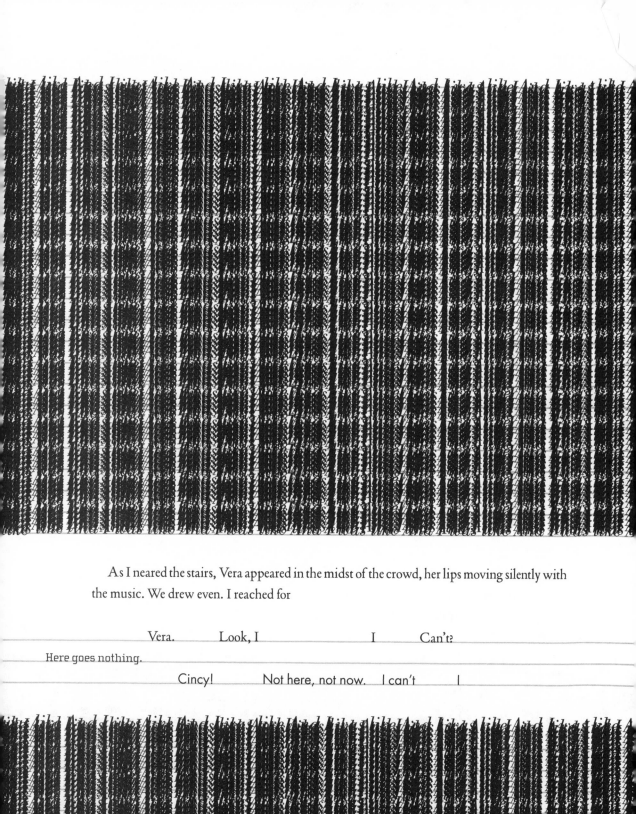

As I neared the stairs, Vera appeared in the midst of the crowd, her lips moving silently with the music. We drew even. I reached for

Vera.   Look, I   I   Can't?

Here goes nothing.

Cincy!   Not here, not now.   I can't   I

She broke away from me. The club's woofers roared as the crowd closed in between us. She was light-years away in a second, absorbed in the sounds.

I followed after her, through the crowd, up the stairs.

Back out onto the Boulevard, into the late-August night. She was gone.

I turned into the alley outside Chambers and rested my head against the wall. The sound of cars parked along the curb and crawling up the block mingled with the music pouring from the system inside.

When the beat bang then you know we clear the block out

"Not now." She won't listen to me.

She rocked back and forth to the jukebox. A smile played across her lips. "Just listen." | She grooved in her seat. She moved so well. | Her lips moved silently with the music.

Get em up nowHIGH Turn it up now   HIGH

She smiled. "So you just keep quiet?"   No.   Turn it up.

She rocked back and forth to the jukebox.

Even in the midst of all the noise, she

heard it. A smile played across her lips.

"Just listen."

the truth

(OG ROCK THE MIC REMIX)

That night, when I finally made it home, the record player in my room was spinning. The needle arm hung close over the vinyl, white noise crackled from the speakers as Tom worked through his next bars in the living room, his song taking shape through the fragments and repetitions of his earlier strummings, notes layering over themselves, building: the song was the songs were the sounds. It was exactly how it should be. It was what we'd all been waiting for him to do.

A wave of static washed out from the speakers, threatening to drown out his song.

So I pulled the needle out.

Then I pulled my chair out, picked up a pen, and began to write.

I wrote every night for weeks. I wrote through my hand jitters, I wrote until my vision blurred, until I had every scrawl, every loop down. Until I finished. It was the first thing I'd written in months. It was the first thing I was proud of, the first thoughts that didn't feel like they needed more proof. It was chaotic; it was contradictory. And it was the whole truth.

■ ■ ■

When I finally finished, I walked into the living room with an armful of sheet music of my own.

Yo, is the mic still hot?

"   "

Tom tapped the mic, sending short pops out of the speakers.

Yeah, I know where to start.

Yeah.   **You know where to start?**

Tom dragged the mouse over the red RECORD button and clicked. I took a deep breath and stepped up to the mic.

At the beginning.   When the university   :‖

ACKNOWLEDGMENTS

I've benefited tremendously from the goodwill and great ideas of many outstanding people while working on *Sound*. So much so, I fear I'll miss someone in the process of trying to thank everyone. That said, I'll try.

Christian Ayers, Eric Bennett, Dave Cohen, and Ross Perlin provided much-needed advice, criticism, and encouragement from the time *Sound* was a bunch of scribbles on napkins. Sorry for inflicting that stuff on you. Thanks for indulging me.

Bonnie Nadell challenged me to elevate my writing and has been *Sound*'s champion for years. Mitzi Angel and Lee Brackstone believed in my vision for *Sound*, showed me how much farther I needed to go to realize it, and made sure I got there. Jeff Clark of Quemadura turned in a virtuoso design performance and has been an energizing collaborator. The folks at FSG and Faber and Faber, U.K.—Lisa Baker, Chantal Clarke, Kathy Daneman, Mark Krotov, Jonathan Lippincott, Sean McDonald, Jeff Seroy, and Charlotte Strick—have given me great homes on both sides of the pond.

My teachers at Harvard College—Ann Blair, Peter Gordon, James Hankins, James Kloppenberg, and Eric Paras—introduced me to many of the ideas at the core of *Sound* and helped me find the words and spaces to pursue them. The Marshall Scholarship Commission kept me sheltered and fed while *Sound* was germinating in the U.K. The crew at Okayplayer, the editors of *Stylus*, and others gave me free rein on the Web for years; somewhere in that time, I found my voice. My teachers at Yale Law School—Jack Balkin, Heather Gerken, and Reva Siegel above all—recognized the odd road I have been trying to travel and have guided me since I arrived at YLS.

Hip-hop has helped me go many places. Shout out to the originators and the innovators.

Further respect is due to all those who talked through my ideas with me, read sketches and drafts, assured me I had something worth saying, made sure I kept at it, and/or provided point-ers, perspective, pillows, and/or placidity while I wrote: Blake Brandes, Isabel Bussarakum, Jay Carey, Julie Cerf, Jacob Eisler, Cliff Emmanuel, Gary Geissler, Adam Goldfarb, Ariana Green, Sophie Hood, Patrick Hosfield, Okechukwu Iweala, Nick Josefowitz, Paul and Ellen Josefowitz, Valarie Kaur, Jeremy Kessler, James Kwak, Matthew Maddox, Rafi Moreen, Chukwudum Muoneke, Tim O'Connell, Nick Osbourne, Barry and Lois Ostrow, Ann Phelps, Sasha Post, Gabriela Rivera, Lauren Schuker, Ryan Sweeney, Kenny Townsend, Michael Ugwu, Jonah and Joshua Vincent, and Rebecca Wexler.

Finally, my family—Bill, Mary Kate, and Nora—have been the foundation for everything I've done. Thank you.

PERMISSION ACKNOWLEDGMENTS

"Make 'Em NV," words and music by James Yancey, copyright © 2003 by Universal-Polygram International Publishing, Inc., and E.P.H.C.Y. Publishing. All rights controlled and administered by Universal-Polygram International Publishing, Inc. All rights reserved. Used by permission. Reprinted by permission of Hal Leonard Corporation.

"Me and Those Dreaming Eyes of Mine," words and music by D'Angelo, copyright © 1995 by Universal-Songs of Polygram International, Inc., 12 A.M. Music, and Ah-Choo Publishing. All rights controlled and administered by Universal-Songs of Polygram International, Inc. All rights reserved. Used by permission. Reprinted by permission of Hal Leonard Corporation.

"Is That Enough," words and music by Marvin Gaye, copyright © 1978 by Jobete Music Co., Inc. All rights controlled and administered by EMI April Music, Inc. All rights reserved. International copyright secured. Used by permission. Reprinted by permission of Hal Leonard Corporation.

"The Party," words and music by Anne Erin Clark, copyright © 2009 by Chrysalis Music and Nail Polish Manifesto Music. All rights administered by Chrysalis Music. All rights reserved. Used by permission. Reprinted by permission of Hal Leonard Corporation.

"The Neighbors," words and music by Anne Erin Clark, copyright © 2009 by Chrysalis Music and Nail Polish Manifesto Music. All rights administered by Chrysalis Music. All rights reserved. Used by permission. Reprinted by permission of Hal Leonard Corporation.

"Cruisin'," words and music by William "Smokey" Robinson and Marvin Tarplin, copyright © 1979 by Bertam Music Company. All rights controlled and administered by EMI April Music, Inc., on behalf of Jobete Music Co., Inc. All rights reserved. International copyright secured. Used by permission. Reprinted by permission of Hal Leonard Corporation.

"Atlantic City," by Bruce Springsteen, copyright © 1982 by Bruce Springsteen (ASCAP). Reprinted by permission. International copyright secured. All rights reserved.

T. M. WOLF IS TWENTY-NINE AND GREW UP ON THE NEW JERSEY SHORE. HE HAS WRITTEN FOR A VARIETY OF MUSIC PUBLICATIONS, PARTICULARLY ON HIP-HOP. HE RECENTLY GRADUATED FROM THE YALE LAW SCHOOL. ////////////

9/13